THE ENDORPHIN CONSPIRACY

To Abby

THE ENDORPHIN CONSPIRACY

A NOVEL

FREDRIC
STERN

To Ana, my soul mate, for her never-ending support, faith and love.

"*In the councils of government, we must guard against the acquisition of unwarranted influence, whether sought or unsought, by the military-industrial complex. The potential for the disastrous rise of misplaced power exists and will persist.*"

—PRESIDENT DWIGHT D. EISENHOWER, in his Farewell Address to the Nation, January 17, 1961

PROLOGUE

The pungent odor of incense assailed him. His temples pounded, his sinuses thickened. Cameron Daniels cleared his throat, set the current issue of *Life* on the night stand next to his bed, and scanned his hospital room for the source of the cloying smell. As usual, there was nothing. Why incense? Why did it always start the same way?

The doctors told him it was an olfactory hallucination from deep within the recesses of his brain—the temporal lobes—an association from his childhood. They said he must have been regressing, reaching back to a safer and more secure time in his life. Cameron Daniels, altar boy. They said the stress of working as a technical analyst for the CIA must have gotten to him, that it happened to a lot of people.

It just didn't make sense. He hadn't felt unusually stressed until after the first time it happened at the agency retreat in Virginia. Since then he had had no peace. His life was hell. It was no consolation there were others like him, and he didn't buy the doctors explanation. Neither did his wife, who had been left a widow—at least emotionally—to care for their baby daughter for the last six months.

The chiming of bells nearly jolted Daniels out of bed. Church bells ringing, just as they had every Sunday during his childhood in Montreal. Now they were so numerous and loud they seemed to rattle his very skull.

He placed his palms over his ears. "God, not again. Stop. Stop ringing those damn bells! I can't take it anymore!"

The ringing continued.

"Please!" His eyes clamped shut. His head moved painfully from side to side. He cried like a child, rocking back and forth in bed. "Why? Why me? What did I do to deserve this?"

Then silence.

Daniels waited for a full minute to be sure—often they came back suddenly—then opened his eyes and removed his hands from his ears. The silence remained unbroken. He thought it was over. Then a voice cut through to his consciousness: "Cameron. Cameron, do not despair."

The voice was familiar, feminine, one he could not place but soothed him. Each time it had become stronger, drawing him in by degrees.

"Cameron, I can help you find peace. Let me help you."

Daniels wiped his eyes and looked towards the window. Rays of early morning sunlight streamed between the slats of the blinds, projecting a kaleidoscope of dancing shapes and colors that seemed to coalesce into human form.

"Why do they torture me like this?" His mouth twisted in pain.

Features formed into a human face, smiled. "I am here to give you salvation. Come to me." A hand stretched out to Daniels, beckoning.

He threw off the sheets, picked up *Life*, eased himself out of bed, and staggered toward the window, swatting at the face before him with the magazine. "Get out of here! Go away! I want my mind back! I want peace!"

The bells resumed, hundreds, perhaps thousands of bells, chiming more and more loudly until Daniels felt his head would burst. He clamped his hands over his ears. "No, God no!"

He opened the blinds, the bright light causing him to squint, and pressed his forehead against the pane. "Stop, please stop. I'll do whatever you say!"

"Come to me Cameron, and you will be free."

The voice came from outside. He could see her clearly now, hovering just beyond the window.

Frantically, Daniels tried to open it. But like all the patient windows in the psychiatric wing at Bethesda, it was locked. The ringing continued, echoing madly inside his head. The pain was past endurance. Desperately, he searched the room, his gaze coming to rest on the chair.

The sound of the chair smashing the window echoed eerily through the room, along the corridor. Seconds later, a young male orderly burst into the room, but it was too late. Cameron Daniels had found his peace.

***

The encrypted cable arrived by special courier late in the afternoon at the Human Ecology Institute in Montreal. Dr. Rudolph Schmidt, the Director, was clearly shaken as he read the decoded message.

"SEPTEMBER 13 1967, 0600. EFFECTIVE IMMEDIATELY MK ULTRA IS TERMINATED. ALL DOCUMENTS TO BE DESTROYED. DO NOT, REPEAT, DO NOT ATTEMPT CONTACT. END OF MESSAGE.-BLUEBIRD"

Schmidt slumped down in his chair, his hand still grasping the cablegram.

"Dr. Schmidt, are you okay?" Josef Balassi asked with concern.

Schmidt stared blankly across the room.

His young research assistant reached across the desk for the cablegram. "May I?"

Schmidt nodded.

Balassi read the note, his fiery brown eyes narrowed in anger. "How could they do this? Ten years of research snuffed out in an instant by fools who know nothing of what you've accomplished! We can't do it, we *won't!*"

"We don't have a choice."

"Yes, we do." Balassi stood, stared down at Schmidt. "Yes, we do."

CHAPTER 1

JULY 1, 2010

HIS PULSE RACED AS HE SPRINTED DOWN FORT WASHINGTON Avenue towards the New York Trauma Center. Dr. Geoffrey Davis checked his watch. Six-thirty a.m. He was running late on his first day back. Bad form. There'd be hell to pay with Dr. Pederson before he even had a chance to meet his team at rounds. Of all days to oversleep, this was the worst.

Even at this hour, Washington Heights bustled with activity. Cab drivers honked their horns at anyone or anything that got in their way, shopkeepers swept yesterday's rotting garbage off their sidewalks into the street, people rushed to subway stations, likely everyone, like him, breaking an early sweat in the sultriness that lingered from the night before.

Geoff stepped off the curb at 175th Street, passed the entrance to the George Washington Bridge. He was jolted by the intrusive beeping of his pager. "Shit," he muttered. He despised the stupid beeper. It made his gastric juices gurgle and his muscles tense every time it went off. Even after all these years. Geoff reached down with his right hand, depressed the grey button and glanced down at the pager at his waist. His attention was diverted from the road ahead barely a second when he was startled by the shrill horn from a rusted, brown Camaro headed directly at him, not more than three feet away. He dodged quickly to his right, tripped over the curb on the south side of the street, and lost his balance. His right shoulder crashed hard into the buckled sidewalk as he attempted to break his fall. His face landed next to a fresh pile of dog shit.

"Look where you're goin', man!" yelled the driver. "You tryin' to get yourself killed?"

Geoff flipped him off. He couldn't wait to get out of this rat trap of a city. Just one more year.

He lifted himself up off the sidewalk, picked up his backpack and swatted away the flies that hovered over the pile left by one of the scores of neighborhood mongrels. His shoulder ached, and a few drops of blood trickled from his elbow. He brushed off his shoulder and tested his arm by moving it back and forth. Nothing broken. He was lucky and he knew it; he could have been killed.

Geoff reached down and felt for the knife he kept strapped to his right shin. It was secure in the sheath. His fellow residents thought he was paranoid to carry the thing everywhere he went, but for Geoff it was more than a habit. His days as a Navy Seal had taught him many useful things, one of which was being prepared for any situation that might arise. Ironic. Washington Heights had become more like a war zone than a neighborhood, potentially more dangerous than a number of training missions he had been on.

The Navy had been good to Geoff, though in the end he found it all too macho and regimented. He appreciated the skills he learned, the education loans, the freedom it afforded him from financial dependence on his father. His family could easily have afforded to send him to any med school in the country. In fact, his surgeon father had secured a place for him at his own alma mater, Columbia. As proud—not always a virtue he'd been told—and independent as he was, Geoff had wanted to do it on his own, without anyone's help. Least of all, his father's.

If he became a physician, he had decided, it would be on his own merits, and he would pay his own way. And he had. Admitted to Harvard Medical School on a Navy scholarship, he had deferred his neurosurgery residency to complete his obligation to the Navy as a medical officer in the Seals. His father never seemed to understand his decision, though seemed oddly proud. Geoff's wife, Sarah, thought he was crazy, but supported his decision. Geoff was his own man.

Geoff straightened his tie, smoothed his sweat-soaked shirt and resumed his brisk pace towards the Trauma Center, trying to act as if nothing had happened. Then he remembered the pager. What a way to start the day. Late and limping like some lame first year med student. Goddamn.

Geoff removed the pager from his waist, depressed the button, and held it up in front of him, keeping his gaze fixed on the road ahead. The number was all too familiar: the Neurosurgical ICU at the Trauma Center. His first call as Chief Resident. Whoever it was would have to wait a few minutes. At least it wasn't a stat page.

Geoff crossed 168th Street, rushed past drug addicts lined up to exchange their needles at the old National Guard Armory building, now a drug rehab clinic, then the Center's ER entrance, aid cars crowding it's parking lot. He climbed the marble stairs leading to the main entrance of the Trauma Center.   Over the entrance was an inscription, the only remaining vestige from the old City Hospital: "For of the Most High Cometh Healing."

Geoff paused momentarily to catch his breath and compose himself, then checked his watch. Six-forty. Despite his eventful commute to work, he was only fifteen minutes late for rounds. Things could have been worse. All would be forgotten by later in the morning.

The automatic doors parted, freeing cool, dry air, refreshing after the sprint from his apartment. Geoff removed his bar-coded ID card from the backpack slung over his sore right shoulder and clipped it to his breast pocket, able then to pass to all areas of the Medical Center.

"Welcome back, Dr. Davis. We missed you around here," said Sergeant Randall Johnson. He grabbed Geoff's hand and shook it vigorously.

Johnson, black, tall and muscular, with closely cropped graying hair and keen eyes, had been recruited to join NYTC security from the New York City Police Department several years ago. Street smart and stern, he showed his underlying warmth to only a few. Geoff was one.

There was a good reason, aside from chemistry and respect. Geoff had saved Randall Johnson's ass big time a few years back, treating him for a disease he wouldn't want to have taken home to his wife Martha. The consequences might have been far more fatal than the disease. Geoff didn't file the report with the department of health. He just gave Randall the shot of penicillin in the behind, along with a lecture, and never once mentioned the incident again.

"Thanks, Randall. Good to see you, too." He glanced at his watch. "Hey, I'm running late for rounds. How about lunch one of these days?" he said, realizing even as he said it the odds of his having the time to actually meet someone for lunch during his year as chief resident were practically non-existent. He was about to re-enter the Twilight Zone.

Johnson guffawed. "Yeah, let's pack a lunch and picnic on the GW Bridge! Hey, good luck, man. I'm sure you'll be the best chief this place has ever had."

"Thanks. Gotta go."

Geoff hurried up the long corridor that lead to the bank of elevators. Lithographs dotted the walls illuminated by soft lights, all a blur to Geoff as he raced to get to rounds. Nearing the elevators, he couldn't help but notice a rapidly approaching pack of young men and women in newly starched, white coats, stethoscopes dangling around their necks like amulets, mouths chattering. Med students and new residents.

Geoff hit the elevator call button, checked his watch again, tapped it twice with his finger. Six forty-two. Damn. He paced, waiting for the elevator to arrive. An overhead page cut through the white noise in the corridor. "Dr. Geoffrey Davis, emergency room. Dr. Davis, emergency room."

A rush of adrenalin hit him. He turned and ran back down the hallway towards the ER. He had no idea what train wreck awaited him there, but whatever it was, he was prepared to handle it. This was what he loved about medicine. Making order out of chaos, saving lives, being resourceful. It was a lot like his days in the Navy. Rounds would have to wait.

A woman's voice tugged at him from behind. "Dr. Davis, wait up!" Geoff stopped and turned to face a young woman with bright eyes and a friendly smile. She wore a white coat with a stethoscope draped around her neck. "My name's Karen Choy," she said, extending her hand. "I'm the new resident on the neurosurgery service."

Geoff shook her hand. "Nice to meet you, Dr. Choy. Have you done a neurosurgery rotation before?"

She hesitated. "Yes, well, only as a med student. Not as an intern."

"Hope you like crash courses. I'm on my way to the ER. Let's go."

CHAPTER 2

"WELL, DR. DAVIS, NICE OF YOU TO PAY US A VISIT. FOUR MINutes to answer a page—you better cut that in half. Dr. Spiros has been setting his stopwatch again.

"Don't forget, it's July first." Jan Creighton, head nurse on day shift, spoke with more than a hint of sarcasm.

"Jan, you look great. New hairdo?" Geoff asked.

"Twenty-five pounds off, five more to go and counting. Oh, you mean the perm? You're the first guy around here to notice."

In truth, Geoff didn't care much for Jan Creighton, though he respected the way she ran the ER. Forty-five, never married, sarcasm was her trademark.

"Where's the action?"

"Trauma room one. Want me to take you there, or do you remember the way?"

Her words grated. "Good to see you, Jan. I'm sure I'll be seeing you again real soon."

From the strategic viewpoint of the nursing station, a central, Plexiglas-enclosed area about twenty by fifteen feet in dimension, Geoff could see all areas of significance, from the ambulance entrance to the trauma rooms. The nursing station functioned as traffic control, flow directed by the head nurse, visibility providing her the ability to monitor all ER activity and assign treatment rooms and staff as indicated by patients' apparent conditions.

Geoff left the nursing station, Karen Choy in tow. He turned, collided with a passing medic, knocking him into one of the portable crash carts that dotted the hallway adjacent to the nursing station. Like a quarterback sacked from the blind-side, the medic sent his clip-board flying and crashed helplessly to the floor.

"Sorry, I didn't see you coming." Geoff was physically unscathed but embarrassed.

"Hey, man, where the fuck you brains at!" the medic said as he got up off the floor. He reclaimed his clipboard and brushed his behind.

When the medic looked up, Geoff instantly realized who he was, embarrassment giving way to pleasure. "Santos, you son-of-a-bitch! I couldn't have knocked you on your butt better if I'd tried!"

"*Ay, Dios mio!* Geoffrey Davis, I thought you had died and gone to heaven without me. The laboratory is no place for a fine doctor such as yourself."

"I'm back."

The two men embraced warmly. Geoff turned towards Karen Choy, who stood by, obviously unsure what to make of it all. "Dr. Karen Choy, this is Enrique Santos, the best damn medic in the City of New York."

Santos blushed, extended his hand. "Don't believe anything he tells you, Dr. Choy, but it is a pleasure to meet you. You've got a fine teacher."

"The pleasure is mine. I've heard a lot about you from the other residents." Karen looked at Geoff. "Why don't I meet you over by the trauma room?"

"Sure. I'll be right over."

They couldn't have been from more different worlds: Geoffrey Davis, blueblood son of a surgeon from Connecticut, and Enrique Santos, blue collar, Puerto Rican medic from Spanish Harlem. Thirty-eight years old, of medium height with broad, dark features and a trim mustache, white shirt with its short sleeves rolled up above bulky biceps, the shirt's top buttons left open far enough to expose a large, silver crucifix resting comfortably between well defined pectorals, Santos appeared the prototypical macho Latino. It was a well-honed facade, a means of protecting his sensitive, caring nature. Street smart and self-made, Santos was a living example that growing up in Spanish Harlem did not inevitably lead to a broken life.

If only his younger brother, Jose, had allowed Santos into his life, Geoff knew Santos could have gotten him off the streets and made him a productive member of society. But the lure of a street gang seduced him, stole him away. Higher than a kite one night on angel dust, he ended up in the NYTC ER, a victim of a hit and run. A younger Geoffrey Davis, the trauma doc then, spent a good part of the night with Jose, desperately trying to save his life. The bond between the doctor from Connecticut and the medic from Spanish Harlem was forged by sharing that personal tragedy.

"How's everything going?" Santos asked, his warm, brown eyes searching Geoff's.

"About as well as it can around this place."

Santos slapped him playfully on the cheek. "*Bueno, bueno, mi amigo*. Hey, we'll have you over for dinner real soon. Gloria will fill you up so good we'll have to wheel you home in a barrel."

"I'd love to. Maybe one day next week. You just getting off shift?"

"Yeah, long night. You see that cop Ceravola and I brought in—Smithers?"

Geoff looked toward trauma room one. "I was just on my way there."

"He's in bad shape. Looks like he was attacked by a pack of

wild dogs. Good luck."

An overhead page pierced the air. "Dr. Davis, trauma room one, stat!"

Geoff glanced back toward the trauma room. "I'd better get going. Good to see you, Santos. I'm sure we'll be seeing a lot of each other this year."

"*Hasta luego,* Geoffrey."

Geoff bolted to the trauma room area, met Karen. Trauma room one contained four beds, each separated from the others by curtains suspended from the ceiling. A young black man, in the far bed, diagonally across the room, obviously quite intoxicated, was tied to the bed by four leather restraints and was being tended by an intern, who was grappling to suture his face back together while at the same time dodging the patient's attempts to bite his hand.

"Makes you feel appreciated, doesn't it?" Geoff said, pointing to the struggling intern at the far bed. As he neared the room, it became obvious where the real action was. Just beyond bed one stood four New York transit cops, one with sergeant's stripes.

Geoff knew right away the patient was a cop. Stat calls took on a heightened level of urgency when a cop was involved. Dr. Spiros made sure all residents understood this from day one in his ER.

An organized tumult of activity buzzed around bed one—blood spurting into color-coded test tubes, IV's dripping frantically to keep up with blood loss, stethoscopes and lights probing for answers. Medicine in the trenches. An army of doctors, nurses and technicians in their green scrubs, each with a task, all coordinated by the trauma doc, a second year surgery resident who acted as field commander, barking out orders, triaging when necessary.

"Get a blood gas, stat," called out the trauma doc, Dave Flynn. He turned to Lynn Graves, the nurse. "How are his vitals doing?"

"Pulse one-forty and thready. BP holding at ninety over fifty."

"Run those IV's wide open, or we're gonna' be starting a do-pamine drip real quick. Type and cross him for five units whole blood, stat!" Flynn ordered.

"They're running full bore now."

"Is the blood gas drawn yet?"

"It's already gone to the lab," said an intern.

Lynn Graves glanced at Geoff and Karen approaching the bedside. "There's no place like home, is there Dr. Davis?"

"There's definitely no place like this home, Lynn. I missed the ER." Geoff smiled at Lynn, then turned to Dave. "Need some help?"

"I'd love some, Geoff. You know how it is on July 1." He looked at Karen. "Too many rookies on the trauma team."

"What's the story here, Dave?" asked Geoff.

"Forty-two-year-old transit cop attacked while on duty this morning. Here at the 168th Street subway station, in the elevator, going down to the IRT. Fucking animals out there. He's been in and out of consciousness. Bad head injuries, as you can see, may have a basal skull fracture. Hard to believe this was done by one fucking lunatic," said Flynn, shaking his head from side to side.

"Did you do a peritoneal lavage? Any internal bleeding?" Karen asked.

"Do you think we've been sitting around playing Xbox, Dr. Choy?"

"Cool down, Dave. Karen's question was a good one," said Geoff.

"Sorry. It's been a long night." Flynn's hand massaged his brow. "We did a lavage. Fluid was bloody. He's probably got a lacerated liver or spleen. We're waiting for the general surgeons to evaluate that. Best we can do here is keep up with the blood loss."

Flynn was a good man, but obviously under a lot of pressure already today. A cop on his first day in the trauma unit. A lot for anyone to handle. Still, he was doing what he had to do. Geoff stepped back and let him work.

Geoff remembered his own days in the ER all too well. Call nights eternal, living in a time warp. The world went on outside the glass cage—people laughing, playing, loving—but for the resident on call in the ER, the world was a constant barrage of the downtrodden and abused—heads slashed, bashed and blasted away, limbs busted and dangling, faces contorted in anguish. Stealing life back from the brink of death, a day's work in the ER. Days with little sleep, few breaks, irregular meals. Geoff loved the adrenalin, the camaraderie.

What he hadn't liked was the toll it had taken on his marriage. Sarah had been his lifeline to humanity, had forced him to remember his priorities daily. A part of him seemed to have died with her.

"Better get a central line in right away," Geoff said. "You're going to need it to keep up with his fluid—"

"Pulse 150, BP's down to 70/palp."

The cardiac monitor alarm sounded. "He's in V-fib! One milligram of epi,stat!"

Flat line. Nothing. Geoff grabbed the paddles out of the intern's hands, placed them on the cop's chest. "Set it at two hundred. Stand back, everybody clear?"

"Two hundred," Lynn said.

"Clear!" Geoff pressed the button. The patient's torso arched in the air and flopped back down on the bed board with a thud. The monitor did not change.

"Continue chest compressions!" said Flynn.

Still no pulse.

"Charge it again!" ordered Geoff.

"Ready."

"Hold on," said Geoff. The silence was broken by rhythmic beeping. Smiles broke out all around.

"Pulse 110, BP 95/60."

"Looks like he's stabilizing for now," said Flynn.

From the corner of the curtained area, Dr. George Spiros quietly observed the frenetic scene. His belt weighed down by three pagers and two cell phones marked his rank as commander-in-chief. He was a short man with graying black hair, stocky build with a soft middle. Spiros watched every move keenly, his small but intense, dark brown eyes peering through thick lenses set in tortoise-shell frames, his expression severe as he waited for someone to make an error in judgment.

Think clearly, but act quickly and instinctively, he constantly told his residents. He drilled this into their minds every morning during five a.m. rounds, when he reviewed aloud every single case from the night before, red grease pencil in hand. No one escaped criticism; no case was handled well enough. There was no place for error in judgment in his emergency room, no place for hubris—except his. Fear and respect motivated the residents passing through his ER. It worked remarkably well.

A nurses aid entered the room, bags in hand. "Blood's arrived."

"Hang two units and run them in full bore," said Flynn. He turned to Geoff. "Thanks for the help. You don't have much time to do your neuro evaluation. The OR will be ready for him in ten minutes."

"No problem. Dr. Choy and I will take it from here. Why don't you take a break." Geoff motioned Karen to approach the head of the bed, while nurses and interns continued about their work.

The victim was fair-skinned, somewhat overweight. His face was swollen to marshmallow puffiness, the white flesh of his cheeks and forehead marked by deep crimson lacerations, as if something had attempted to gouge out his eyes. Sanguineous fluid oozed from his nose and right ear. Dark bruises encircled both eyes, giving him a raccoon-like appearance. Around his neck was a stabilizing neck brace to protect his upper spinal cord from excessive movement. Possible spinal fracture. His blue uniform had been cut away, revealing numerous, large bruises, abrasions, and bite marks on his chest and arms. Were this an ER in Montana, he could have been the victim of a grizzly bear attack. But this was New York, where transit cops patrolled the dusky, fetid bowels of the subways, often in perilous isolation, where the animals were most frequently two-legged.

Penlights and reflex hammers in hand, Geoff and his apprentice evaluated their patient.

"The bloody fluid coming from his nose and ears, that's spinal fluid, isn't it?" asked Karen.

"Sure looks like it. That, along with the raccoon's eyes pretty much point to a basal skull fracture. We'll know when he has his MRI scan. He must have been smashed on the back of the head with a hard object or fallen down, hitting his occiput. He's in a bad way."

"He seems to be losing the little bit of consciousness he had." Karen checked his pupillary responses.

"What would you say his coma scale rating is?" Geoff asked.

"Moderate to severe head injury. Fair to poor prognosis."

"Very good. Of course that's all meaningless in the face of what his PET scan will show us regarding the actual extent of his brain injury."

"Thorough evaluation, doctors," interrupted Dr. Spiros, restless with his role of observer. "Now would you like to let me in on his neuro status is and your treatment plan? I don't think I can put off the mayor, the police commissioner, and the press much longer."

Karen Choy gladly deferred to Geoff.

"Probable basal skull fracture, brain swelling due to diffuse head injury. We'll know for sure after his scans. Numerous contusions, lacerations, and probable internal injuries. His neck's been stabilized with a cervical collar in the unlikely event there's a spinal fracture. Plan is to take him to the OR for an exploratory laparotomy, place a head bolt to monitor his intracranial pressure, then when he recovers, take him to neuroimaging for his PET and MRI scans. If he makes it, he'll be spending at least several days in the ICU. Did I miss anything?"

Spiros wore his usual deadpan expression. "No."

"Then we'll be taking him now. Can we borrow a nurse for the trip to the OR?" asked Geoff. He raised the bedrails and unlocked the wheels.

Spiros nodded his head affirmatively, turned to leave, then paused. "Good job, Dr. Davis, but try and get here more quickly next time." He left the trauma room.

Karen exhaled. "So that's *the* Dr. Spiros."

"Astute observation, Karen. You'll go far. Stay here with the patient. I'll go find a nurse to help."

Geoff stood at the nursing station, listening to the scramble of activity around him. The interminable electronic ringing of telephones, overhead pages, sirens of police vans and aid cars, the voices of patients, families, and staff. While he had been working it had been tuned out of his conscious awareness by that part of the brain responsible for selective attention. The cacophonous agglomeration of sounds had melded together, nothing more than a symphony of background sound, white noise.

"Any nurses free to help transport a patient?" asked Geoff.

"Only one free is Nurse Creighton," said Bea Mendelssohn, the ER clerk, gazing up at Geoff over her reading glasses.

"That's okay, I don't want to take her away from her more important duties here," replied Geoff. "Dr. Choy and I will take care of it ourselves."

"That's probably the wisest decision you've made in your two hours as chief resident, Dr. Davis." Bea smiled knowingly.

"Thanks Bea. I'll be seeing you."

"Oh, Dr. Davis, one more thing. There's a message from Dr. Howard Kapinsky. He wants to know if he should start rounds without you. He says the team's been waiting for an hour."

CHAPTER 3

Detective Donald O'Malley steadied his elbows on the makeshift command post in the Central Park Zoo and peered through the high power binoculars for the tenth time in the last hour. He scanned the red brick facade of the Penguin Building, then focused on the doorway, watching for the slightest hint of movement. Nothing. Four hours broiling in the midday sun, breathing the stench of filthy animals, and not a goddamned thing.

The trumpeting of an elephant cut through the heavy air. The splash of a sea lion in the mammal pool nearby made him flinch. He felt like he was on a fucking safari, instead of a stakeout.

O'Malley lifted the binoculars from around his neck and resolutely placed them on top of the stand. He removed his dusty NYPD baseball cap, wiped the beads of sweat from his brow with his handkerchief. Reaching into his pants pocket, he removed what had been a large pack of Juicy Fruit and stuffed another stick of gum in his mouth—number ten to be exact—adding it to the wad that already produced a large bulge in his cheek. O'Malley's ritual. The binoculars, the cap, the Juicy Fruit. He had repeated it ten times in the last hour. It usually made him feel secure, in control, though the latter state had thus far eluded him today.

Donald O'Malley, decorated veteran of the NYPD and Commander of the City's Tactical Response Unit had been involved in scores of stakeouts before, but the waiting still drove him crazy.

Next week he would write his last chapter on the TRU after ten years as unit commander. Though he had a perfect record, it was time to hang it up. His ulcer and his wife, Stella, had convinced him of that. He wouldn't miss the waiting, that's for sure.

The TRU was ready to be handed over to a young buck like Valdez. For O'Malley, it was back to homicide. Not exactly what Stella had in mind, but she'd live with it as she had with his entire career. Some of his best years on the force had been on homicide, and he had decided that was where he would finish out. Three fucking years to go! He couldn't believe it.

"Get the full background check yet? We got a sheet on him?" asked O'Malley as he turned toward Lieutenant Valdez, who had just returned to the command post.

"Best we can tell, sir, he's clean. Nothing, not even a parking ticket. Married, five kids, goes to church on Sundays, worked in the Parks Department for fifteen years. Same place, right here in the Zoo. Personnel record's clean, too."

O'Malley shook his head in disbelief. "You mean this loony tune's been chugging along on the straight and narrow for the last forty-nine years of his life and all of a sudden he goes bananas?"

"That's right, sir."

"Doesn't make sense."

"No, it doesn't seem to, sir."

"Check the city hospital logs?"

"Yeah. No psych admissions. Hit by a car going home from work a few months ago. Spent a week in the intensive care unit at the Trauma Center, but I guess he came out okay."

"Except for his scrambled brains." O'Malley glanced at his watch. "When's his old lady getting here? It's already 1310."

"The guys at the service entrance are expecting her any minute."

What better way to smoke out a hot-headed, crazy man than to bring in his *esposa*. Get his emotions revved up, cloud his thinking, force him to make a careless move. The wife was O'Malley's catalyst.

"If she doesn't arrive soon, my men are in a good position to take him out—"

"Goddamnit, Valdez!" O'Malley crumbled up the wrapper from the last stick of Juicy Fruit and threw it to the ground. "When I'm ready to sacrifice that little girl, I'll know who to call! That lunatic has a grenade and is loco enough to blow up both himself and the girl. We have to let him think he's making the first move. Get it straight *now*, Valdez. Next week you're on your own!"

Although angry at Valdez' impatience, O'Malley had been in enough of these situations to sense there was a healthy tension building. Something would happen soon. The impasse was nearing an end.

"Commander O'Malley," crackled the voice over the walkie-talkie, "Señora Romero is at the gate."

"Well, Rispoli, roll out the red carpet." O'Malley replaced the radio in his holster. "Valdez, alert the sharpshooters. No one moves until I give the word." O'Malley watched the woman approach with her police escort.

"And, Valdez, get on the radio and tell the men to let her walk to us alone. We don't need to make Jesus any more paranoid than he already is."

"Yes, sir!"

O'Malley and the men of the TRU tracked Maria Romero as she turned right and passed between the weathered stone eagles on her way to the makeshift command post, which had been just four-and-a- half hours ago merely another hot dog stand at the zoo.

O'Malley knew the Romero woman was forty-eight, but she looked ten years older. Her bright yellow tent dress rippled with each step as she walked anxiously past the sea lion pool and headed toward them.

The shrill call of a macaw pierced the air.

Señora Romero was speaking in Spanish—a language O'Malley never quite grasped and therefore considered babble—rapidly and loudly. Her plump face was beaded with sweat, her hair flying wildly as she walked past them, not to them. She dropped to her knees in a position of prayer.

"Jesus, *mimosa*, what's gotten into you? Let the *pobrecita* go, please! Think of our own little Juanita!"

O'Malley was worried. His catalyst had turned out to be more of a runaway nuclear reaction. There would be a goddamn meltdown if they didn't control the situation now.

"Grab her, Valdez! Say something to her in Spanish and shut her up! She'll blow the whole thing open."

Even as she spoke, O'Malley knew it was too late. Jesus Romero had heard his wife's unexpected plea. How he'd react was anyone's guess. O'Malley had to make a move. His mind whirred into high gear as he grabbed the megaphone from Valdez.

"Jesus, your wife Maria is here. She wants to talk to you."
An eternal second passed.

"Man, you get that *cochina* out of here, or I blow myself up and take the girl with me! Time's running out, you know man? You got five minutes, then it's bye-bye!"

O'Malley heard Jessica's whimper echoing inside the Penguin Building. He'd never even seen the girl, but her pitiful cry triggered an emotional association in his brain and summoned deep feelings of sadness.

Filthy animal. Donald O'Malley, the ultimate professional, tried his best to suppress his simmering emotions. Donald O'Malley, the grandfather, unfortunately could not.

"Jesus, we've got the money, but you know we can't land a plane here."

"You just deliver what you said, man, or it's over. You got that?"

Maria broke loose and ran toward the Penguin Building, her fists stabbing the air in defiance. "You son-of-a-bitch, I'm no *cochina*!"

The men in black fatigues on the rooftops and behind the columns were ready, laser sights trained on the entryway to the building. *Goddamn meltdown*, thought O'Malley.

To everyone's astonishment, Jesus appeared in the doorway, his green Parks Department uniform hanging over his corpulent frame like a soggy sheet, drenched with the sweat of the oppressive New York summer and his raging emotions. His beefy arms were wrapped tightly around little Jessica. Between his hands he clasped the grenade. His dark brown eyes danced wildly.

"I told you to get the bitch away from here. Now! Or I pull the pin!"

Maria stopped dead in her tracks, barely ten feet from the doorway. "*Dios mio—*"

O'Malley saw an opening. "Take him. Now!"

The first shot came from the sharpshooter stationed on the roof of the restaurant. The bullet hit Jesus just above the right brow, blew out the back of his head and splattered bloody fragments of brain tissue on the stone facade of the building behind him.

It was the second shot, though, O'Malley would live to regret. Fired from the Tropic House walkway, the bullet pierced

Jesus' right hand, the index finger of which had been wrapped securely around the grenade pin. The fiery explosion propelled Jessica violently backward. Her head smacked against the brick column by the entrance. Jessica Humphries lay on the cement like a limp ragdoll.

***

The blue and white Airlift Northeast helicopter maneuvered between the trees and landed with a blast of wind on the slate walkway in front of the Penguin Building. Medic Enrique Santos was the first out of the chopper door, followed closely by Rosey Ceravolo. Rick Davidson, the pilot, remained in the cockpit.

Santos and Ceravolo raced up the walkway, Ceravolo dragging the stretcher behind her. Now ten minutes since the explosion, Jessica had been left untouched by the police. Feeling frustrated and impotent, they knew better than to move a patient with serious head and neck injuries. Jessica's head was cocked obliquely, resting in a pool of blood at the base of the column. Her extremities, no longer limp, had assumed a rigid, mannequin-like attitude, wrists and toes extended downward. Her skin was a pale, waxy yellow, her cheeks and lips drained of life-sustaining blood and oxygen.

The look of death. Santos had seen it all too many times before.

Her little chest heaved ever so slightly, but with great rapidity, as her brainstem automatically directed the muscles of respiration to suck every bit of precious air they could into her lungs. The two medics knelt on either side of Jessica and went to work.

"Pulse 130 and thready, blood pressure 60/palp," said Ceravolo as she released the Velcro on the undersized blood pressure cuff. "She must be hemorrhaging internally."

"Good bet she is, but that may be the least of her problems." Santos removed his flashlight from the red tackle box and gently pried her lids open. "Pupils are mid-dilated, barely reactive. Not a good sign. How are her breath sounds?"

"Okay on the right side, decreased on the left. She may have a collapsed lung. Could be from a rib fracture." Ceravolo examined the large bruise over the child's left rib cage.

"Large scalp laceration, but her skull seems all right," said Santos, carefully wrapping her head with gauze.

Ceravolo started a saline IV and ran it in as fast as it would drip. She got the neck brace and the backboard out of the chopper.

Gently, they lifted their fragile cargo into the compact, high-tech quarters of the helicopter. As the chopper began its ascent, Santos and Ceravolo applied the electrodes that would monitor all of Jessica's vital signs, including her heart rhythm. Rick momentarily glanced over his shoulder and signaled for them to put on their headsets. There was no other way to communicate easily over the thunderous noise of the helicopter.

"She gonna make it?" he asked.

"Too soon to tell, but her chances are better than they were ten minutes ago," Ceravolo said.

"Her vitals seem to be stabilizing," said Santos.

"Looks like you two have things under control. Don't you think it's time to call in? Wouldn't want to piss off the boss on a Sunday night," said Rick.

"Guess you're right. I'm sure he's going nuts waiting to hear from us. Patch us in. Tell him the radio was out for a while," said Ceravolo.

"You tell him. He's on the line now," said Rick. "Good luck."

"Shit," muttered the medics in unison.

"What the hell's been going on? How's the girl?" boomed the voice of Dr. George Spiros.

"Vitals weak but stable. Probable closed head injury, pupils five millimeters and sluggish. May have a collapsed lung and internal hemorrhaging. This *pobrecita* has had better days, Dr. Spiros," Santos said.

"Have you given her any dopamine?"

"No. Just normal saline, as much as her little vein can take. Her pulse is regular at 120, her BP 75 over 35. We're bagging her at 24 breaths per minute."

"Ceravolo, you there? I haven't heard from you today. How's the girl's cardiac rhythm?"

"A little fast, but regular."

"Sounds like we'll need the neurosurgeons as well as the general surgeons on this one. What about that crazy Parks Department guy? Anything left of him?"

"The coroner's picking up the pieces," Santos said.

"Can't say I'm upset about that. What's your ETA, Davidson?"

"Two minutes, sir."

"Good job. But call me sooner next time. See you at the landing pad in two."

"Roger."

They breathed a shared sigh of relief, and the helicopter thundered north, flying high above the once- majestic Hudson River.

Enrique Santos, seasoned medic, devout Catholic, and father of five, reached into his pocket, and clutched his rosary beads in one hand, caressed little Jessica's blood-stained, bandaged forehead with the other. *Dios mediante—God willing—you will make it, pobrecita.*

CHAPTER 4

"Nice job assisting in the OR, Karen," said Geoff. "You've really gotten your feet wet in a big way on the first day."

Geoff looked at his wrist, checked his watch. One-thirty p.m. So much for morning rounds. He inserted his ID card into the security panel outside the NSICU. A green "enter" sign illuminated, and with a whoosh, the doors parted.

"Thanks. I really like being in the OR, and it helps to have a good teacher."

Geoff and Karen entered what amounted to a decompression chamber, where white coats had to be removed and kelly green jumpsuits donned. They cleansed their hands with the disinfectant soap, then put on surgical gloves.

"Ready?" Geoff asked. The door opened and he stepped into the room, Karen following right behind him. The antiseptic aromas of iodine cleanser and surgical adhesive wafted their way, the distinctive scents reassuring, familiar, to Geoff.

"Well, Dr. Davis, I thought you'd never get here," said Cathy Johannsen, charge nurse of the day shift. Cathy was about thirty-eight, had long white hair pulled back in a pony tail, sparkling blue eyes and a fine, chiseled nose emphasizing her Scandinavian decent. She was a bit too big bottomed for Geoff's taste, though many of the male residents considered her a knockout.

"Cathy, with you in charge, I knew everything would be under control. All I have to do is sign the orders."

"I wish it were that simple," she said, "It's good to have you back, Geoff. I hear you had a long morning."

"A typical day at the Trauma Center. Good experience for Dr. Choy, here." He motioned to introduce Karen Choy. "Sorry. Let me introduce you two properly. Cathy Johannsen, Dr. Karen Choy, first year resident."

The two women shook hands. "Pleasure," said Cathy. "You're lucky. You have a great teacher."

Geoff smiled, cleared his throat. "Where's the team? We need to be briefed on recent admissions."

"Over by bed eighteen, the little girl with the head injury," she said, pointing to the opposite end of the ward.

Geoff looked around the room. It had been a long time. The scene was surreal, not unlike a modern version of Dr. Frankenstein's laboratory. There were rows of bodies, all ages, shapes, sizes and colors, in various states of consciousness. Most were comatose, having lost control of their bodily functions to machines—machines that did their breathing, filtered their blood, regulated their IV infusions, monitored their core temperature, pulse, and blood pressure. Other machines measured the pressure inside their skulls caused by brain swelling from injuries. Connecting these bodies to each of these machines were tangles of tubes, wires, bolts, and needles protruding from skulls and every natural and man-made orifice imaginable. All of the machines and monitors were linked by cables to a central computer at the nursing station staffed by a team of monitor technicians twenty-four hours a day. No bodily function escaped detection and control.

Except the brain. Brainwaves had been studied for years with the electroencephalogram, and changes in brain pressure could be followed with intracranial pressure monitors, but the physiology of consciousness had remained a great mystery. Until the

PET scan. Geoff and Karen drifted toward bed eighteen, where they joined up with the rest of the team.

"Ah, Geoffrey, my friend, good to see you back in the saddle," Kapinsky said. "We almost gave you both up for lost." He put his arm around Geoff's right shoulder.

Geoff stiffened, grabbed Kapinsky's arm and removed it from his shoulder. "Sore shoulder. Hurt it working out the other day."

"Sorry, chief. Hey, let me introduce you to your team."

Introductions were made all around, Geoff analyzing the new group of doctors he'd be responsible for. There were two first year residents: Karen Choy, whom he had already spent half the day with, and Brian Phelps, bearded, intense, humorless, and at thirty-two, older than usual for a first year neurosurgical resident.

Geoff acknowledged the two medical students assigned to the team. Both were women, wide-eyed, uninitiated to a brutal, clinical rotation like neurosurgery. Then there was the gnat, Howard Kapinsky. Short,with thinning, frizzy brown hair, mud brown eyes, a substantial nose, and his perennial, pencil-thin attempt at mustache. Kapinsky, the momma's boy from Sheepshead Bay.

The rift between Geoff and Kapinsky had developed over the years, Kapinsky envious of Geoff's strapping good looks, accomplishments and family background, Geoff disgusted with Kapinsky's servile behavior and endless brown-nosing.

Kapinsky had a photographic memory for minutia and could reference obscure journal articles and list differential diagnoses *ad nausea*. This behavior was nurtured by the system at an institution like the NYTC, but the bottom line was he was an horrendous surgeon, all thumbs in the operating room, even after six years of surgical training.

It wasn't as if Geoff hadn't tried to befriend him early on. Their first year working together Geoff had tried to loosen up

Kapinsky's tight-assed personality, taking him out on the town, to bars and nightclubs, even a foray to Geoff's favorite Times Square strip joint—The Palomino—a place that would rouse a hard-on even with a eunuch like Kapinsky. But to no avail. For a while, Geoff had wondered if Kapinsky was gay, but he finally wrote him off as just an asexual bookworm with a fudgy nose.

Mark Jackson, the only black in the program, joined them, having finished his note on the patient in bed seventeen. Mark had a sharp mind and excellent surgical skills. He exuded a quiet confidence, not unlike Geoff in the early years of his residency.

"Well, Mark, it doesn't look as though you got much sleep last night," Geoff said.

"Sleep? What's that? I spent yesterday afternoon in the OR with some poor junkie named Jose whose friend shot him in the face, last night with an unfortunate twenty-five year old hang-glider who got in the way of a telephone pole. This little girl with a head injury just came in. The good news is someone else is on call tonight."

"Tell us about the hang-glider first," said Geoff. He looked to his right, at the patient next door in bed seventeen. The man was tall, probably about six-two, muscular. A surgical dressing was wrapped around his ribs and upper torso. He had bruises around his eyes, and the lids were swollen shut. Sprouting from the top of his shaved head was a metal bolt with IV tubing connecting to a toaster-size box, on the front of which was a modulating digital readout. "By the looks of things, seems like he's going to be off to the ward pretty soon."

The team drifted next door and assembled around the hang-glider in bed seventeen. The medical students raised pens to clipboards, their attention focused on Mark Jackson.

"In a nutshell, John DeFranco is a twenty-five year old man

who was in his usual state of good health until yesterday afternoon when he was hang-gliding up in Westchester County and caught a bad wind that sent him crashing into a utility pole. He was taken to Basset Hospital, where he was stabilized, then transferred here for observation. On admission, he was noted to be in a moderately deep coma due to a closed head injury. Amazingly, there was no spinal fracture or any other life-threatening injuries. Just a few broken ribs and a ruptured spleen."

"What did his admission PET scan show?" asked Geoff.

"Moderate brain edema with a low level of endorphins in the brainstem." Mark pointed to the intracranial pressure monitor next to the head of the bed. "His ICP has been hovering around fifteen all morning. That's an improvement from yesterday. All in all, a decent prognosis," said Mark.

"Then why is he still comatose?" asked Karen Choy.

"We have him snowed in a medically induced coma on phenobarbital to lessen his brain cells' metabolic rate and need for oxygen. Once we drop the phenobarb level, he should wake up, hopefully by tomorrow." Mark grasped the metal bolt protruding from the top of the patient's head between his thumb and forefinger. "Then we can remove this ICP bolt and transfer him to the neuro ward where his rehabilitation can start."

"Good job, Mark," said Geoff. "Let's hear about the new patient in bed eighteen."

The team members regrouped around the little girl's bed, Mark holding the clipboard, Geoff standing next to him near the head of the bed.

"This one's not so rosy." Mark cleared his throat. "I'm sure we'll hear about this on the news tonight, if not sooner. Jessica Humphries, an eight-year-old girl, was in otherwise good health until she was taken hostage earlier today by a lunatic at the Central Park Zoo. He threatened to blow himself and the girl up. The grenade exploded ripping him to shreds—that's all that remained of the guy according to Suzanne Gibson in pathology—and throwing Jessica twenty feet in the air. Unfortunately, she landed on her head."

Geoff felt a pang of sadness. He studied the patient carefully. Her face was round and moon like, features swollen and distorted. Dark, bruised lids were taped tightly shut, and her lips were dry and cracked at the corners of her mouth where an airway tube had been taped to one side connecting her to the respirator that controlled her breathing. A patch of her fine, blood-crusted hair had been shaved on top for the ICP bolt, which had been inserted through the hole drilled in her skull, to monitor her intracranial pressure, as with the hang-glider in the next bed.

"What is the extent of her injuries?" asked Karen Choy.

"Her primary problem is the closed head injury," replied Jackson. "Pupils are mid-position, but sluggishly reactive, eye movements spontaneous. She responds to localized painful stimulation, and over the last few hours seems to be attempting to make some sounds—"

"Sounds? You must be exhausted Mark," interrupted Kapinsky, "this girl is deeply comatose."

"What's her coma scale rating, Mark?" asked Geoff. He fixed his gaze in Kapinsky's direction.

"Nine out of fifteen, consistent with moderate head injury."

"Hardly deep coma, Dr. Kapinsky," Geoff said. "How has her intracranial pressure been, Mark?"

The group's attention shifted to the ICP monitor and its ever-changing digital readout.

"Doing better now, twelve to thirteen. Was a bit high earlier. After some intravenous mannitol and hyperventilation, her ICP seems to have responded well. Brain swelling must be lessening."

"Any other significant injuries?" asked Brian Phelps, briefly lifting his head out of his three by five cards.

"Collapsed right lung. The chest tube was placed by the general surgeons in the ER, and the lung seems to be re-expanding slowly. I repaired her scalp laceration. Spleen's okay. No internal bleeding. A smattering of superficial shrapnel injuries, nothing too significant. Just the brain."

Just the brain, thought Geoff. A biochemical mass the size and weight of a cantaloupe, the essence of what makes us uniquely human, the seat of our intellect, creativity, and emotions. Containing ten billion nerve cells, its labyrinthine pattern of axonal wiring and peculiar chemical balance of neurotransmitter substances were what distinguished an Einstein from a simpleton, a man of sound mind from a psychopath.

"Does that imply that if her brain swelling dissipates, she will come out of her coma?" asked one of the medical students.

"You're assuming her nerve cells are only swollen, not permanently injured," blurted Kapinsky. "Only thirty-eight percent of patients with her type of injury have a good recovery. Thirty-two percent have a moderate to severe permanent neurological or psychological deficit. Twenty-five percent die in the hospital."

"Thank you, Professor Kapinsky," said Geoff, no longer able to conceal his annoyance. "How about the PET scan results, Mark?"

"Her admission scan revealed a grade two out of five level of beta-endorphin flooding her brain's receptors. Again, consistent with her coma, but with a fairly good prognosis."

"That is, if you buy that PET scan endorphin data," Kapinsky interrupted. "PET scanning is where CT scanning was thirty years ago—in its infancy with crude resolution and lacking standard means of interpretation. And endorphins, well, I don't see how you can make any reliable statement regarding their relation to brain functions, let alone any clinical prognostication. The data is shaky, all conjecture. The only truly predictive model is Bayesian statistical analysis, utilizing the Glasgow Coma Scale, and according to this patient's profile—"

"What do you know firsthand about PET scanning or endorphins?" Geoff tried to contain his rising anger. "I spent last year studying endorphin patterns in the brains of head injury patients using the PET scan. There is an excellent correlation between endorphin levels in the brain and coma prognosis. Dr. Kapinsky, one day you'll learn all truth does not come neatly packaged in formulas."

The medical students ducked behind the safety of their clipboards to avoid the verbal crossfire.

Kapinsky smacked his lips. "Why do runners all have this irrational, almost fanatic belief in the power of endorphins to control every aspect of the human mind? I can buy the claim they're natural, morphine-like endogenous analgesics, but when you start telling me, without citing any data from controlled studies, that these compounds are responsible for everything from the anesthetic effects of acupuncture to the runner's high in trained athletes and paranoid delusions in schizophrenics, well I think it's a bunch of bullshit! I'm surprised as a physician and scientist you can accept such conjecture."

After six years of almost constant conflict, Kapinsky knew precisely how to push Geoff's buttons. What Geoff could never understand was what pleasure it gave him, except to compensate for Kapinsky's feelings of inadequacy. To respond at this point would only escalate Kapinsky's warped need for conflict, make rounds ever more counter-productive. "I'll be more than happy to share my research data with you at another time, Kapinsky, but we have rounds to conduct."

Beads of sweat dotted Kapinsky's whitened upper lip. His jaw was clenched, his face gnarled in frustration.

Geoff turned his attention back to Mark Jackson. "Let's talk about your treatment plan."

"Sure. With her vital signs stable, I think we should concentrate our efforts at further resuscitation of her brain—"

Cathy Johannsen arrived from the nursing station and interrupted their discussion. "Geoff, Dr. Pederson's secretary just called. She wanted to remind you about the three o'clock meeting in his office."

"I thought it was four. Is she still on the phone?"

"No. She said she sent you an e-mail about it. She just wanted to remind you to be on time."

"E-mail messages. God knows how many I have stacked up." He looked up at the clock on the wall. "It's two-thirty, and I haven't even signed onto the system yet. Is the terminal in the staff room free?"

"I think so."

Geoff looked over at Mark Jackson, waiting to discuss his treatment plan on the girl. "Mark, why don't you and Kapinsky finish leading rounds. I've got to check my messages before the meeting with Pederson."

"No problem."

Geoff followed Cathy back to the nursing station and sat down at the vacant computer terminal. He enjoyed playing with computers, though he was hardly an expert. Nothing like his computer geek kid brother, Stefan. The extensive computerization at the Trauma Center dazzled Geoff. Even Stefan thought it impressive.

Geoff booted the computer, signed on, and entered his password.

Hello, Dr. Geoffrey Davis. Welcome to the Traumanet System.

You have three new e-mail messages. Would you like to view them?

Geoff manipulated the mouse and clicked on the e-mail icon.

MESSAGE #1 DATE: JULY 1, 2010 TIME: 0721

FROM: Alpha Micronet.org/syssad

Received: NYTC.org, 1 July 2010 0718.

MESSAGE: Hey bro. Good luck today. I know you'll do a great job, as always! Stefan.

P.S.- How about dinner tonight?

Geoff smiled, appreciated the irony of Stefan's message. His kid brother urging him on, the way Geoff had always been there for Stefan. He clicked on "Reply" and entered his response:

Thanks. I'll call you later. Geoff.

Geoff clicked on message number two.

MESSAGE #2 DATE: JULY 1, 2010 TIME: 0900

FROM: L. EVERS; NYTC-A1/NSGLEE

MESSAGE: Dr. Pederson would like to see you today at three p.m. in his office for chief residency orientation meeting. Please be prompt. The doctor does not like to be kept waiting.

Thank you.

Geoff smiled, shook his head. It was probably going to be the same pep talk Pederson gave the last seventeen chief residents. He clicked on the third message.

MESSAGE #3 DATE: JULY 1, 2010 TIME: 1037

FROM: Received by: Mercury, NYTC.org, 1 July 2010, 10:36; received: gopher/nih.gov, 1 July 2010, 10:33; received: relnet/ info.umd.edu, 1 July 2010, 10:30; received: telnet/nasa.gov, 1 July 2010, 10:21; received: ber2759.USDA.gov, 1 July 2010, 10:17; received: cobalt, telnet/locis.loc.gov, 1

July 2010, 10:15.

MESSAGE: *Keep your eyes open. Nothing is as it appears. Proteus.*

Geoff stared at the cryptic message. What the hell did that mean? He noted the time it was sent: 10:15 a.m. He had been in the OR. Proteus. Obviously a code name. Geoff examined the extensive path the message had taken. It was from somewhere outside the medical center. The message must have been an error or simply meant for someone else.

Geoff clicked on the "Help" option of the e-mail screen then entered the Traumanet address book just for the hell of it and clicked on "search for sender address." The search came up empty. The Traumanet address book didn't include Internet addresses.

"Everything okay?" Cathy Johannsen asked.

Geoff continued staring at the cryptic message on the screen. "Yeah, fine. Just got someone else's e-mail. It's not the first time."

Geoff moved the mouse and deleted the first two messages.

CHAPTER 5

R. Phillip Lancaster sat in the rear of his black limousine gazing out the window, his mind lost in thought. He hated Washington in the summertime—the oppressive heat and humidity—and this was the most blistering summer of the last decade.

Worse yet, it was next to impossible to accomplish anything of substance during the summer months. Key staffers as well as elected officials on the Hill often took their vacations in July, and when they weren't physically away, their minds were elsewhere, wilting in the heat or wishing they were playing somewhere, anywhere but here. Even the President, a man he had known since their college days at Yale, with whom he shared a reasonably close, but necessarily guarded friendship, seemed less interested in what Lancaster felt were important matters of national security and more interested in going fishing. Might as well close down the shop and hang up a sign: "Sorry, closed 'til after Labor Day."

Frustrating indeed for Lancaster, paragon career intelligence officer, a role he had played for over thirty years, a role that had augmented his value throughout numerous administrations of both political parties but limited his ascendance as well.

With last year's election of his long time associate William Cabot to the White House, Lancaster had made the erroneous and atypically naive assumption that friendship would transcend politics and he would be at the helm at Central Intelligence. He felt it, visualized it, tasted it. Political debts intervened, and he was passed over for an inexperienced dolt, Dick Bennington, the President's former campaign chairman.

Cabot appointed Lancaster Deputy Director for Science and Technology, but Lancaster wasn't ready to throw in the towel just yet. His years of training had taught him there was a solution for every seemingly no-win situation. He was resourceful and willing to adjust rules if need be.

Sixty- two years old, tall, but by no means willowy, his silver, perfectly coiffured hair and aquiline profile telegraphed his blue-blood Bostonian roots. Lips taut, cleft chin resting on his fist, Lancaster peered through the limousine window down the tree-lined street of Alexandria, Virginia. Today, while the rest of Washington was on vacation, R. Phillip Lancaster worked to solve his no-win scenario.

"Sir, you did say 761, didn't you?" asked Frank Leber, Lancaster's bodyguard and personal chauffeur.

"What's that, Frank? Yes, 761. You remember which house that is, don't you?"

"Yes, sir, Mr. Lancaster. The brick colonial with the white columns, second from the end on Pendleton Street. The same house where the Russian Federal Security Service officer—Solenko was his name, I believe—was debriefed last year."

"Your memory constantly amazes me, Frank, though he was a member of military intelligence—not FSS. That defection was quite a coup for our CIA Special Op boys—" Lancaster caught himself mid-sentence, wondering whether Frank Leber really needed to know so much. One slip of the tongue could blow open the entire project. Lancaster was close to his rightful position, the one he was destined to fulfill. He would guard his bits of knowledge like precious gems.

The limousine turned the corner and paused briefly at the outer gate to the residence, a pause long enough for the young marine guard to recognize the occupant of the back seat and wave the car through. Already parked in the circular drive of the sterile house on Pendleton Street were two generic government vehicles, blue Ford Explorers, standard issue of the federal government that year. Background on the streets of Washington with thousands of similar vehicles on the road at any one time. Contrary to common belief, not all upper level bureaucrats were chauffeured in stretch limos, a trapping of office the patrician deputy director demanded at all times.

Lancaster stepped from the car and bounded up the red brick path, Leber carrying his briefcase, and as always one step ahead, to the rear entrance of the old colonial. Lancaster adjusted his striped tie, pulled down his heavily starched white sleeves from inside his suit jacket. He entered the vestibule of the elegant structure and greeted the guard posted at the doorway. Lancaster and Frank exchanged a glance and a nod, the silent command, wait here until I finish. Lancaster grabbed his briefcase and crossed the main hallway to the meeting room. Sunlight streamed through the large stained glass window at the end of the corridor, projecting an iridescent kaleidoscope on the dark parquet floor beneath his feet. Resolutely, he entered the study.

"Hell of a spy, Phil," blurted Joe Franklin, Deputy Director for Operations at the CIA, still staring out the window at the parked limo resting like a beached whale on the circular drive. "Remind me never to offer you a job in Ops."

Lancaster despised being called Phil, a salutation used only by Joe and the President. He indulged Cabot by nature of their longstanding friendship and, more importantly, his position, but with no one else did he comfortably allow such a breach of familiarity, particularly with Joe Franklin, whom he considered a somewhat vulgar, though deceptively brilliant, tactician. Unfortunately, Franklin was a necessary ally, and the plan was all that truly mattered. With pursed lips and great restraint, Lancaster let it go. "Glad you could make it on such short notice, Joe." He extended his hand. Always the diplomat. "Did the boss question where you were going?"

"He's outta town at the moment. I'm covered, don't worry about me. I drove myself here, let my driver have a couple of hours off to take care of paperwork, errands, all that. No one asked any questions." Joe Franklin paused awaiting a response that never came. "This place brings back such warm memories. Ironic, isn't it?"

"How's that?" Lancaster asked with a hint of impatience.

"Remember 1962, the Company retreat for the Technical Services Staff? This was the place, wasn't it?"

Lancaster shifted uncomfortably in his chair. "We were young and inexperienced then. I'm the first to acknowledge my mistakes."

"Damn costly one, Phil," Joe Franklin said, his thin lips forming a sneering grin. "Almost got you canned."

Lancaster's spine stiffened. He turned to the third member of the camarilla. Lancaster flashed a smile and offered a firm handshake to General Robert "Bulldog" Townsend, Deputy Director for National Intelligence. "Good to see you, General."

Fifty-eight and a decorated veteran of G2—Army Intelligence—the nickname could not have caricatured the closely shorn, heavily jowled general any more precisely.

"What's going on, Phillip?" Townsend asked in his usual cut-through-the-bullshit style. "We weren't supposed to meet until next month, then I get this coded message via courier to meet you here in broad daylight, no less risking the entire project and my ass!"

Lancaster set his stainless steel briefcase down on the mahogany and leather desk, and using his personal electronic code, unlocked it. He removed three identical folders, each sealed with red tape and stamped, "Top Secret: Eyes Only," with a Greek upper case sigma underneath. He handed each man his copy, cleared his throat.

"Gentlemen, a certain urgency has forced me to call this meeting sooner than we had planned. We're in a code yellow situation." Lancaster paused, more for dramatic effect than from a loss of words. "There's been a breach of security. I have reason to believe the project has been infiltrated by the Inspector General's Office."

The words fell like laser-guided bombs, the ramifications of the potentially devastating information clear to the conspirators.

"Do we know who the agent is?" asked Franklin. "I can take care of that."

"We have our suspicions, but nothing concrete yet," Lancaster said.

"How about the Boss? Does Bennington know about the Project?" asked General Townsend, his eyes fearful.

"If he does, so does the President, and if he knew, we'd be history, especially with the goddamn lawyers running the country these days."

"I thought *the man* was a good friend of yours, Phil?" prodded Franklin.

"He was," Lancaster said. His voice was bitter.

"Is Papa Bear safe?" asked Townsend.

"He is, for now."

"How's he taking it?" asked Townsend.

"Okay, but with him, you never know. We need to watch him very carefully."

"So, what's the containment plan?" Franklin asked, impatiently chewing on the stem of his pipe.

Lancaster stared at each of the two men in turn, his lips forming a steely smile. "Open your files and read, gentlemen. We've waited too long to allow this project to fail again."

Franklin glanced at the first page of the document and flashed a grin back at Lancaster. "I hate to admit it, but you'll make a great director, Phil."

CHAPTER 6

"Doctor Pederson has been expecting you, Doctor Davis," said Lynn Evers as she peered at Geoff over the top of her reading glasses. "You know how much Dr. Pederson dislikes waiting."

Geoff glanced at his watch. Two fifty-nine p.m. Good thing he was early.

Every department chairman had his enforcer, his hit man, or woman—usually it was a woman. Of late middle age, moderately overweight, humorless, Lynn Evers epitomized the role. The Terminator, the residents called her. She either loved you, which was rare, or hated you, and while she couldn't directly affect your career, she could make life over a seven-year period pretty damn miserable. Somehow, Geoff had managed to sneak up on her good side, which was to say she acted resoundingly neutral toward him. Good thing. The past several years had been miserable enough.

Geoff answered with a smile and a nod, quashing a stinging retort. Mrs. Evers reached over to the phone panel with her right hand, depressed the intercom. "Dr. Pederson, Dr. Davis has finally arrived," she said in a tone loud enough to be heard through Pederson's office door and probably down the hall as well. A forced smile. "You may go in now."

Geoff thanked Evers politely, brushed quickly past her desk, and knocked softly on the dark-paneled door.

"Come in," replied the familiar baritone voice, muffled by the door. Geoff entered the inner sanctum, treading lightly as he always did with "the Colonel" in the intimidating surroundings of what the residents referred to as "headquarters."

Richard Pederson was an imposing man. In many ways, he reminded Geoff of his commanding officer in the navy. Tall and lanky, with thinning, reddish-brown hair strategically combed to camouflage his baldness, his large hands and long, thin fingers seemed made for gripping a basketball as much as a surgical instrument. Indeed, he had played college ball for a while, a fact he freely share with the residents when in a particularly chummy spirit, which occurred twice a year—at the departmental Christmas party and at the annual reception he hosted at his home for the new residents.

Pederson had a tremendous need to exercise control over himself and those around him. This was exemplified by his annoying habit of strategically dropping his voice so that he could barely be heard, forcing the listener to strain to hear exactly what he was saying.

Exceedingly formal, Pederson vented his perpetually bridled carnal desires by telling lewd jokes, though never in the presence of female residents. His equally stilted wife, Corinne, the only daughter of a Presbyterian Minister, played the role of officer's wife as closely to the script as humanly possible, the only apparent paradox being her spirited interest in her husband's base jokes. Two seeming Puritans in public, every resident that passed through over the years was convinced it was all leather, whips, and chains behind closed doors. Even if it wasn't true, the notion made Pederson seem at least somewhat human.

At sixty-two, Pederson had been Chairman of the Department of Neurosurgery for eighteen years, having been named to the position at forty, then the youngest department chairman in the country in his field of specialty. A brilliant clinician, superb surgeon, and equally keen politician, he had honed his skills in the Army Medical Corps during the first Gulf War, attaining the rank of Colonel after only four years. He had come to NYTC—then the old City Hospital—from the Massachusetts General Hospital and immediately established himself as a force to be reckoned with at the medical center as well as on a national level.

Surgically, he had pioneered a new laser treatment for epilepsy, which complemented the powerful information provided by Balassi's PET scanner. The two had begun collaboration on the epilepsy project while Balassi was at the NIH. They had revolutionized the surgical treatment of seizures.

Pederson's political acumen was neatly documented on office walls replete with meticulously oak-framed certificates, diplomas and all the right photos with civilian and military VIP's shaking hands and smiling.

Seated in a high-back, swivel chair, reading glasses resting half-way down his long nose, Pederson's profile was silhouetted by hazy sunlight diffusing through the large window that overlooked the GW Bridge. He appeared thoroughly absorbed studying a PET scan on the light box above his side table when Geoff entered the room. Geoff approached the desk and stood for what seemed like minutes.

"Welcome, Geoff," Pederson said. He stood reluctantly and turned his attention away from the scan. "Didn't mean to ignore you there—just a fascinating and most significant scan." Pederson extended his large hand. "I'm sure you've been dreaming about this day for seven years. I know I did when I was a resident. Come, sit down." He gestured toward the wingback chair opposite the desk.

Geoff sat down, his posture held erect by the vertical incline of the chair's back. The room smelled of polished leather. Geoff was reminded of the time in high school he'd been called to the principal's office to receive a commendation but had assumed he was being summoned to answer for an offense he couldn't remember.

"Thank you, Dr. Pederson, but I must admit I'm a bit anxious." At that moment, the strange e-mail message played across Geoff's mind. Obviously not to be so readily dismissed as he had thought.

"Well, I can certainly appreciate that, Geoff," replied Pederson quite matter-of-factly. "But you have nothing to be anxious about. Your selection as chief resident was unanimous among department members. Your record at Harvard and during your residency here is beyond reproach, your surgical skills far beyond your years. Equally as important for this position—and I think you know this—you have a leadership quality, an innate gift few men have, fewer still in medicine. Whether or not you realize it, you are a future leader should you decide to stay in academic medicine. I hope you will."

Pederson swiveled in his chair and gazed at the slightly yellowed, black and white photo of his own residency class, his full lips and hooded upper lids forming an ever-so-slight, nostalgic smile. "You remind me of myself at your age, Geoff. Top of my class, called upon by the great Dr. Bedrossian, then Chairman at the MGH, to do the same honor as yourself. I was terrified! It wasn't until I was about halfway through my chief residency that I realized my worth. You will feel the same shift, though I don't think it will take you as long."

Geoff was taken aback by the flood of compliments. Pederson was a man who rarely let you know where you stood. When he did offer praise, it was usually gilded with sarcasm. Geoff was glimpsing an entirely different side of "the Colonel," and he felt privileged.

Had Pederson forgiven the events of the last year so quickly, so easily? Geoff had to know, clear the air at the start. "I appreciate your confidence, sir, but my performance at the end of my last clinical year was far from stellar."

"Geoffrey, Geoffrey," Pederson said, his towering frame leaning forward over the desk. "I haven't forgotten. We all go through major crises in our lives, emotional traumas so great we feel as if we can't go on. The death of a loved one is the most traumatic of human experiences. Believe me, I know."

Another glimpse beneath the armor. Pederson was human after all.

"The bottom line is, it's over. Your life is back on track. Balassi tells me you did a superb job in the lab, and now you're back in the saddle. Let's forget the past and look to the future, which seems bright indeed."

Geoff's anxiety melted away, leaving him with a peace he had not felt in a long time. He began to feel excited about work, something he had not experienced since his early days as a resident. "Thank you, Dr. Pederson."

Pederson stood up and removed a large three-ring binder from the top shelf of his mahogany bookcase. On the side was printed, "Manual of the Chief Resident of the Department of Neurosurgery," and on the front the seal of the NYTC, a melding of both the new and the old: the ancient caduceus—serpents intertwined around a staff—a picture of the new medical center, and an inscription from the old one: "For of the Most High Cometh Healing."

He handed the notebook to Geoff, the baton passed from mentor to apprentice, the same ritual repeated each of the last eighteen years. "Everything you need to know as chief is in this manual. Read it completely. I know you will do a fine job. Any questions?"

Geoff's mind was clear, his attention focused. He felt relieved of the burden of the past, encouraged by his prospects. He felt he might as well start clean right now, get it all off his chest. "Not a question, but something you need to know from me before you hear it from someone else."

"Oh?" said Pederson, his right brow elevated, his curiosity aroused. Obviously, he hadn't heard yet.

"It's Howard Kapinsky, sir. I'm not sure how it's going to work out. We've had trouble working together in the past, and my year off doesn't seem to have changed anything. Now I'm his boss, and I'm sure that bothers him even more."

Pederson chuckled. "I wouldn't lose any sleep over the situation, though I must admit you're going to have your hands full reigning in Howard Kapinsky over the next year. He's a smart boy, but he's different."

Different? Geoff couldn't understand why Pederson had let the fool into the residency, nor why he didn't have the guts to let him go. "That's for sure. I'll do my best to keep him out of trouble."

"If anyone can do it, you can. Kapinsky respects you a great deal."

Geoff did his best to contain his incredulity, but knew his facial expression betrayed him. "Your confidence is appreciated." Pederson failed to detect his reaction. Something else was occupying his thoughts.

"Enough on that subject," Pederson said. He gazed through his large window into the distance, his weighty hands in the pockets of his heavily starched white coat. "There is another, more important, matter you need to be made aware of—your first official duty as Chief Resident."

Pederson returned to his desk chair, sat down, and removed his reading glasses. His voice dropped, barely a whisper, forcing Geoff to strain forward. "Next Monday we will be hosting an international delegation of scientists from PETronics Corporation's headquarters in Copenhagen lead by Dr. Yuri Zelenkov. Dr. Zelenkov and his party will be spending the week here as our guests, learning firsthand the intricacies of our PET scanning program and observing in the operating room."

"Do you know Dr. Zelenkov personally?"

"Yes, quite well, but I'd like him to get to know you, and you, him. I think you'll find it a rather rewarding experience. There might even be a free trip to PETronics Headquarters in Copenhagen if you play your cards right."

Geoff was perplexed. He hadn't ever heard of Zelenkov before.

"Next to Balassi and his technician," Pederson continued, "you know as much or more about the clinical applications of PET scanning than anyone else in this medical center. I want you to share freely whatever knowledge you have with Dr. Zelenkov and his group. By the time he leaves, he needs to feel completely comfortable with our program, particularly its applications in the diagnosis and surgical treatment of seizures. That's his area of special interest."

Pederson paused, as if sensing Geoff's hesitance. He leaned forward in his chair, his voice rising just enough for Geoff to hear without straining. "Geoff, I know you feel your clinical duties are far more important, that you might view this as simply an administrative pain in the rear, but this is a potentially monumental visit for our Medical Center. I needn't remind you of the important role PETronics has played at the NYTC. If it weren't for their generosity, we wouldn't be here."

"Yes, sir," Geoff replied. Pederson never offered choices.

"Good," Pederson said. He stood abruptly, a broad, deep grin on his face. He patted Geoff's still-sore shoulder. "Then get back to work. Keep your nose to the grindstone this year, and your future will be golden."

CHAPTER 7

Geoff completed evening rounds in the NSICU with great swiftness, delegating most of the basic patient management work to Karen Choy and Brian Phelps, who in turn delegated the scut work to their assigned medical students.

Happily, Kapinsky was out of the way, working up a patient in the ER, his assigned med student in tow. Geoff sat in the staff workroom of the NSICU, staring at the patients' lab values on the computer screen. He removed the three by five cards he kept on each patient from the breast pocket of his white coat and studied them one last time, checking to see if he had missed anything. He hadn't. He glanced at his watch. Six-thirty.

The e-mail message still gnawed at him. He knew it was probably just a crank or misdirected, but it bugged him. When he had time, he'd try and track down the sender. If he couldn't figure it out, he was sure his brother Stefan could. Geoff had promised Stefan he'd come over for dinner.

"Geoff, I think we're okay here if you want to go home," Karen Choy said. "I'm on call tonight anyway. My hot date is right here in the ICU."

"Sure you're okay?"

"Everything's under control. Smithers 'and little Jessica's vitals have stabilized. Their brain stems are on autopilot. DeFranco's coming out of his phenobarbital coma and the nurses are getting ready to ship him off to the ward. There's nothing for me to do but babysit tonight."

"Guess you're right," Geoff replied. He stood up and walked to the door. "If you run into any problems—"

"I have your cell phone number. Just don't turn it off," Karen replied. She smiled.

"Thanks, Karen." Geoff turned to leave, then paused. "Good job today. See you in the morning." Geoff grabbed his backpack and headed for the elevator. He left the hospital through the main entrance, avoiding the ER. It was never wise to leave through the ER when your goal was to get home. After this morning's eventful sprint to the Trauma Center, he decided to take the subway instead of walk the fifteen blocks as he usually did.

The sultry, summer night smacked him in the face like a wave of steaming, stagnant water as he left the controlled environment of the medical center and descended the marble steps onto Broadway. New York in the summer was New York at its worst. People, from local shopkeepers and apartment supers to gangs of teenagers, escaped the sweltering confines of their homes, apartments, and stores and simply hung out—on the stoops of their buildings, out their windows and doors, on street corners. People hanging out meant more boozing on the sidewalks, more noise, and when the thermometer rose high enough and tempers flared, more crime. The worst of New York magnified by a factor of ten.

Geoff entered the 168th Street subway station doing his best to avoid the scraggly panhandler who stood by the entrance to the station. The fetid smell of rotting refuse nearly overwhelmed Geoff. He descended the stairs, passing beneath an overhang splattered with posters, and whisked down the long, dimly lit corridor that lead to the IRT elevator.

The subway, New York's netherworld. Eight hundred miles of tracks spanned five boroughs, served twelve million people. A city within a city with its own unique sub-culture and population. Street people, like the tattered panhandler, lived in the subways all year round. For a buck, the subway delivered you from one end of Manhattan to the other, or if you were in the wrong place at the wrong time, swallowed you up like an insect in a Venus fly trap.

The faint but distinctive and pungent aroma of marijuana hung like a cloud in the air about mid-corridor, then it was over-powered by an acrid mixture of cheap whiskey and vomitus. Geoff's nostrils flared at the assault on his senses. The floor was littered with evidence of last night's events: an empty bottle of Thunderbird wrapped in a well-worn brown paper bag lay on the floor by the elevator door, next to it a used condom, a crumpled *Penthouse* centerfold, a half-eaten bag of Cheetos.

Geoff scanned the area. No one lingered behind the riveted steel columns or in the dark, shadowed corners of the corridor— at least no one he could see. His hand reached up to press the IRT elevator button, then he paused.

A crunching sound. Movement off to his right. Geoff's adren-alin surged, and he spun in the direction of the sound, reached down for his knife. He knew he was as prepared as possible for whatever was coming his way. He was as skilled in hand-to-hand combat as anyone around.

Only no one was there.

His gaze was caught by the bag of Cheetos, by its movement. Geoff gave a swift kick at the bag with his right foot, and a huge grey rat squealed in pain and scurried off to some dark crevice by the stairs.

"Fucking rats," he muttered aloud. He wiped the sweat off his brow with the back of his hand and exhaled. He shook his head from side to side and began to laugh. "Fucking rats in the god-damn fucking subway!"

"What'd ja expect to see down here, buddy? Cuddly little guinea pigs?" boomed a voice from behind Geoff.

Geoff turned around swiftly to see the reassuring, bulky form of a New York Transit cop.

"Never seen a rat that big," Geoff said. "It looked more like a raccoon."

"Then you ain't been in the subways much," said the officer, whose name tag read *Dumbrowski*. He raised his left brow, twirled his nightstick. "Where you from, Vermont or somethin'?"

"No. Connecticut. Been living in New York for the last seven years, though. I just stay out of the subways when I can." Geoff stared at the cop's deft handling of the stick, the large revolver strapped to his waist. A New York cowboy. A New York ranger riding the rails.

"And you ain't seen rats before?"

"Just in the lab," Geoff said with some embarrassment.

The officer guffawed, his protuberant, middle-aged gut twitching. He raised his heavily equipped belt over his jutting abdomen, let it slide back down to its natural resting place. He paused and looked down, then glanced thoughtfully towards Geoff.

"Well, let me give you some free advice. Dumbrowski's rules of riding the subway. Rule number one: don't make no eye contact. Rule number two: go about your business as quickly as possible. Rule number three: don't take the IRT elevator. It's the most dangerous ride in the whole goddamn city this side of the Port Authority. Patrolman Dumbrowski here's been around this jungle and survived. I seen things down here you'd never imagine. Stick to Dumbrowski's rules, you should make out okay."

"Thanks for the advice."

"So where you goin'?"

"Uptown, 181st Street."

"Well, good thing you ran into old Dumbrowski here then, cause you'd be taking this dangerous ride for nothin' and end up in Fort Apache." Dumbrowski smiled widely, clicking his gum. He patted Geoff on the shoulder—the good one—with his bulky hand. "IND's over that way, down those stairs." Dumbrowski pointed his stick down the corridor to the left.

"Thanks."

"Dumbrowski. Joe Dumbrowski. Friends call me the Brow. Sure beats the first part of my name, huh?" he said with a chuckle. He slid his nightstick back in its holster. "Don't forget the rules, now. This world down here ain't forgivin' to foreigners."

Geoff nodded, checked his watch as Dumbrowski walked away, then heard a thunderous rumble in the distance. The floor began to shake. A train was arriving down below on the IND platform. Geoff broke into a trot and along with a handful of people who came seemingly from nowhere, headed to the uptown platform. He descended the stairs quickly. Just as his foot touched the platform, the shrill honk of the train sounded and its twin beacons emerged from the murky depths of the tunnel. The long graffiti-smeared train screeched to a halt and opened its doors, allowing passengers to exit.

Instinctively, Geoff looked up at the sign on the side of the train to make sure it was the "A" train, though he didn't need to check since no other subway line ran this far north. He entered the second car.

Geoff had his own "rules of the rails," born of his generally cautious nature. He made it a practice never to get into the first car, since he'd surely be crushed to death if there was a collision, or the end car, since that was the least occupied and presumably the most dangerous. This strategy had worked well for him over the last seven years. In spite of the considerable amount of crime in the subways, not only had he never been accosted, he had never even witnessed a serious incident.

Geoff sat down on one of the long benches just inside the doorway. The car was about half full, mostly people on their way home from work downtown. The neighborhood north of Washington Heights, known as Fort Tryon Park, remained a fairly stable enclave for elderly German Jews as well as those of the Hasidic sect, an ultra-religious group of Eastern European descent whose literal interpretation of the scriptures often put them at odds with the rest of Judaism.

A young, heavily-bearded man with a pasty complexion, wearing a wide-brimmed black hat, a white shirt, the tails of which hung below the border of his drab, black jacket, flew through the doors, large briefcase in hand and horn-rimmed glasses ajar, narrowly escaping the capture of his shirt tails in the double-doors as they slammed shut. The man took a deep breath, adjusted his glasses, and sat down with a loud thud next to Geoff.

"Almost got me that time," he said with a sigh as he wiped his sweat-beaded brow.

Geoff smiled and nodded. The last thing he ever did in the subway was strike up a conversation. Not that he felt threatened by the man in any way, but conversations attracted attention, and that was not what you wanted to do in the subway, unless of course you were looking for trouble.

Across from Geoff was seated an elderly Italian woman, black kerchief on her head. Protruding out of a Macy's shopping bag at her feet was a copy of the evening's *New York Post* with its usual sensational headline: "Central Park Psycho Explodes." The caption underneath read, "Girl Hostage Clings to Life," and was followed by a large, somewhat grainy picture of a man.

It was not the headline so much as the picture that attracted

Geoff's attention. It was obviously an old photo taken in happier times. The man was tall, big-boned, easily six feet plus. He wore a kelly green Parks Department uniform and stood holding a rake in front of the Tropic House at the Central Park Zoo. His dark-skinned face was plump, somewhat pockmarked, and it bore a spirited, broad smile. Hardly the look of a psychopathic killer.

Geoff knew that man. He could not remember the details, nor the man's name. Geoff was poor with names, but his visual memory was excellent, bordering on photographic. He'd remember soon enough. The specifics about the face would abruptly interrupt whatever else he was thinking about like a flashing neon sign. Simpler yet, he'd grab a copy of the paper on the way out of the station and find out who the man was.

The train pulled away from the station with a great lurch and accelerated, its jerky movements causing the heads of the passengers to sway back and forth like erratic metronomes. The rhythmic chugging of the steel wheels on the ancient tracks created an almost hypnotic beat and set Geoff's mind wandering. His thoughts raced through the day's events, a veritable kaleidoscope of visual images. He thought of Jessica clinging to life, tubes extruding from every orifice, a bolt sprouting from the top of her head. All because she had convinced her grandmother to take her to the Zoo that day. All because some lunatic, some lunatic Geoff knew, snapped and went into a murderous frenzy the instant their paths crossed.

Geoff's mind drifted to bittersweet thoughts of Sarah. She had kept him emotionally honest all the years they were together, in touch with his human side. Geoff had felt torn between his real desire to help people and the analytical approach to disease he was taught in med school and residency, patients readily sorted into lists of differential diagnoses, operative procedures. The gall bladder in bed one, the brain tumor in the ICU. A faceless ward of patients, their lives layed out on three by five cards. Geoff worried that without Sarah, he was becoming the prototypical surgeon, becoming cold and clinical like his father had been.

Geoff met Sarah at Harvard, at a Christmas party, their junior year. Geoff was attracted to her at first glance. Tall, about five-ten, with smooth, olive complexion, Sarah's golden blonde hair was tied back in a French knot. She wore a strapless, black and teal dress that accentuated her broad shoulders, curvaceous bust and long, slender back. She carried herself with confidence. Sarah's physical attributes aside, the beauty of her personality was what finally most attracted Geoff. She was bright, caring, sensitive, down to earth. And unlike Geoff, spontaneous. Life with Sarah had been intimate and exciting. They moved in together their senior year, stayed in Boston to attend their respective graduate schools, their relationship stronger for having survived the rigors of medical and law school.

Sarah chose to become a public defender right out of Harvard Law and was assigned to the Superior Court in lower Manhattan. Highly principled, a champion of social causes, she was some-what left of center politically. She challenged Geoff to remain in touch with his patients as people first, forced him to pause and reflect when he became detached.

He thought back to one particularly stressful time, an ER rotation at the end of Geoff's first year at the NYTC. She'd pulled him out of the ER, away from the house staff lounge—fortunately Dr. Spiros wasn't around—dragged him home for a candlelight dinner, made him watch a film, "The Doctor," then, her lips soft and sensuous, the warm glow behind her hazel eyes, ripped off his scrubs and made passionate love to him on the living room couch. Sarah had always known, better than he, just when he needed her most. Their life together seemed like a dream to him now, a mirage evaporated into thin, desert air.

"Lousy *shvartze!*"

Without warning, Geoff was yanked from his sweet daydream back to the grimy, cacophonous reality around him. A black teenager, boom box resting on his shoulder, untied Air Jordan's on his feet, had just entered the subway car through the end door and turned up the volume. He danced around the car to the rap tune, timing his pirouettes to jive with the haphazard jolts of the train as much as with the music. A captive audience. Several of the passengers watched with curiosity, but most—Geoff included—looked downward or at their newspapers and avoided eye contact.

Dumbrowski's Rule Number One.

The man sitting next to Geoff became more restive. He smacked his lips in disgust, grabbed his briefcase off the floor, placed it securely in his lap. His mumbling became a thunderous command. "Turn down that music!"

The other passengers cringed. The youth turned up the volume full blast and continued his elbow-flailing, finger-snapping lip-synch.

Those who had attempted to ignore the situation now glared at the teenager, hoping he'd walk through to the next car and make himself someone else's problem, though most knew better. He was seeking disruption and recognition. He had achieved his goals here in this car.

He continued his routine, meandering toward Geoff and his seat-mate. Geoff's pulse began to race. A confrontation was brewing, and he had the unenviable ringside seat. Squat and soft in the middle, the Hasidic man was obviously no match for the brawny teenager with the box.

The youth was barely two feet away now, music blasting. He sauntered forward, paused in front of Geoff and the Hasid, removed the boom box from his shoulder and thrust it in the older man's face. "Hey, mutha' fuckin' Jew, don't you dig rap?"

Geoff looked at the man next to him. His face had turned a deep crimson, and the veins in his neck bulged so far they appeared ready to burst. His entire body quivered with something more than fear, and his hands clutched something inside his now partially open briefcase.

Geoff caught the man's eye. His gaze was maddened beyond mere anger, a frightening stare. Was Geoff sitting next to a lunatic, or was this just an irate citizen whose tolerance had reached flash point? Geoff knew the wisest thing for him to do now was to get up and walk through to the next car, but the man might need his help.

"This is what I think of you and your rap, filth!" The man jumped up from his seat and fired an Uzi sub-machine gun at the black youth, propelling him to the opposite side of the car, splattering blood onto walls and nearby passengers. The teenager landed with a loud thud at the feet of the Italian woman with the shopping bag, who was now wailing and praying aloud.

Shrieking men and women rushed to still-closed doors, knocking each other down, trampling those who had fallen. A five-year-old child, who had escaped her mother's grasp, ran and hid under a bench, screamed wildly. Utter chaos.

Pop-pop-pop. Another round of machine gun fire and loud howling. Geoff, behind the man, held onto a pole in the corner of the car. He looked about to see if anyone else had been hit. The sound of the automatic weapon pierced the air again, followed by more screams and crying. A goddamned war zone.

"Everyone sit down!" yelled the man as he fired the machine

gun over their heads, blowing out the windows and sending shards of glass flying. The wind rushed through the car, blowing papers all around. The sounds of screeching wheels on the old tracks and the train rushing through the tunnel at high speed reverberated loudly off the narrow tunnel walls and into the car.

Geoff had to do something. He needed a plan. His knife was no match for an Uzi, and he had no intention of dying in a New York subway. He looked at the Hasid. Throughout it all, his wide-brimmed black hat had remained in place. He stood in the center of the car, his foot on the shoulder of his conquered adversary, the machine gun resting on his knee. His face was still reddened, his shirt saturated with sweat. His breathing was labored, and saliva sprayed from the corners of his mouth as he exhaled. He appeared for all the world like a rabid dog, only instead of just teeth, this madman had a machine gun.

"All of you are gentiles, heathens, believers in a false God. The day of judgment is upon us! The Lord spoke and proclaimed to the Children of Israel that on the Day of Judgment the Messiah would deliver you to the Promised Land. Your time is now! Who will be the first to join the fallen Goliath and meet your maker on Judgment Day?"

He slowly panned the room with his machine gun, his right index finger twitching as it curled around the trigger.

The subway jolted to the left as it turned. The deranged man stumbled, but quickly regained his balance. Geoff lost his footing and fell to the floor. He stood and grabbed a commuter strap. Something red caught his eye, and he knew what he had to do.

"Well?" said the man, his maddened eyes now staring in Geoff's direction.

Geoff stabilized himself against the corner wall, reached upward, grabbed the emergency brake, and pulled with all his strength, ripping the handle off its cord.

The train screeched to a halt. The occupants of the hijacked car flew violently forward. There were more screams, passengers hid under seats and behind whatever they could find. The Hasid fell to the ground, his back against the wall, but he still clutched the Uzi.

Geoff released the commuter strap and lunged at the deranged man. The gun was aimed in Geoff's direction. Geoff deflected the barrel upward, and it fired as they collided, bullets piercing the ceiling. More shots went off, fired wildly around the car as they struggled for control of the weapon. Geoff was amazed at the madman's strength.

A loud crash exploded through the door to Geoff's right, and the Hasidic man pulled free from Geoff.

"Everyone hit the deck!" A man burst into the car, his service revolver drawn and aimed at the Hasid. "Drop it, pal!" The officer approached the man slowly, arms extended, his revolver aimed directly at him all the while.

Geoff stared in disbelief. Fucking Dumbrowski. The Texas Ranger.

The Hasid let go of the Uzi, and Geoff grabbed it. The man lunged at Dumbrowski. "Send me to my maker!"

"Hold it right there, Goddamnit! I said freeze!" Dumbrowski had no choice but to fire his service revolver.

The man's body jerked backward spasmodically with each shot. Blood frothed from the corner of his mouth as he slumped to the floor of the subway car.

CHAPTER 8

"A Hasidic Jew, can you believe it?" Geoff stepped out of the shower at Stefan's apartment in SoHo, exhausted and still astounded by the evening's events.

"Not just any Hasidic Jew, Geoff." Stefan raised his voice enough for Geoff to hear him on the other side of the bathroom door. "The crazy man who blew away that poor black kid and almost killed you was a *rabbi*. Samuel Levinow was a prominent leader in the Hasidic community."

Geoff put on a pair of surgical scrubs, entered the living room. Stefan handed him a tall glass of ice water. "How did you find that out so quickly?" he asked. He drank half a glass of water, set the glass down on the coffee table.

"I heard about it on the news just before you came. I was worried sick about you." Stefan removed a Kleenex from his pocket, wiped his forehead, adjusted his wire-framed specs. He sat down on the couch next to Geoff. "I called the hospital, and Karen Choy told me you had left hours ago. Then the news bulletin came on TV. I knew you were involved in some way. I called the police. They told me you were there giving a statement."

"A statement? Is that what they told you?" Geoff shook his head with annoyance. "It was more like an interrogation. I was beginning to wonder who the criminal was."

Stefan looked Geoff squarely in the eyes. "You're safe. That's all that matters now."

The two brothers were remarkably different. They had grown

closer after their father's death several years before, first by necessity, then by mutual desire. Geoff—handsome, successful, Rhodes scholar, ex-Navy Seal. Mister perfect, his brother called him. Stefan—brilliant, albeit eccentric, computer whiz, M.I.T. drop-out. Bill Gates with a pony tail.

Stefan had been his mother's favorite—she had died while they were in college—in spite of his sexual orientation. Ostracized by his surgeon father, whose paternal focus had been on Geoff's medical career, Geoff had tried to fill the void, acting as much as a father to Stefan as a big brother. With both their parents and Sarah gone, Stefan was the only immediate family Geoff had left.

Geoff stared off into space, shook his head. "I just don't get it."

"Don't get what?"

"The guy seemed normal when he sat down next to me. He even tried to strike up a conversation. Now you tell me he was a rabbi? The last kind of person in the world I'd expect to do something violent or crazy."

"You said he was taunted by that black kid playing the loud music," Stefan said. "Maybe he was mugged in the subway once before and felt as though his life was in danger. The old fed-up-citizen-transforms-into-subway-avenger story."

"It's not normal for a rabbi to carry a machine gun in his briefcase for protection. Besides, in another minute and he would have blown us all away. The man was crazy. He simply snapped. I saw it in his eyes." Geoff leaned forward, reached for the glass of water, downed the remainder.

"Does it really matter why the man went nuts, Geoff? It's over, and you're alive to talk about it."

Geoff took a deep breath, rubbed his temples. "I guess you're right," he said.

Stefan patted Geoff on the leg. "Look at you. You're exhausted. Let me put you to bed. You have rounds in five hours." He stood, walked to the linen closet, removed a blanket and a pillow, set them down on the coffee table. Stefan pulled Geoff up off the couch, and they opened the bed. Stefan unfolded the blanket, fluffed the pillow.

Geoff collapsed onto the couch. "This has been a very strange day," he said. "I haven't even told you about how things went at the Trauma Center, especially the odd e-mail message I received. I need you to look at it. I don't know where to begin." His lids were now at half mast.

"You can tell me all about it in the morning. Now get some rest." Stefan stood, turned out the light, left the room.

Sleep ignited dreams so vivid and powerful, Geoff's heart began to race fiercely, his breathing becoming labored. Sunday afternoon at Central Park Zoo. The sun's rays bathed Geoff and little Jessica with warmth and brightness. They were sitting on a grassy field playing games, having a picnic lunch. Jessica's favorite, peanut butter and honey on white bread, crust removed.

The sky turned black and an ominous, dark funnel appeared on the horizon. The wind blew fiercely as the twister wound its way toward them. Adrenalin surged, and Geoff reacted instinctively. He threw their lunch into the basket and swept Jessica up into his arms all in one motion, then ran for the safety of the Penguin House at the north end of the zoo's esplanade.

As he neared the fountain at the center of the walkway, a wave of panic spread over him: Jessica was gone. He dropped the basket. No Jessica. How could it be? A moment ago she had been securely tucked under his right arm.

He looked around frantically. The zoo was deserted.

Geoff broke out in a cold sweat. She was missing. He cupped

his hands to his mouth and yelled her name at the top of his lungs, but gusty wind drowned out the sound of his voice. Geoff spied a phone by the lamppost.

The police, damn it, call the police!

A sweet, little voice echoed downwind. "Dr. Davis, Dr. Davis. Where are you"?

Geoff's attention focused in the direction from which the voice seemed to come. He looked toward the Penguin House. No one. He looked all around. Deserted. "Jessica, I can't see where you are. Call me again."

"I'm in here. With the penguins," she cried. "There's a man in here, too."

Geoff's nerves were raw. He began to sweat profusely. A man. His dread worsened. Was she being molested? He ran towards the Penguin House. "I'm coming, Jessica. Hold on."

A figure suddenly appeared in the doorway. A large man wearing a Parks Department uniform, a bomb strapped to his body, stood clutching Jessica in his arms.

Geoff stopped dead in his tracks. He looked at Jessica. She was smiling peacefully.

"It's okay, Dr. Davis. This nice man found me."

Geoff's gaze shifted to the kidnapper's face. It was a peculiar face, not like any he had ever seen. At first Geoff did not realize what was so strange about the man, then it suddenly became evident. His skull was as transparent as glass. Contained within, Geoff could see the psychedelic convolutions of the man's brain, its vivid colors radiating through his transparent skull. His brain was like a living PET scan, the outer shell emitting a royal blue, the deeper zones emerald green and chartreuse, all mapping out the man's endorphin receptors. At least his pattern appeared normal, Geoff thought with some relief. In his fascination, Geoff momentarily forgot about Jessica.

Then Geoff saw something, and a state of total fear overwhelmed him. Deep at the base of the man's temporal lobes, an area of searing vermilion the shape of a horseshoe pulsated brilliantly, like the core of an uncontrolled nuclear reactor about to go into meltdown. The man's limbic area was saturated with endorphins. He was schizophrenic. There'd be no reasoning with him. Geoff looked at Jessica, who continued to smile, as if to reassure him everything would turn out all right.

Trying not to make any sudden moves, Geoff approached.

"Don't come any closer, Doc, or we both go sky high." The man's left hand grabbed the detonator strapped to his waist.

Doc. The accent. The way he said Doc.

"Just relax and be cool about it. That's my patient you've got there. Why don't you just put her down, let her go." In a flash, the man's face transformed and assumed definition. "Doc, you fucked up my brain once. You're not gonna have a chance to do it again!"

Geoff was confused. His gaze was again drawn to the man's brain. The red hot horseshoe area was pulsating at a crescendo, its crimson glow spreading to adjacent areas of the brain like creeping molten lava.

Movement over to the right of the doorway. Another person. A cop was sidling toward the man and Jessica, gun drawn. Dumbrowski.

"Hold it right there, pal!" he commanded, his gun aimed at the man's pulsating brain.

The man turned abruptly, yanking Jessica as he did so. "You were too late last time, cop. You're too late this time, too!"

A feeling of helplessness engulfed Geoff. His gaze darted frantically from Dumbrowski to the man holding Jessica, back to the cop. "Take me instead of the little girl," Geoff said. He continued advancing toward them.

"It's over, Doc. You put that horseshoe in my brain, and now you pay the price!"

"What are you talking about?"

"My brain, man. You poisoned my brain!" the man yelled hysterically, his entire brain now a bright orange-red like a pulsating sun about to explode. His right thumb reached the detonator button.

"No!" Geoff screamed.

A white-hot firestorm erupted around him.

Geoff sat up in bed, his body sopping with sweat, his heart pounding.

"Geoff, are you okay?" Stefan sat down on the edge of the sofa bed. "You must have been having a nightmare."

Geoff wiped the sweat off his brow and searched the blackness of the room. "How could I have forgotten that face? That voice?"

"What are you talking about?"

"The man who went nuts at the zoo."

"I'm beginning to wonder if you're losing it now," said Stefan. He rubbed his eyes.

"He was the first head injury patient in our PET scan/endorphin study a couple of months ago."

"Must have had a lot of brain damage."

"Obviously more than I thought at the time." Geoff reached over, turned on the light on the end table, grabbed a pad and a pencil.

Stefan squinted his eyes at the offending light.

Geoff scribbled down a single word: *Romero.*

CHAPTER 9

"You look like hell, Geoff," Cathy Johannsen said. They sat at the ICU nursing station. Geoff had recounted the bizarre events of the night before.

"Could I make up a story like that?"

"You have a pretty active imagination, but I have to believe you were there. Your name was all over the papers. 'Dr. McDreamy of the A-train saves the day.' You're the hero of Washington Heights."

"How's Karen doing?"

"She's doing great. She handled herself like a pro. Mark, well, he's smart but a bit green. No new admissions, by the way, and they were able to get little Jessica off the ventilator."

"So soon?" Images from his dream flashed in his mind. Jessica clutched tightly in Romero's arms, the white-hot firestorm engulfing them all.

Karen Choy approached the nursing station. "I guess you heard the good news," she said with a broad smile.

"Don't get me wrong, Karen, I think it's great, but didn't you take her off the ventilator a little prematurely?"

Karen shifted her weight, massaged the back of her neck, as if she was surprised by his question. "Well, it wasn't my idea entirely. Howard suggested we do it."

Geoff was upset. "Kapinsky? He should know better than that. Where is he now?"

"Over there, by Jessica's bed," Cathy said. She rolled her eyes, pointed to the far corner of the room. "He's doing his clown routine."

Geoff left the nursing station, Karen behind him, and walked towards Jessica's bed. Kapinsky was standing at the bedside blowing up balloons and twisting them into the shapes of animals. He playfully set each one on Jessica's table after he made the corresponding animal's sounds.

Geoff watched the scene in amazement. His anger abated and his instinctual dislike for Kapinsky melted away, however briefly, as he observed the tender interaction. It was hard to believe this was the same abrasive tight-assed geek he had come to loathe over the years.

"And do you know what this one is, sweetie?" asked Kapinsky in his best kindergarten voice. "I'll give you one hint. Hee-haw, hee-haw."

Jessica's eyes were open, like slits. She cracked half a smile, made a feeble attempt to mouth the word donkey.

"Great!" Kapinsky replied. "Now I have one last animal friend for you to meet."

"Looks like you've found a cure for endorphin-coma, Kapinsky," Geoff said as he and Karen approached the bedside.

Kapinsky smiled and continued about his business of creating a balloon giraffe. "Now, Dr. Geoff, let's not frighten our patient. She's never seen you before."

Geoff's initial reaction was to get pissed off at Kapinsky's tone, be he realized immediately Kapinsky was right. "Would you like to introduce us?"

Geoff approached Jessica cautiously, noting the frightened look in her eyes. She was a different child from the grotesque, bloodied little girl he had seen the other day. The endotracheal tube had been removed, and one of the nurses had made braids and tied them together over the shaved area on the top of her head. She was no longer a faceless victim.

"Jessie, this is my friend, Dr. Geoff. He's your friend, too, so don't be afraid of him." Kapinsky placed his arm around Geoff, who had softened enough to tolerate the contact.

Jessica nodded slowly, and her frightened expression relaxed. She attempted to mouth words—obviously using every bit of her strength to do so—words Geoff picked up on right away. "Daddy. Where's my daddy?"

Geoff turned to Karen with concern. "Have you spoken with the family?"

"Her dad and grandmother spent most of the night here," Karen said. "They went home to rest about an hour ago. Her mother died a few years ago."

Geoff grasped Jessica's hand firmly with his own. "Daddy went home to nap, Jessica. He'll be back soon."

He turned to Kapinsky. "I think it's time to let her rest."

Jessica nodded slowly as her eyes closed.

The team, lead by Geoff, walked toward the nursing station. "Looks great, doesn't she?" Kapinsky said with a smug smile.

"Sure does. Tell me how you weaned her off the ventilator so quickly, Karen."

Karen rubbed the back of her neck and took a breath. "Her vitals had remained stable for almost thirty-six hours and her intracranial pressure had dropped to normal levels. When she became arousable and her pupils were normal and fully reactive to light, we had respiratory therapy evaluate her pulmonary functions. Her $pO2/CO2$ levels were normal. After checking her chest x-ray and seeing her lung had re-expanded, and after repeating the PET scan, we—Howard and I—thought it was safe to try to wean her off the ventilator."

"I understand your desire to help her recover as quickly as possible, Karen, but I hope you realize how potentially dangerous what you did was. She could have died. Surely you, Kapinsky, should have known better."

Karen looked down, avoiding eye contact with Geoff.

"It was done under very controlled conditions, Geoff. I would never have taken the risk with this little girl otherwise," Kapinsky said.

"Did you check her PET scan first?"

"I haven't seen the most recent one. I think the hard copy is still in Neuroimaging," Kapinsky said.

Geoff looked him squarely in the eye, saw insecurity behind the defiant stare. "Just be more cautious and follow standard protocol next time. I don't want any unnecessary morbidity on our team."

"Sure, chief," Kapinsky said.

Geoff looked over his shoulder at the empty bed next door, bed seventeen. A newly vacant bed in the NSICU meant one of three things: the patient was in neuroimaging, on the ward, or in the morgue. Geoff felt a twinge of concern. "Where's the hang glider?"

"Transferred to the neuro ward around five this morning. He came out of drug-induced coma during the night, and the staffing in the NSICU was a little short. The bed control supervisor asked if it was okay to move him a few hours early," Kapinsky said. "I mean, I knew we planned on sending him down to the ward today anyway, right?" Kapinsky seemed to sense Geoff's annoyance.

"Who's the chief resident, here, Kapinsky? The bed control supervisor is supposed to clear requests like that with me, not with the senior resident." Geoff glared at Kapinsky.

"Well, she was going to, but I was here, so I told her not to bother calling you. I didn't think it was that big a deal."

"You thought wrong. Next time, bother me." Goddamned Kapinsky. This year might be even longer than Geoff had imagined.

"Whatever you say, chief."

Something seemed different this morning to Geoff. He wasn't quite sure what. Maybe it was that the NSICU was quieter than usual at early morning rounds. Phones rang, nurses and medical students chatted, techs came and went, respirators hissed. Smithers. That was it. "Where's Smithers?"

Geoff looked around the room for the cop he and Karen had admitted from the ER yesterday. The three possibilities flashed through his mind again.

"Neuroimaging," Kapinsky said. "You wanted him to have a PET scan as soon as he was stable, right?"

"He just had major surgery yesterday and came this close to crumping." Geoff gestured with his fingers. He felt really uneasy about this one. "He didn't seem stable enough last night to stand the hour it would take in neuroimaging." He gave Karen a questioning look. "Who went with him?"

"Brian Phelps and a medical student," Karen said.

"Great. A first year resident and a med student. I hate July," Geoff muttered.

"What?" asked Karen.

"Forget it. It's not your fault." Geoff looked at Kapinsky. "Did you okay this?"

"Well, yes. I mean he was stable enough to be transferred with a portable respirator—"

"Stable enough?" I don't like you taking risks with our patients, Kapinsky." Geoff locked stares with Kapinsky. "You had better get your act together real fast, or this is going to be a long year. For both of us."

Kapinsky bit his upper lip, squinted, looked down. "Sorry. I was just trying to be helpful, chief."

Geoff tensed his jaw, nodded. He turned to Karen. "I've got some test results to check on the computer. It shouldn't take me long. Skip the rest of rounds and head down to neuroimaging, check on Smithers. I'll meet you down there in five minutes."

"Sure," Karen said. She grabbed her clipboard off the bedside table and left.

"Kapinsky, I'll be in the lounge. Don't extubate or discharge anyone in the next five minutes, okay?"

"Don't worry, chief."

"I *do*," Geoff said. He turned and headed to the front of the NSICU, entered the house staff lounge, and sat at a vacant terminal. He had been curious all morning to find whatever records he could on Romero, search for any hint of mental illness, schizophrenia specifically. He didn't remember much about him. The face, the name, his accent. The way he said 'doc,' just like in the dream. His thoughts flashed back to the disturbing nightmare, and a pulsating horseshoe appeared brightly in his mind's eye. Geoff wanted to pull Romero's scan, if for no other reason than to satisfy his curiosity and put the strange dream to rest.

Geoff signed on to the Traumanet system and entered Neurad, the neuroimaging database. Reviewing patient records and test results required a second level security clearance, PET scan data, third level. Geoff viewed this as a tremendous inconvenience. PETronics Corporation insisted it was essential to preserve patient confidentiality.

WELCOME TO THE NEURAD SYSTEM, DR. DAVIS. YOUR ACCESS IS CLEARED. PLEASE ENTER THE

PATIENT'S NAME AND BIRTHDATE OR HOSPITAL NUMBER.

Geoff entered the patients name: Romero, Jesus.

He waited for the digitalized image to appear on the screen. The cursor pulsed for what seemed like minutes before delivering the response.

NO SCAN OR FILE WITH NAME: ROMERO, JESUS. PLEASE TRY ALTERNATE SPELLING OR ENTER HOSPITAL NUMBER.

Geoff re-entered the name using different spellings. All resulted in the same response. He switched to the patient record system, tried to pull up Romero's medical chart and got the same message. There was no record of a Jesus Romero having been to the New York Trauma Center. Geoff rested his hand on his chin, stared blankly at the screen, tapped his finger on the desk. He knew the man had been a patient at the NYTC. Now it was as if he had never existed. Must be a computer error. Geoff made a mental note to see if there was a hard copy of the scan filed in neuroimaging, a chart in medical records. They couldn't have vanished into thin air.

CHAPTER 10

Having maneuvered through the maze of limited access elevators and corridors leading to the labyrinthine sub-basement of the PETronics Research Center, Geoff paused at the entrance to PET Scanning. Over the main doorway a large sign, its illuminated red block letters pulsating brightly, issued a stern warning. "Scan In Progress. Do Not Enter."

"Who designed this medical center, anyway?" a voice reverberated through the hallway.

Geoff startled, turned around. "Karen? I thought you'd be inside with the patient by now."

"So did I." Karen shifted her stance, smiled in seeming embarrassment. "I kind of got lost. You'd think that with all of the head trauma that comes through this place, PET scanning would be right next to the ER, not in the outer reaches of Siberia."

"It all comes down to money," Geoff said. "And control."

Karen wrinkled her brow. "What do you mean?"

"The reality of healthcare in the new economy, Dr. Choy. Private-public partnerships, that's what I mean. It wasn't a government grant or some grateful benefactor that built this research wing, Karen. PETronics Corporation bankrolled it. They designed it. They control it."

"A medical equipment company owns this place?"

"That's right," Geoff said.

"So we sold out? Is that the answer?"

"I wouldn't exactly call it that, but control is tied to purse strings. I felt the same way at first, but I spent all of last year working in Balassi's laboratory, innumerable hours here working with the PET scanner. I was never aware of any attempt on the part of PETronics to control the basic research that was taking place. Dr. Balassi says they're the ideal silent partner.

"I know it's hard to believe, but they built this building, donated this state-of-the-art PET scanner, and gave Dr. Balassi, the world pioneer in PET scan research, total freedom to run the program as he sees fit. No more mountains of paperwork, grant applications to the National Institutes of Health, or competition for scant research dollars in Washington. Life's a tradeoff. So is medicine these days."

"Maybe," Karen said. But it just doesn't feel right. The same way free black bags and stethoscopes from the drug companies didn't feel right when I graduated medical school. I donated mine to the Nicaraguan Red Cross."

The lighted "Do Not Enter" sign extinguished.

"So did I." Geoff smiled. "Let's go in." Slowly he opened the oversized door and entered the imaging room, Karen following behind.

A waft of cool air swept over them as the heavy door clicked shut securely behind them, locking out the mustiness of the basement corridor. Their eyes adapted to the change in luminosity, the only light provided by the auxiliary controls on the PET scanner and two dimmed, overhead LED fixtures.

The room was about twenty-five by thirty feet, roughly the same size as the usual CT scan suite. There was nothing conspicuously unique about the place. It could have been, except for the size, any imaging room in any medical center in any city in America. But of course, it was anything but that.

The PET scanner was located at the far end of the room, a

white metallic, box-like structure extending from the floor to just below the ceiling, with a central opening large enough to allow entry of any body part to be imaged, the patient being positioned on a retractable exam table. Massive cables surrounded by specially insulated ducting extended from the unit to the ceiling, all wires converging in the complex computer that choreographed the examination and processed the images.

The most unusual aspect of the suite was in what went unseen to the casual observer. Though the PET scanner was the most obvious and most talked-about piece of hardware, the adjacent room housed the cyclotron, a particle accelerator necessary to produce the radioactive compound used in each PET scan study, its close proximity dictated by the short half-life of the materials. A sixteen-ton, Rube Goldberg-like device composed of huge magnetic coils, stainless steel cylinders, vacuum chambers, hoses, and thousands of feet of tubing all surrounded by vast, retractable lead-shielded walls, the cyclotron provided the lifeblood of the PET scan. Like a mad scientist's garage creation, it was an engineering marvel constructed for the essential function it performed, without regard to form or aesthetics.

The room was deserted, which surprised Geoff given the "Do Not Enter" sign had been turned off just moments ago. No patient, no tech, not even a sign that a scan had recently been performed. Where did everybody go?

Over the quiet hum of the nearby scanner's cooling system, Geoff could make out the muted voice of a technician in the control room beyond the Plexiglas enclosure.

"Let's go let the tech know we're here," Geoff said, feeling reassured.

Geoff rounded the corner of the Plexiglas partition and was surprised to discover two techs instead of one in the control room. Only one was not a tech. Seated behind the master imaging computer console, frenetically typing in commands, was Dr. Josef Balassi. The brightly colored images on the screen cast a peculiar vermillion hue across his full-bearded face, setting his normally intense, close-set, brown eyes afire. His collar-length, grey hair danced to the symphony of the flickering light of the CRT. Twenty Thousand Leagues Under the Sea, Captain Nemo at the keyboard. He was totally immersed in studying the three dimensional images of the brain appearing on the screen.

"Great images, Walter!" said Balassi in his thick Slavic accent. "The new C-11 isotope compound is labeling the brain just where I thought it would." Balassi hit the table with his fist triumphantly, nodded his head in self-approval.

Intensely loyal to Balassi, whether out of admiration or fear Geoff didn't know, Walter Krenholz, the archetypal worker bee smiled his mortician's smile. "Looks like we have company," he droned, acknowledging Geoff's presence at the station.

Balassi hit the enter key, instantaneously storing the data and clearing the screen, then looked up, and recognizing the doctor standing at the console, offered a smile.

"Geoffrey, you've only been out of the lab one week, and already the monkeys and I miss you dearly!" He stood up and grabbed Geoff's hand, shaking it firmly. Things going okay?"

"It's been interesting. We've got a couple of tragic cases in the NSICU."

"You mean that poor little girl injured at the zoo?" Balassi pursed his lips, nodded his head side to the side.

"She's one of them. The other one's the cop whose PET scan I thought you'd still be doing." Geoff looked around for his patient, puzzled about where he was. It wasn't that easy to move such a severely injured patient on and off the scanning table. "Where is he?"

"You just missed him. We completed his scan moments before you arrived, Geoff." Balassi shot a glance at Walter. "He must be in the service elevator by now."

Walter nodded affirmatively as he busied about the scanner getting it ready for the next study.

"Were there two residents with him?" Geoff felt uneasy, not knowing his patient's status after the precarious trip from the NSICU and the physical stress of the scan.

"Two or three, I'm not really sure. One had a beard, though, if that helps. What happened to the poor man?" Balassi asked.

"Must be Phelps."

"What?"

"Brian Phelps, the new resident. He was the one with the patient," said Geoff.

"A new resident. I understand your concern. If it's of any re-assurance coming from a simple scientist, your patient seemed stable during his scan. I'm sure he'll be all right. What happened to him?"

"A transit cop, attacked in the 168th Street subway station. Basal skull fracture on MRI. He's in a bad way."

"Packs of wolves roaming the subways. I stay out of them whenever I can, and so should everyone else." Balassi shook his head, stroked his beard. "How's the little girl doing?"

"Holding her own so far, coming out of her coma. I haven't seen her admission PET scan yet, but I was told she graded two out of five on the endorphin-coma scale."

"Actually, I haven't had a chance to review it yet, either. I'll have Walter dig it up before you leave," Balassi said. "Let's review the study on the last patient, Smithers. Looks like the computer just finished processing the images." He entered a command on the keyboard, stared at the screen. Balassi looked up at Karen

Choy, and as if suddenly aware of her presence, stood and seized her hand. "You must be one of the new residents, as well. A very *beautiful* one."

"Dr. Balassi," Karen said, blushing. "It's an honor to meet you. I'm Karen Choy."

Balassi smiled. Fifty-eight, divorced twice, now a sworn bachelor, he had an uncanny ability to engage any woman in his presence regardless of her station or marital status. "Beautiful hands, the hands of a fine surgeon, I'm sure, Dr. Choy."

Karen awkwardly withdrew her hand. "Thank you."

Balassi motioned towards the work station. "Come in, both of you. Sit down. Let's look at the results."

Balassi's large right hand enveloped the mouse and began clicking a series of commands to the computer, dramatically altering the fuzzy, two-dimensional images that appeared on the screen. A Technicolor, three-dimensional reconstruction of the brain appeared, rotating slowly on its axis, all of its convolutions and fissures in full, finely detailed view.

More than an anatomical study, what was being displayed on the screen was a dynamic, physiological blueprint of the endorphin distribution in the brain, all of the inner workings of the mind potentially visualized on a computer screen, specific patterns and neural pathways mapped out in intricate detail like a genetic map of the human chromosome.

The rotation ceased at a view from above, looking down on the major lobes of the brain, frontal and parietal, separated by a central fissure. Click-click. A fine slice through the brain's lower regions appeared, bringing the temporal lobes and limbic region—the deep-seated areas responsible for memory and emotion—onto the screen. Central areas of searing vermilion were enveloped by regions of yellow, emerald, and a deep, royal blue, a psychedelic map of the brain's endorphin receptors.

Click-click. The brilliantly colored patterns dissolved, and a new image emerged, a large central blotch of orange-red, the brainstem, a more primitive area of the brain, responsible for controlling bodily functions, breathing and heart rate. Click-click-click. The central image magnified, honed in on the reticular formation, the gatekeeper of the brain's conscious awareness, burning red on the CRT, its neuronal endings saturated with beta-endorphins.

"Well, that explains his coma," said Geoff, pointing out the high concentration of endorphin receptors in the patient's reticular formation. "Can you quantify it?"

Balassi answered the question with a click, positioning the cross hairs on the center of the hot spot on the screen by manipulating the mouse. Numbers appeared above the image corresponding to the color-hue scale at the top of the screen. Blue areas contained the smallest concentration of receptors, red the largest.

"Fifty picomoles per gram, about two-and-a-half times the normal density of endorphin receptors," Balassi said matter-of-factly.

"That places him somewhere in the middle on the endorphin coma scale, about a three out of five, I'd say. Prognosis for coming out of his coma, fair," Geoff said.

Balassi nodded affirmatively, manipulating the mouse and reducing the image magnification to review the slices higher in the brain at the level of the temporal lobe.

"What do those hot spots correspond to?" Karen asked, pointing to two faintly red, almond-shaped islands in a sea of chartreuse surrounding the central red of the brainstem.

"The amygdala, the area of the brain thought to be responsible for rage and fear. It probably contains the highest concentration of endorphins in the brain of a normal subject. But as you can see in our comatose patient, it seems faint relative to the sky high endorphin levels in his reticular formation, the endorphins suppressing his consciousness much the way a drug addict overdosed on morphine or heroine would be comatose. Morphine, heroine, and most narcotics bind to pretty much the same endorphin receptors, except, interestingly, PCP or angel dust, which binds to a class of newly discovered *sigma* endorphin receptors," Geoff said.

"And the yellow-green area surrounding the amygdala? That indicates a moderate level of endorphin activity?"

"You're catching on, Karen." Geoff smiled. "That area is the limbic region, seat of our moods and emotions. The shrinks love to talk about this part of the brain. His limbic endorphin level appears normal. Good thing. The last thing you'd want out on the street is a schizophrenic cop.

"I'll try and dig up a recent scan of one of the psych patients. The pattern's completely different. The limbic area glows like a forest fire, and the reticular formation is blue as the ocean, just the opposite of what we see here. Looks kind of like a bright red horseshoe. Once you've seen the pattern, you won't forget it," Balassi said.

Geoff hadn't been able to get that horseshoe out of his mind. He had to check for Romero's scan before he left neuroimaging.

"Easy for you to say. Could just as well be psychedelic photos of the Beatles on the cover of *Life* to me. It all looks so foreign," Karen said, shaking her head.

"Interesting scan, Geoff. Good case," said Balassi. He turned to face Geoff. "Be sure to let me know how he does clinically so we can correlate the PET findings. Let's be sure we keep within the project's protocol."

"Will do," Geoff said. "You said you wanted to review the scan on the girl. There's another scan I wanted to check for, also, a patient we scanned several months ago."

Balassi raised his brow. "Oh?"

"His name is Jesus Romero. Ironically, he's the crazy guy who held the girl hostage at the zoo. I tried to pull his scan up on the Neurad system from a terminal in the NSICU, but the system couldn't find his record."

"Why the interest in this Romero, Geoff?"

"Academic interest. That's all."

Balassi stroked his beard, hit the intercom button. "Walter, we need your assistance here."

Seconds later, Walter Krenholz entered the control room. "Yes, Dr. Balassi," he said, his face an expressionless mask.

"I need you to check the file room for two PET scans. One on Jessica Humphries, the other on a fellow named Romero, Jessie Romero."

"Jesus is the first name," said Geoff.

"Sorry. Jesus Romero."

Bald as a cue ball, Walter's deep-set, blue eyes appeared deeper still due to the dark circles below them. Sullen and seemingly devoid of personality, not many people at the NYTC, even those who worked directly with him day to day—as Geoff had for a year—knew much about Walter. Except of course, Balassi. The two had worked together for the last twenty years, Walter having accompanied him to the NYTC from the National Institutes of Health.

Walter nodded and left the control room.

"You know, Geoff, the Neurad system hasn't crashed once yet. If it doesn't show a scan on Romero, one was probably never done. You must be confusing him with someone else," Balassi said. "But, if you like, I'll try a search myself."

Geoff shrugged his shoulders. "Sure."

Balassi typed in a command to search for a scan on Jesus Romero. No image. No file. No such patient existed in the system. "Well, let's see what Walter comes up with. If anyone can dig it up, he can."

Their conversation was interrupted by Walter, who returned from the file room.

"I checked the files and the log books. There are no records of any scans on a Jesus Romero. The girl's scan was signed out earlier today," Walter said.

"Signed out?" Balassi asked. His face reddened, his gaze narrowed. "No one signs out a PET scan from here before I have a chance to review it! No one! Who signed that out?"

"Dr. Kapinsky," said Walter.

"Who the hell does he think he is?" raged Balassi. His fist crashed down on the table, launching pencils into the air like aborted ballistic missiles. Walter scampered to pick them up and return them to their proper place.

"We have rules down here for a reason. If we let just anyone sign out an unread scan, they'd be all over this medical center! Besides, he doesn't even know what he's looking at."

"Not that I'm defending his action, but we had a discussion about her scan on rounds this morning, and he probably wanted to review it himself. Maybe he's becoming a believer," said Geoff.

"Whatever the reason, his behavior is inexcusable. When you get up to the ICU, tell him I want that scan returned to me here—personally—or Pederson will hear about it!"

"I'll take care of it," Geoff said.

Balassi turned and headed out the door, leaving a gust of air in his wake. Walter Krenholz followed behind him.

Geoff was surprised by Balassi's sudden outburst over the girl's missing scan. It didn't seem like a big deal to Geoff, but Balassi was a perfectionist. After a year in Balassi's lab, Geoff was used to that side of him and knew how to handle his sporadic outbursts.

Geoff was more puzzled by the lack of a record of any kind on Romero. He was sure Romero had had a scan just months ago. Damn the Neurad system. He'd check the medical record file room himself.

A shrill, beeping tone pierced the air. The alarm stopped, and a voice boomed from the overhead speaker. "Code 999, seven east, code 999 seven east!"

Geoff startled, sprang from the chair. He looked up at the speaker on the ceiling, waited for the "all clear" signal. Must be a drill. The alarm resumed, followed again by the urgent page. "Code 999, seven east, code 999."

"Shit. Let's go, Karen!" He grabbed her arm, pulled her up from the chair.

"What's a code 999?"

"Disaster code. This is no drill."

CHAPTER 11

GEOFF DASHED OUT OF THE ELEVATOR FOLLOWED BY KAREN Choy and a cadre of residents and technicians. He raced down the hall toward the mob of people congregated at the nursing station on seven east, pushed his way through until he ran into a wall of security guards. A woman's scream echoed from a distance, penetrated the babble of confusion at the nursing station, but Geoff could not make out her words.

Geoff turned to Gail Ross, the head nurse, who stood at the nursing station, anxiously biting her lower lip. "What the hell's going on?"

"I can't believe this is happening." Gail nodded her head in denial.

Geoff grabbed her by the shoulders. "What's happening, Gail? Tell me."

"A patient flipped out and is holding one of the nurses hostage in his room. I was just in there half an hour ago to give him his meds. He seemed okay, just a little anxious. Nothing unusual, at least for a head trauma patient."

"Who's the patient?" asked Geoff.

"His name is DeFranco. John DeFranco."

"John DeFranco? The hang glider we sent down from the NSICU earlier today?" Geoff was incredulous.

"That's right," she said.

"What medication did you give him?"

"Just his usual dose of IV cimetidine."

"Any sedatives, narcotics, new medications he might be allergic to?" asked Geoff.

"Nothing else," Gail said.

Karen Choy was standing nearby, listening to the conversation. "Cimetidine has been reported to cause rare hallucinogenic reactions," she said.

"Anything's possible," said Geoff. "I've got to get in there and see what's going on. Wait here." Geoff walked over to the security guard nearest the nursing station. "I'm Geoffrey Davis, Chief Resident. That man's my patient, I need to be in there. I think I can help."

"Strict orders from Sergeant Johnson. No one goes in," said the guard.

"Tell him Geoff Davis is here. Please."

The guard called in on his radio and waited for a response. The human chain of security guards parted, allowing Geoff to pass through. "Go ahead."

Geoff ran down the hall to room 719. The door was closed. He heard loud voices, the words muffled by the door. The guard outside the door glanced at Geoff's ID badge and nodded, allowing him entry. "I'd open it slowly if I were you. The guy's crazy. He's got a fork to her throat."

Geoff acknowledged the advice and slowly entered the hospital room. There were three people inside. Randall Johnson stood next to the sink, attempting to negotiate with the man to release the hostage. John DeFranco stood by the far side of the bed, his head shaved, face beet red, beads of perspiration rolling down his forehead, his ribs wrapped in surgical tape. With his left arm he grasped a Philippine nurse around the neck. His right hand held a fork to her jugular. Geoff couldn't believe this was the same man. Last time he saw DeFranco, he was comatose.

"Who the fuck is this? I told you no one else comes in!" yelled DeFranco, his voice quivering. His maddened gaze met Geoff's.

"This is the doctor I told you about, John," said Johnson calmly. He gestured towards Geoff. "He's here to help you."

DeFranco became more agitated, tightened his grip on the nurse's throat.

Her chest heaved, her eyes widened like those of a petrified child. "Please let me go, I have a family, children who need me! They're just babies!"

DeFranco pressed the fork more firmly, indenting her neck. The nurse whimpered uncontrollably.

"Shut up, just shut up! I've got a wife, kids, a family too, you know. You've screwed up my head so badly they don't even know who I am!"

"Mr. Defranco, I'm Geoff Davis, one of your doctors. No one wants to hurt you. We want to help you get better, make things the way they were before your accident—"

DeFranco laughed. "Accident? You expect me to believe that, just like that cop over there, don't you? It's all part of the plan, isn't it? You've kept me here, drugged me and fucked up my head, and now you tell me I had an accident! You think I'm that stupid?"

Geoff glanced for an instant at Johnson. Their gazes met, Johnson motioning with his eyes toward the window. That must be the plan. "Nobody thinks you're stupid, Mr. DeFranco. But you did have a bad accident, hit your head in a hang gliding crash, and you have amnesia. You've been in a coma for a few days in the New York Trauma Center. Now, please put the fork down and let the nurse go. She didn't do anything. If you're angry at anyone, it's me you should be angry at, not her."

Geoff walked slowly toward DeFranco, extended his hand.

"Take me instead."

DeFranco backed up toward the window as Geoff approached, then he began to tremble. "Stay where you are! Don't come any closer!" His tremor increased, his grip loosened on the nurse enough for her to break free. She ran toward the door, sobbing. DeFranco's face paled, his legs wobbled. Geoff lunged forward to catch him.

Johnson grabbed his radio microphone, yelled, "Hold your fire! We've got it contained in here."

John DeFranco collapsed into Geoff's arms. His eyes rolled up into their sockets, blood frothed from his nose and mouth, his entire body convulsed in one final, gigantic spasm.

CHAPTER 12

"When do you think DeFranco's path report will be ready, Suzanne?" Geoff asked. Suzanne Gibson, the neuropathology fellow, had completed her pathology residency at Georgetown University Hospital. She had to have done exceptionally well to get this plum of a fellowship at the NYTC. Two hundred applicants for one position. To the best of Geoff's knowledge, the NYTC had never taken anyone from Georgetown before. Harvard, Yale, Columbia, but not Georgetown.

At a table in the corner of the cafeteria, they were trying to converse above the din of the late morning crowd. Geoff washed down a bite of gooey blueberry pie with a gulp of black coffee. The Trauma Center was noted for many things, but the cafeteria's cuisine was not one of them. Geoff, otherwise health conscious, had a penchant for blueberry pie, even the kind so full of corn starch and sugar one could barely taste the blueberries.

"I did the gross sections this morning," Suzanne replied. "Nothing out of the ordinary. Just neuronal swelling, probably secondary to his initial head injury. The microscopics should be ready tomorrow, the amygdaloid electron micrographs the following day."

Suzanne paused, lifted her cup with both hands, sipped her green tea. She looked at Geoff over the top of the cup, smiled. "It's a pretty amazing story, Geoff. If it wasn't all over the hospital, I'd have a hard time believing you. First the crazy rabbi on the train, now this guy. You've had quite a time lately."

"That borders on understatement."

"I'm still not sure what you're after, Geoff. I mean, the guy just plain flipped out."

"I think there's something more going on here—what I'm not yet sure. John DeFranco had no prior history of mental illness. He was recovering from his head injury in a normal way, had come out of his coma just fine. Before we transferred him to the ward, he was oriented enough to his surroundings to know he was at the Trauma Center. He wasn't agitated in the least. That's why I'm confused."

Suzanne set down her cup, rested her chin on her hand. "I assume you've already poured through his chart, lab tests, scans and all. Anything stand out as out of the ordinary?"

"Nothing. His labs, vital signs, admission MRI and PET scans were all pretty ordinary, consistent with his injury and course while he was on our service in the NSICU. Only things I haven't had a chance to review yet are his pre-transfer ICP readings and PET scan. I'm sure there aren't any surprises there. That's why I'm so interested in what you may find."

"It's a rather unusual request you're making, to do electron microscopy on the amygdaloid area of the brain in a routine post mortem," Suzanne said.

"It's not a routine post mortem."

"Okay, the protocol's not strictly routine since the medical examiner's office has to be involved, but this is simply an autopsy, not a research project. Who's going to fund the electron microscopy work? You know the Medical Examiner's office won't buy off on it."

"Put it on the Neurosurgery Department's tab. I'm sure Dr. Pederson won't mind."

"You can sign *your* name to that one, Geoff. I don't need any trouble with Pederson. He's a pretty powerful guy around here. I still have another year to go on my neuropathology fellowship, and I'd like to—"

"Suzanne, I'm not talking about robbing a bank. Just doing some additional testing."

"I doubt you're going to find anything structurally abnormal on the micros or the EM. I didn't see any evidence of neurological disease or a brain tumor."

"What about any abnormal biochemistry?"

"Biochemical assay? You mean drug levels—cocaine, amphetamines, that sort of thing?"

"I was referring to neurotransmitters. Dopamine, serotonin, GABA, endorphins."

"Neurotransmitters? Now you're really reaching. There are hundreds of potential neurotransmitters in the human brain. That's a research project in and of itself. It would take weeks just to isolate the ten most active substances, several weeks more to quantitate them. If you knew specifically what you were looking for, and we got hold of the brain tissue soon enough, I might be able to identify—."

"What's 'soon enough'?"

"All depends which substance you're after."

"How about endorphins?"

"Fifteen, thirty minutes. Tops." Suzanne paused for a moment, studying Geoff with her keen brown eyes, then added sardonically, "So, the hang glider was a runner, was he?"

"Might have been."

"What's with the endorphin assay?"

"Just a theory," Geoff replied.

"And what might that be?"

"Something to do with endorphin levels and schizophrenia.

It's a bit obscure, but it's in the literature, and we confirmed it in the PET lab. It seems that some violent schizophrenics have exceedingly high levels of endorphins in the limbic area of the brain, particularly in the thalamic and amygdaloid regions."

"Interesting," Suzanne replied. "Are you saying that DeFranco was schizophrenic? You just told me he had no history of mental illness."

"No, but what if his head injury, or the coma, or some medication given to him, inadvertently caused an imbalance in his brain's endorphins, resulting in a schizophrenic-like pattern in his amygdala? His behavior was just like a violent schizophrenic's in those final moments. I saw it in his eyes. Just like the rabbi on the train. I bet if we were able to assay both their brain's endorphins, they'd be out of whack."

"Well, you may be right, but we never look at that fine a level of detail on autopsies," Suzanne said. "I might be able to run an endorphin assay on DeFranco's brain tissue, but unfortunately what's left of the rabbi's brain has long since been pickled. There's no way to do any biochemical assays at this point. Nothing in his chart indicated any history of mental illness, either."

"Chart?" asked Geoff. "What are you talking about?"

"The rabbi was admitted for twenty-four hour observation a few months ago after a minor head injury. A concussion sustained in a scuffle with some skinheads at a JDL rally."

"Do you still have the chart?"

"Of course. I will until I'm done with his report."

"Do me a favor, Suzanne. Don't send it back to medical records."

"Another favor. Now you owe me two."

"You name it."

"I have tickets to the Joffrey Ballet next Friday night—"

Their conversation was interrupted by the shrill beep of Geoff's pager.

"Can't even have a cup of coffee around here without that stupid thing going off." He removed the pager from his belt and lifted it to his ear to hear the garbled message.

"Dr. Davis, NSICU stat. Dr. Davis—"

"Guess I'm wanted."

"You certainly are. Think about Friday."

"I will." Geoff rose abruptly from the table, grabbed his tray.

"Just as friends, Geoff, nothing more." She looked up at Geoff, brushed back her shoulder-length auburn hair, smiled.

"Got to run, Suzanne. Call me when you get the final report on DeFranco, and please don't forget about the rabbi's chart."

"It's a good thing I have a strong ego. I'll call you."

Geoff slurped the remaining drops of coffee, dumped his tray on the conveyor, and bolted through the cafeteria door and up the back hallway towards the service elevator.

There were only two patients still on the critical list, Smithers and the girl. His mind clicked off their most recent status reports, system by system. Jessica was further along in her recovery, stable for several days now. Smithers was not. There had to be something wrong with the cop. But what? His vitals and intracranial pressure had been stable. Geoff had yet to review yesterday's PET scan personally, but the preliminary report Karen had given him this morning indicated a waning level of endorphins in his reticular formation. All evidence pointed towards recovery. Geoff was puzzled. It just didn't jive.

Geoff's thoughts were interrupted by the voice of the hospital operator through the intercom in the elevator: "Code blue, NSICU. Code blue, NSICU".

"Shit, I'm too late," he muttered aloud as he pounded the elevator wall with his fist in frustration. *Smithers seemed to be doing so well.* Geoff stared up at the floor numbers as the elevator rose skyward toward the tenth floor for what seemed like an eternity. Six, seven. His jaw was clenched, his leg muscles tensed. Nine, ten! The elevator leveled off at the tenth floor with a bounce, and the doors slid open. Geoff dashed across the hallway, nearly flew through the double doors and into the NSICU.

"What the hell's going on with Smithers?" he blurted aloud. There was a flurry of activity around the bed in the far corner of the room. No one responded, let alone turned around to acknowledge him. IV bottles were dripping, the drawers of the red crash cart opening and slamming frantically shut. Geoff heard Kapinsky's voice bark an order from across the room. "Pulse is slowing to fifty. Give her another 0.5 mg of atropine."

Her?

It was only then Geoff realized Smithers was resting comfortably in the bed to his left. *He* was not the one in trouble. Geoff pushed his way through the mass of interns and medical students crowding around the bed of the little girl.

He turned to Kapinsky. "What the hell's going on?"

"Must be massive cerebral edema. One minute she was sitting up, playing games in bed, then wham! She let out a violent shriek and started babbling incoherently. Her pupils blew, and she went into cardiac arrest."

"Why didn't you call me right away?"

"I paged you stat as soon as it happened, Geoff. It all came down in just a few minutes."

"Mannitol's here, Howard," announced an out-of-breath Karen Choy who had just run up five flights of stairs from the pharmacy.

"Run it in full blast," Geoff said, taking charge.

The monotonous beep of the monitor suddenly slowed.

"Pulse dropping to forty!" announced one of the interns.

Geoff looked up at the cardiac monitor. She was about to go into complete heart block. "Give her an amp of epi. Stat!"

Kapinsky withdrew the six-inch cardiac needle from the package and attached it to the palm-sized vial of epinephrine. Outlining Jessica's small sternum with his index finger, he carefully guided the huge needle through the chest wall and into her heart with a pop. He withdrew the plunger, and seeing the ominously dark blood fill the syringe knew he was in the ventricle. He pushed the vial with the palm of his hand and injected the epinephrine directly into her heart chamber just as the monitor alarm sounded, indicating her heart had stopped beating. He withdrew the needle quickly and stared at her chest, looking for a sign her heart was starting to beat.

"Start compressions," Geoff ordered, alternating his gaze between Jessica and the monitor.

Flat line. No change. What the hell went wrong?

Suddenly the horizontal line of the monitor began to dance wildly.

"V-fib!" said Kapinsky.

"Give her fifty milligrams of lidocaine!"

An intern popped the vial and pushed the lidocaine as fast as the IV line could take it. Geoff studied the monitor for any hint of a normalizing heart rhythm.

"No change. Keep the compressions going, Karen," Geoff said. "Lets give it another minute."

"Geoff, you know that cardiac arrest secondary to massive cerebral edema and brainstem compression is irreversible. We're treating the symptoms, not the cause."

"Damn it, Kapinsky. I don't need your lectures now! This isn't an exercise for your neurosurgical boards. She just got the mannitol a few minutes ago. We need to give her brain a chance to respond."

"Something made her brain swell suddenly like that, and mannitol's not going to help."

Geoff turned away from Kapinsky and looked at the monitor. V-fib. No change. He knew Kapinsky was right, but he had to do *something*.

"Charge the defibrillator. Set it at 100." Geoff grabbed the paddles, rubbed them together to spread the conductive gel. "Stand back!"

Karen Choy stopped her chest compressions, and everyone backed away from the bedside as Geoff applied the paddles.

He squeezed the red button, and Jessica's little body wrenched violently upward, then fell. Geoff looked at the monitor. No change.

"Again!" he yelled. "At 200."

"Isn't that kind of high for a child?" Karen Choy asked.

"Just do it!"

Geoff applied the paddles, pressed again. With a jolt, Jessica's back arched and her jaw clenched in one massive spasm of muscular contraction. She landed with a muffled thud off the edge of the bed board.

"Still flat, Geoff. Nothing." Karen was still poised over Jessica.

Geoff stared at the monitor for what seemed an eternal minute. He looked at Jessica, whose once rosy cheeks were now blue. Pink, frothy saliva foamed from the corner of her mouth. He approached her cautiously, reached down and stroked her forehead, brushing blonde curls off her brow. Her skin was cool and clammy. With his thumb and index finger, Geoff raised her lids to check her pupils with his penlight. Fixed and dilated. She was likely brain dead. The only thing keeping her "alive" was the CPR being administered by the code team. They could go on for hours like this but—a movement!

"Oh, my God!" exclaimed a startled Karen Choy as she stopped her chest compressions and jumped off the bed. The intern who had been breathing Jessica removed the mask and ambu bag.

Suddenly, Jessica's head arched backwards, and her mouth gaped, every muscle of respiration in her neck and chest trying to suck in life-sustaining air in one final gasp.

"Agonal breathing, Karen," Geoff said.

"Right, I forgot," she replied, a little embarrassed. "A death reflex."

Geoff knew it was over. He had already made the decision, but the words did not flow easily. "Let's call it," he said, defeat permeating his voice.

"I'll go talk to the father." Kapinsky started to leave the bedside.

Geoff grabbed him by the arm. "No, I'll do it. I need to get his permission for an autopsy. I want to know what the hell happened here."

CHAPTER 13

GEOFF SAT ALONE IN THE MEDICAL STAFF ROOM OF THE NSICU. He had signed on to the computer to check for Jessica's PET scan one more time, but the digital image of her most recent scan was still missing from the computer's data banks. Strange, he thought. It had been two days since the scan and still nothing entered.

Even stranger was the latest, cryptic e-mail message. The sender was the same, Proteus, as were the convoluted gates the message had passed through to reach Geoff's computer. The words pulsed brightly, burning an afterimage on his retinas.

There are no accidents in life.

What the hell was that supposed to mean? If this was a prank, Geoff failed to see the humor in it. He printed the new message along with the first one, so he could provide his brother with something from which to work to help him track down this Proteus. When he found out who it was, there'd be hell to pay. Geoff would turn whomever it was in to Dr. Pederson. Pederson had no tolerance for this sort of thing.

A knock on the door interrupted his thoughts. "Mind if we come in?" asked Karen. Kapinsky followed close behind her.

Geoff cleared the e-mail screen and swiveled his chair. He rubbed his eyes, took a sip of cold, black coffee. "No, of course not. I could use some help trying to piece all of this together." He waved his hand over the hundreds of pages of chart notes and lab printouts spread over the surface of the table. On the corner of the table was a grease-stained box of pizza, one slice remaining.

Karen and Kapinsky sat down across from Geoff. "Have you made any sense of this stuff yet?" asked Karen.

"Two things stand out here. The nursing notes indicate she was a bit agitated during the night. The nurse reported she sat up in bed and let out a shriek in the middle of the night."

"Don't forget she is—was—just eight years old. The ICU is a pretty scary place," said Kapinsky. He grabbed a stack of lab test results and flipped through the pages.

"She was too sedated to be scared like that." Geoff picked up the medication record, pointed to an entry at the bottom of the page. "Says here she was given 250 milliliters of chloral hydrate at 2200, an hour before her fight or flight reaction.

"Fight or flight reaction?" asked Kapinsky. "What are you talking about? Either she was having a nightmare because the chloral hydrate hadn't kicked in yet, or she had an adverse reaction to the medication."

"I doubt it was the medication. Just like DeFranco, she'd had the medication—in this case, chloral hydrate, in his cimetidine—before without any adverse reaction."

"Then what's your explanation?" asked Kapinsky.

"The description of her behavior, her vitals and neuro exam all coincide with the fight or flight reaction. Look," Geoff went on, plopping the relevant chart notes and vital sign flow sheets down in front of Kapinsky. It's all right here. She had a massive sympathetic outpouring of adrenalin at around eleven o'clock last night."

Kapinsky studied the flow sheets one at a time, scanning the log of her vital signs and her bedside neuro checks. It was all there in black and white. "Okay, let's say she did have this outpouring of adrenalin affecting her nervous system. That still doesn't explain her sudden, massive brain swelling."

"No, but this does," said Geoff as he unrolled the printout of her intracranial pressure monitor from the night before. "Look here. Her ICP had been stable in the twelve to sixteen range for several days, then *this* happened."

Geoff unrolled the tape carefully, his gaze gliding along the even line until it abruptly changed course and climbed upward beyond the thirty millimeter mark.

"My God, her intracranial pressure spiked to thirty-five in a matter of seconds! I've never seen anything like this." Karen Choy's eyes widened in awe.

Geoff studied the tape further. "Looks like her intracranial pressure spiked from fifteen to thirty-five, then leveled off at twenty-five and stayed there until she became bradycardic and her heart rate slowed dramatically."

"What could cause such a sudden rise, Geoff?" asked Karen.

"Uncal herniation, herniation of the base of the temporal lobes due to an expanding mass like a brain tumor, can cause a picture similar to this—agitation, sympathetic nervous system changes, then cardiac collapse. But the intracranial pressure rise is generally more gradual, over hours, not minutes. Short of cerebral hemorrhage, and she had no evidence of that by her MRI, done earlier in the day, I honestly don't have a good explanation for what happened."

"There is one other possibility we need to consider, Geoff," said Kapinsky.

"I'm on the edge of my seat, Kapinsky."

"What if Jessica and DeFranco were killed?"

CHAPTER 14

"Murdered! I think you've lost it, Kapinsky."

"Who said anything about murder? Mercy killing is more what I had in mind," he said in a hushed tone as he leaned towards Geoff.

"She had great nursing care, Howard. You said that yourself," interjected a perplexed Karen Choy.

"That's not the point."

"Then get to the point, Kapinsky."

"At 2200, she was supposedly given chloral hydrate. At 2210, her intracranial pressure spikes, and at 2300 she has her massive adrenalin surge. Obviously, it was a result of being given some sort of medication."

"That's easy enough to determine," said Karen. "Chloral hydrate is a controlled substance. All we have to do is check the log in the pharmacy."

"Logs can be altered, Karen," Kapinsky said.

"Why would anyone do something like that?" Karen asked.

"Don't you remember the Brookshire Nursing Home Killer? A nurses' aid working on the night shift knocked off eight patients over a three-month period by injecting lethal doses of potassium. She thought she was doing them a favor, speeding them along to God's Kingdom and—"

"Kapinsky, don't you start talking about a mercy killer on the loose in the hospital, or the next thing you know we'll all be on the front page of the *New York Post*, and you'll be bounced out of this residency, with me close behind!"

Kapinsky persisted. "Let me check the medication log. The only thing that could have caused her ICP to spike like that was a drug."

"I think it would be best if you stayed out of this, Kapinsky. I'll check the log."

"You mean the pharmacy still lets you do that?"

The jab came seemingly from nowhere and hit Geoff hard. *So much for confidentiality.* Anger and resentment welled up within Geoff. Someone had betrayed his trust. His jaw muscles tensed. He leaned forward across the table, then stopped.

To react with anger would be to play into Kapinsky's game. Geoff took a deep breath, leaned back in the chair, his eyes all the while studying Kapinsky's. "Why shouldn't they?" asked Geoff.

"I don't know, Geoff, I mean, I just didn't know if things had—"

"Had what?" Geoff smiled.

Beads of sweat formed on Kapinsky's upper lip. His small brown eyes darted back and forth. He sputtered, then answered. "Changed. That's all, I didn't know if things had changed, you know. I mean, if things were okay between you and the pharmacy after what happened."

"Everything's just fine, Kapinsky. Thanks for asking, but it's not your concern. Now why don't you do something productive like bring us Jessica's last PET scan so we can review it together. Maybe it will corroborate your theory. While you're at it, you better explain why you removed the scan from neuroimaging the other day. You got us in some pretty hot water with Dr. Balassi over it."

"What are you talking about?"

"I'm talking about removing the scan from neuroimaging before Balassi had the chance to review it, and on top of that being stupid enough to sign your name as evidence. Might as well rob a bank and leave a calling card!"

Kapinsky looked confused. "I never removed the scan. I was only going by our discussion of it at rounds the other morning."

"What do you mean? We got blasted by Balassi because you broke the rule and signed out the scan before he read it."

Kapinsky stood his ground like a pit bull. "Like I said, I never saw it. I haven't been down to PET scan in days. Mark and Karen took Jessica down last night for the repeat scan."

Geoff locked stares with Kapinsky, searching for a sign of truth or falsity. "How do you explain your name in the log and her missing folder?"

"Obviously a mistake," he answered matter-of-factly.

"But one you're going to have to answer for to Balassi. I got my ass burned once already trying to protect yours."

"Why don't we check the computer filing system and see if it's shown up?" Karen said.

So simple, thought Geoff, and here we are bantering like kids in the schoolyard. "Good idea, Karen. The bar code on the film plate may have been picked up on the laser scanner on someone's light box."

Karen nodded and they moved to the computer terminal. Geoff sat down at the console, Karen and Kapinsky standing on either side of him. They stared intently at the screen. The multi-colored CRT pulsed brightly as Geoff manipulated the mouse and entered the Neurad system. He typed the command "Petfile tracking" and watched the cursor blink as the computer processed the request.

"Welcome to Petfile tracking. Please enter your security code."

Geoff entered his seven letter code and waited once again.

"Hello, Dr. Davis. Your access is cleared. Please enter patient name and birthdate or hospital number."

Geoff punched in Jessica's name and birthdate. The cursor pulsed as it searched thousands of files for the last time the bar code was scanned.

Then came the answer: PRC-217.

"PRC-217. Where is that, Geoff?" Karen asked.

"PETronics Research Center, Room 217. Balassi's office."

"I don't get it. I thought you said he was pissed off because he couldn't find it and thought I had it," said Kapinsky.

"He was, and he couldn't. Must have found it like Karen said and taken it to his office afterward."

"Except the date and time it was logged in there by the computer precedes the incident," Karen said.

"Someone's trying to make me look bad, and I don't like it," said Kapinsky. "Walter reported my signature in the log book? That son-of-a—"

"Cool down, Kapinsky. I'll clear it up with Dr. Balassi after we finish here." There was clearly no love lost between Kapinsky and Walter. Geoff's thoughts flashed to the cryptic e-mail messages, the strange deaths on his service, Kapinsky's theory, the dig about the pharmacy log. Someone had betrayed him. He felt suddenly uneasy. Geoff shifted in his seat, stood abruptly.

"Where are you going?" Karen asked.

"I've got an important call to make, then I'm going to neuro-imaging to talk to Balassi and find that scan. Somehow, I think it will give us an important clue regarding Jessica's death. If I don't make it back by sundown, call the FBI and tell them Balassi is holding me hostage in his office."

Geoff paused at the doorway, looked at Kapinsky. "Take good care of Smithers. I want to be called for any problems, even a bowel movement that's out of the ordinary. He's the only patient left on our service."

CHAPTER 15

"KAPINSKY SAYS HE NEVER SIGNED THE SCAN OUT, DR. BALASSI."
Geoff stood in front of Balassi, who leaned back in his desk chair staring intently at Geoff over his half-reading glasses.

"The scan's still missing, and Kapinsky's name is in the book. He must be lying to you. God knows why," retorted Josef Balassi sharply. "You're the chief resident, Geoff. Can't you control your flock?"

"Kapinsky says that's not his signature in the log book, Dr. Balassi."

Balassi shifted in his chair, broke eye contact. "Then whose is it, Geoff? Some secret agent forging his signature?"

"That's not exactly what I had in mind."

Balassi leaned forward. "Just what did you have in mind, Geoff?"

"The computer tracked the scan to your office, Dr. Balassi."

"My office? I'm the one looking for the goddamn scan!" Balassi rose from his chair, his close-set brown eyes glaring at Geoff. His voice quivered with anger. "I'm not sure what you're implying Geoff, but I suggest if you want to survive this year you refrain from meddling in my laboratory. If someone in my office misplaced that scan, I will deal with them myself. Is that understood?"

"I'm not implying anything other than what I stated. Pet-file tracked the scan to your office. We've had two very strange deaths on our service, and I believe the girl's PET scan may give us some very important information about the cause."

"Strange deaths, indeed." Balassi leaned back, stroked his beard, motioned Geoff to sit down. "I wonder if you're making it all out to be more than it really is. Looks more like post-head trauma psychosis syndrome and death from cerebral edema to me. The only thing that's strange is your paranoia, Geoff. I think you've been away from this too long."

"I don't think so, Dr. Balassi. These deaths just don't sit right with me, sir. I think there's more to it. I just don't know what at this point."

"We're scientists, Geoff. We act on facts, not feelings."

"That's why I want to review the scan."

Balassi paused, as if in thought, for a moment. "I'll try and track the scan down, Geoff, and as soon as I find it, I'll let you know."

"Dr. Balassi," interrupted Walter Krenholz, now standing in the doorway, "Dr. Zelenkov is here to see you."

Geoff turned toward Walter, stared in annoyance at his intrusion. Walter broke the stare quickly and looked to Balassi for a response.

"Bureaucrats. Great!" He slammed his pencil down on the desk. "That's all I need now, a visit from the PETronics home office. Things have been a mess around here ever since the new residents started July 1!

"You'd better clean up your team's behavior, Geoff, or the main office will pull every dollar out of this place they put into it."

Balassi put his hand to his chin and thought for an instant, then motioned to Walter with his hand. "Tell the good doctor our chief neurosurgery resident will be with him momentarily."

"I thought Zelenkov was due tomorrow."

"Just like the home office to try and catch us off guard. Can't trust them for a minute, which leads me to your role here, Geoff."

Balassi spun around and faced the wall behind the desk, gazing intently at an old photograph, one that Geoff had glanced at with curiosity many times before. It was a photograph of great significance to Balassi, a portrait of a time he spoke of with intense emotion to those who worked in his lab: Balassi, the young scientist, side-by-side with his one and only mentor, who in Geoff's estimation bore an uncanny resemblance to Sigmund Freud, pocket watch and all. Balassi's beard was more closely trimmed, his hair dark brown and closely shorn, but the same fiery intensity had burned in his eyes even then.

"I've worked too hard over the last thirty years to give it all away, Geoff. You can show our friends from PETronics the inner workings of our scanner, even the software for the imaging refinement. But keep them out of the cyclotron. I don't want them near our new isotopes. Once they know the details, every two-bit researcher in the country will try to duplicate our efforts. Understood?"

Geoff nodded in agreement.

"And whatever your thoughts are about the tragic deaths of your patients recently, please don't discuss them with Zelenkov. The last thing we need is PETronics getting involved."

Dr. Pederson's admonition echoed in his mind. *Keep your nose to the grindstone this year, and your future will be golden.*

Geoff had all but accused Balassi of concealing the scan. Geoff had spent his entire last year in Balassi's lab, building a mutual trust. What possible reason would Balassi have to do something so absurd?

"I understand and couldn't agree more, Dr. Balassi. I'm really sorry about my tone earlier regarding the scan. I didn't mean to—"

"Forget about it, Geoff," Balassi interrupted, raising his right hand. "I'll take care of it."

He paused, then gave a smile. "Tell Dr. Zelenkov I'm tied up in the lab now but it will be my honor to meet with him tomorrow."

"Will do." Geoff stood and walked to the door.

"And, Geoff," added Balassi. "Thanks."

CHAPTER 16

"Please tell me about your head injury protocols, Dr. Davis," Dr. Yuri Zelenkov said. "The home office has been most gratified by the work here at the Trauma Center. I'm sure we will be just as generous with funding next year if your success continues."

Geoff and Zelenkov stood by the doorway of the PET scan control room, had just finished the tour of the area. Zelenkov was short, but his broad shoulders filled out his dark blue suit, bulging at the seams. Bald, with a grey fringe of hair impeccably trimmed above his ears, his small mouth neatly framed by a salt and pepper goatee. His eyes were dark, almost charcoal gray, his stare severe, made more so by an intermittent twitch of his left eyelid. His accent was unusual, a mix of Russian and Scandinavian, peppered with a hint of British. Odd. Zelenkov was a Russian name. Must have been his schooling.

Balassi's admonition to tell Zelenkov only what he needed to know echoed inside Geoff's head. "All closed head injury patients get a head bolt placed to monitor the intracranial pressure. They have a PET scan on admission, they're scanned again if there is any change in the mental status, and one last time at discharge."

"And your conclusion from these studies?"

Geoff paused, considered his words carefully. "We're currently analyzing the data. It's to be submitted for publication later this fall."

Zelenkov stroked his goatee, peered at Geoff, seemed to force a grin. "I admire a man who guards his words, Dr. Davis. It shows you can be trusted with things of importance. But I must remind you it is PETronics that funds this research, so you need not fear revealing your preliminary data to us."

Geoff realized Zelenkov was correct. Besides, it was the cyclotron isotopes Balassi seemed concerned about, not the head injury data. "So far it appears there is an excellent correlation with the head injury patients' endorphin levels as demonstrated by PET scan, and the level of consciousness. It's not perfect, but there is a greater correlation than we thought there would be."

Zelenkov nodded approval. "Impressive, Dr. Davis." He paused. "May I call you Geoffrey?"

"Geoff would be fine."

"Very well then, Geoffrey. I don't know if it's been mentioned to you at all, but the home office in Copenhagen has a special educational grant program for chief residents at the institutions we joint venture with. An all expense paid four week trip to Copenhagen. You'd be our special guest, lecture at our medical school, test new isotopes on patients using PETronics' fourth generation PET scanner.

"I can see how much you've learned here, but you can accelerate your training in Europe, where there's no FDA to delay new technology or get in the way of highly experimental research. Unfortunately, the scientific bureaucracy in the United States hampers advancement. It takes an average of seven years in your country to approve a new technology for patient use. In Europe, new medical devices are approved for general use after only one year of testing. Clinical research centers in Europe are once again taking the lead, this time by default."

"The FDA can be a real pain and hinder progress, there's no question about it, but someone has to safeguard the public from potential harm. It's a balancing act, imperfect at times, but necessary."

The spasm of Zelenkov's left eye accelerated, spread to the corner of his mouth. "Don't be so sure, Geoffrey. The history of scientific discovery is replete with risk, researchers and patients risking their health, sacrificing their lives for the public good.

"Louis Pasteur injected himself with his own small pox vaccine, Jonas Salk injected himself with the polio vaccine he developed. New medicines, therapies of all sorts have been tested on AIDS patients, prisoners and the military before being used on the general public. As you can see, there are alternative ways of safeguarding the public other than bureaucratic nuisances like the FDA."

Geoff tensed his jaw. He had no fondness for government bureaucracy either, but the life of another human being was too great a cost for scientific advancement. There was no point in debating Zelenkov further. It would just get Geoff in deeper trouble with Balassi. "I suppose there are alternatives, Dr. Zelenkov."

Zelenkov managed a thin smile, his twitch diminished. He leaned toward Geoff, extended his hand. "I'm glad you can see things from our perspective, Geoffrey. Please consider my offer to visit PETronics. I think you will find it a very rewarding experience."

CHAPTER 17

THE TEAM OF DOCTORS AND NURSES ROUNDING ON THE NEU-rosurgical patients recently discharged from the NSICU paused by the door to room 725. Mark Jackson, the first-year neurosurgery resident, lead the discussion.

"How'd Smithers do last night?" he asked Leslie Rogers, the night nurse coming off shift.

"Considering the extent of his injuries, he's recovering well from a medical point of view. His vitals have been stable, though he hasn't eaten much since yesterday and didn't sleep well at all. The thing I'm more worried about is how much residual brain damage he might have. His psychological status seems a bit strange."

"Strange? What do you mean?" asked Mark, as he looked over the neuro record from the night shift.

"He took a nap after the ICP bolt was flushed and removed yesterday afternoon, but when he woke up around dinner time he started acting a little paranoid."

"Paranoid? All of these head trauma patients act a little weird. You and I would, too, if we had our brains scrambled like he did. He probably has some residual brain swelling, that's all."

Leslie Rogers was annoyed at the young resident's flippant attitude. "I've been a neurosurgical nurse since long before you started medical school, Dr. Jackson. I've seen thousands of post-head trauma patients, and I'm telling you the patient has more than the usual post-head trauma depression or lack of inhibition.

He was downright paranoid during the night."

"I wasn't questioning your experience, Leslie, but he seemed to be coming along fine yesterday when we discharged him from the NSICU," said Mark Jackson. "Why don't you tell me more about this?"

"During the night he kept saying I was trying to drug him and refused to eat or take any medication by mouth. It almost seemed like he was hearing voices, he seemed so agitated and distracted. He had a very fitful night's sleep. We've had to sedate him and give all of his medications and fluids intravenously."

Leslie Rogers checked her watch. "In fact, he's due for another dose of his sedative now."

"What did you give him?" Mark asked.

"Just some Seconal and—"

The startling sound of glass breaking inside room 725 resonated along the hospital corridor. Mark Jackson and Leslie Rogers dropped their charts and rushed into Smithers' room.

"Oh, my God!" screamed Leslie. She put her hand to her mouth.

Standing by the far side of the bed, still holding the chair he had used to break the window, was Smithers. His chest heaved, and his bloodshot eyes danced wildly as the wind rushed in through the gaping window. A fresh cut across his forehead dripped blood on the floor below.

"Stay away from me!" he screamed, saliva spraying from the corners of his mouth. "You're trying to poison me, I know you are!"

Mark Jackson approached cautiously, his shoes crunching on the shards of glass that covered the floor.

"Mr. Smithers, no one here is trying to poison you. The doctors and nurses here—all of us—are trying to help you. You've been in a bad accident. You're recovering, and everything is going to be all right. I think you're just overtired and feeling stressed from the whole ordeal."

Mark continued advancing towards Smithers. "Why don't you get back in bed, and we'll give you a little something to—"

"I won't let you give me any more of your poisons! You're fucking up my head, man!" Smithers threw the chair at them.

Mark and Leslie ducked, and the chair crashed into the wall. Several more people crowded the doorway to the room. Leslie Rogers tried to shoo them away.

"Mr. Smithers, we won't give you anything, I promise," Mark said. He halted in his tracks.

Smithers climbed up on the window ledge. "That's what he told me, too, but he fucking lied to me! Look what's happened," Smithers said, pointing to his head. "But it's not going to happen again. I won't let it!"

"Who told you, Mr. Smithers? Maybe I can talk to him," asked Mark, feebly trying to reason with him by playing into his paranoid delusion.

Mark extended his hand in as non-threatening a way he could. "Why don't you just step back in the room. I promise to tell him never to do it again. Deal?"

Smithers remained on the window sill. His legs were wobbly, barely able to hold up the rest of him. His bloated face was drenched with sweat. He looked down at the street below, then back toward Mark and Leslie.

Ever-so-slowly, Mark Jackson approached, his hand extended, to barely a foot away.

Smithers reached out his trembling hand, then quickly pulled back. He began to laugh like a madman. "I'm free!" he screamed as he fell backwards out of the seventh story window.

Mark Jackson lunged forward, but it all happened much too quickly. All he came up with was Smithers' slipper.

"Holy shit!" he yelled, looking out the window. "He's landed on the third floor overhang! Call a code!"

Geoffrey Davis was on his way to the ER when he was paged stat to the third floor roof. He arrived on the scene just after the code team had started the resuscitation attempt. Unfortunately, they were delayed by the fact the fire exit to the roof had been left locked. They'd had to remove a patient from a third floor room and smash a window to get to Smithers.

Officer Smithers lay on his back, unconscious, bloody fluid oozing from his mouth and nose. Medic Enrique Santos straddled his chest, performing CPR. Mark Jackson breathed him with an ambu bag, and an intern monitored his vitals.

"What the hell happened here, Mark?" asked Geoff.

"We were making rounds on the seventh floor, and Leslie Rogers was just telling me the patient had been acting strangely during the night, when all of a sudden we heard this loud crash, and there he was by the broken window, a chair in his hand, raving like a lunatic." Jackson continued breathing Smithers with the ambu bag.

"Jesus Christ. What the hell is going on with the neurosurgery service?" asked Geoff in frustration. He knelt at the patient's side opposite Santos, placed his stethoscope on Smithers' belly, turned to the intern on his right. "What's his blood pressure?"

"70/40. Pulse barely palpable."

"Doesn't look good, Geoff," Santos said.

"No, it doesn't, my friend. How'd *you* get involved in this code?"

"I was coming off shift, leaving the trauma center. I heard the crash and saw him fall. I ran right up here."

"You've tried to save him twice, only I don't think he'll be as fortunate this time." Geoff removed the stethoscope, felt Smithers' belly, which was rapidly expanding. "Keep the compressions going," he ordered, knowing it was a lost cause.

"Don't you think he's hemorrhaging too quickly for us to keep up with it?" Santos asked.

"I'm sure you're right. In fact, he probably transected his abdominal aorta. His femoral pulses are absent," Geoff said in a hushed tone.

"Should we call it off?" Mark asked.

Geoff panned the surreal scene taking place on the third floor roof around him, then his patient, who just yesterday had been on the miraculous road to recovery from severe head injuries. He thought they had saved him, just like Jessica and DeFranco. The last patient on the NSICU service. Damn. Something or someone was working against him.

Geoff thought of the most recent e-mail message he'd received, the words now holding greater meaning. *There are no accidents in life.*

He looked down at Smithers' corpse, then at Santos, at the intern fruitlessly pumping Smithers' chest.

Geoff turned to Mark Jackson. "Call it off. He's gone."

CHAPTER 18

GEOFF AND STEFAN SAT IN A BOOTH IN THE BACK CORNER OF A smokey coffee house on Houston Street. Geoff wasn't thrilled with the idea of taking the train down to SoHo after his last subway trip, but he had thought it was only fair to meet in Stefan's neck of the woods, since Geoff had called him for help. So Geoff had taken a cab. The irony of the present situation wasn't lost on the two brothers, trying now to communicate above the tavern's din.

"I'm trying to remember the last time you asked me for help," Stefan said. "It's usually the other way around." He sipped his Molson's, placed it back down on the table. "I think it was 1998. You were having problems installing a program on your hard drive. I had to do some re-programming for you. Fixed it pretty well, best I can recall."

Geoff shifted in his seat, took a swig of Stoli. The iced vodka slid down the back of his throat, burning a track in its wake. "Stefan, you make it sound like I don't need you for anything. You know that's not true. I really appreciated being able to stay at your place the other night."

"Don't take it to heart, big brother. I'm just giving you a hard time. Making up for all those times you beat me up in the backyard." Stefan smiled. "Any more news on the rabbi?"

"Nothing I've heard about. The ME's office should be finishing his post pretty soon. I haven't heard any more about his background, any history of mental illness."

Stefan examined the printouts of the e-mails Geoff had brought. He enjoyed being needed by Geoff. "Hmm. Very smart sender you've got here. Each e-mail message passed through at least five different Internet gateways before arriving in your box. Impressive. Has to be a hacker. Or a spy. Almost impossible to trace."

"Can you narrow down the location at all by looking at these gates on the printout?"

"Not really. Could be from the next room, could be from China. Here. Look at this path of origin," said Stephan. "On the surface, the message seems like it came from 'USDA.gov,' an Internet address at the U.S. Department of Agriculture. This may be the case, but I'd bet he's using someone else's address or simply routing the electronic message through the gate to disguise the real origin. That's what makes it so tough to pin down. It's kind of like trying to trace a phone call routed through many different satellite networks. Only tougher." Stefan paused, thought for a moment. "Have you responded to any of the messages?"

"I thought about responding to the last one, but I wasn't sure it would be wise."

"There are two advantages to getting a conversation going. One, just like a phone call, it may make it easier to trace. Maybe the sender will slip up and give us a clue. I doubt it, but you never know. Second, you may get some clues about who this person is just by striking up a conversation. Sex, background, interests. Discerning gender alone narrows it down by fifty percent. You may find out a lot that way.

"I guess it's worth a try."

Stefan studied the text of the message further. "Any significance to the codename Proteus that comes to mind?" He looked up at Geoff, adjusted his glasses. "You were the classics major."

"None I can think of, other than the obvious. Proteus, Greek sea god able to change shapes at will, or in this case, e-mail addresses."

"That's it?" Stefan asked.

Geoff paused, rubbed his brow, thought further. "For what it's worth, the myth is that if Proteus was caught and held onto through his many disguises he'd resume his own shape and be compelled to answer questions."

Geoff sank back in his seat. "Whoever this Proteus is, he or she is behind what's going on at the Trauma Center or is onto it. I've got to find out who it is, Stefan."

"I hear ya, brother. I do. I didn't say it was impossible, just almost impossible. I think I can trace it down if you give me a few days. In the meantime, write back. Give it a try."

Geoff leaned forward, looked around, spoke in hushed tones.

"I don't have a few days, Stefan. Patients are dying for reasons I don't understand."

"Sounds like some pretty heavy shit coming down. I'll do what I can." Stefan smiled, reached into his shirt pocket. He handed Geoff a small black metal object, slightly larger than a computer flash drive. "Happy birthday, big brother."

Geoff held up the device and examined it. He was puzzled. "My birthday's not until November, but I've got a drawer full of flash drives I bought at Costco last week. Any files in particular you want me to download?"

"A little something I put together for you. I think it will come in handy." Stefan grinned, adjusted his wire-frame specs. He leaned across the table, motioned for Geoff to do the same. "When you told me about the problems you were having getting data out of the Traumanet system, I did some analysis of the situation. A system like Traumanet has multiple layers of security.

It has to, given the confidential information that's out there and the large number of users, each person with different information needs and roles. Physicians tend to have a pretty high level of access in healthcare information networks, but I think you've been shut out of the high level information loop, Geoff. The data's out there in cyberspace. You just can't retrieve it."

Stefan pointed to the drive in Geoff's hand. "This will help. It's got a password decoding file I wrote. Very proprietary. If you sign on using a codename with a higher clearance level than yours, the program on this file will do the rest. It will try every permutation possible to figure out the password. Just plug it into one of the usb ports at the network station you're at, and *voila!* But don't let anyone catch you doing it. It's pretty hot property, as you'd imagine."

Geoff weighed the drive in his hand, smiled. "You're too much, Stefan."

"Hey, what are kid brothers for?" Stefan slumped back in his chair, finished his brew. "You sure you're okay at that place Geoff? Beneath your calm exterior, you look worried. Are you safe?"

"I'll be fine. I just wish I knew what was happening, that's all."

"You can stay in my place again for a while if you need to."

"Thanks, little brother. I appreciate the offer, but I'll be okay." Geoff glanced at Stefan's nearly empty glass. "Want another round?"

"No thanks." Stefan checked his watch, finished the last drops of ale. "Ten p.m. Gotta get going. I have a very early meeting tomorrow. I'll be in touch."

Geoff stood, gave his brother a hug. "Thanks for the present."

"Don't mention it," Stefan said. He grasped his brother by the shoulders, looked into his eyes. "Just take it easy, okay bro? You're the only family I have left."

Geoff sat back down, ordered another Stoli before heading back uptown. He'd take a cab at this hour for sure.

Stefan left the coffee house and stepped onto Houston Street, walked east to Third Avenue.

Remaining precisely half a block behind him, a man lurked in the shadows, following the same route. Ice blue eyes watched with keen interest as Stefan Davis entered the apartment building at 321 Third Avenue. Blue eyes waited patiently, then made a notation when the lights went on in the apartment in the northwest corner, fourth floor.

CHAPTER 19

"I don't mean to be melodramatic, Geoff, but I thought you'd want to see this in person. It's pretty damn exciting," said Suzanne, smiling as she handed Geoff the biochemistry report.

Geoff studied the long glossy, white sheets of paper, across which appeared rows of thick blue lines. Some lines were faded, almost clear, others a deep blue. To the left of each row were Greek symbols: *beta*, *delta* and *sigma*. The fourth row was preceded by a question mark. Geoff was confused.

"You paged me here to show me a chromatography assay, Suzanne? What's the big deal?"

"Taken for granted once again. Must be my fate in life, Geoff. Wasn't it just yesterday you were all hot-to-trot about endorphin assays? Or was it my imagination?" She pulled the sheet of paper from his hands. "Guess I'll just file it away."

"Endorphin assays?" Geoff grabbed the report from Suzanne and examined it, his interest rising.

"Our discussion yesterday got me thinking about it, so I ran it on all three patients—DeFranco, Jessica and Smithers. De-Franco's tissue was a bit decomposed, but you can get a feeling for what's going on, nonetheless. I didn't expect to find *this*."

Geoff studied the papers. "It's been a long time since I've read a chromatography assay."

Suzanne motioned Geoff to sit down beside her at her cluttered desk. She adjusted her glasses, brushed back her auburn hair, and crossed her legs, revealing just enough of her upper thigh to draw Geoff's attention. She was an attractive woman.

She cleared her throat. "Here. Let's take a look at the girl's assay first. It's a good representation. Highly abnormal, even considering her previously comatose state."

She pointed to the first row and traced the line with her index finger. "The first row represents her delta-endorphin level. This is really a measure of her enkephalins, similar to but not quite the same as endorphins. Her level is within normal limits, nothing unusual there. I wouldn't expect there to be anything out of the ordinary.

"Same goes for her *gamma* assay, also relatively normal," she said, shifting her attention to the second row.

"Her *beta*-level, the sub-group of endorphins I'd expect to be sky high considering her recent coma, is actually somewhat low, nothing remarkable in and of itself, but suggestive, nonetheless."

Suzanne shifted in her chair, tugged on her skirt. It had inched its way upward.

"Suggestive of what?" asked Geoff.

"Suggestive of competitive inhibition with whatever the question mark represents, and I think it represents something significant, just as you surmised."

"Oh?"

"I think we've discovered a new endorphin!" she said proudly, looking up at Geoff with a victorious smile.

"Look here." She pointed to the third line. "This light blue bar represents her *sigma* endorphin level. *Sigma* endorphin receptors are almost non-existent in normal brain tissue, except in angel dust junkies, speed freaks, and some schizophrenics. As you'd expect, she didn't have much *sigma* endorphin activity.

"But look at this," Suzanne continued, her level of excitement rising with each word, "right next to her *sigma* band is a superdense concentration of a similar endorphin, one thousand times as concentrated as her *beta* level."

Geoff's eyes squinted in doubt. "Are you sure? I mean, could it be a mistake? Tissue from the wrong patient, a contamination on the chromatography strip, something like that?"

"Those were my first thoughts as well, Geoff. I ran a second, independent assay on another tissue sample taken from the same region of the brain. The results were identical, and the other two patients demonstrate similar patterns. This is a major neuro-chemical breakthrough, Geoff!"

"What implication does this have?"

"We may win the Nobel Prize for this if we play our cards right."

"I mean for the cases we're trying to figure out, here, Suzanne. The patients who died so suddenly when everything about their progress pointed toward recovery?"

"I'm sorry for getting so carried away, but this sort of thing doesn't happen often."

She straightened up in her chair, removed her glasses, placed the printout on the desk. "Well, it indicates an exceedingly high level of a *sigma-like* endorphin, emphasis on *like*. One with similar characteristics in some ways, probably different in others than a true *sigma* compound. This is virgin territory here. Your guess is as good as mine."

"How closely related does it seem biochemically?"

"Close enough that someone might have missed it on casual inspection. But as you can see, it's a real entity."

"I mean are we talking about a difference in a single carbon atom or an entire group of amino acids?"

Suzanne studied the printout thoughtfully. "That's impossible to tell from just a chromatography assay. I would guess one or two amino acids and probably a slight molecular conformational change. All it takes is one amino acid substitution to entirely change the functional ability of a protein. Just look at hemoglobin and sickle cell anemia. Valine for glutamic acid, and voila, abnormal hemoglobin."

"Could this have been a mutation?"

"That's possible, but not likely," Suzanne said.

"Why's that?"

"Several reasons. One being that the concentration of this *sigma-like* endorphin—let's call it *sigma-b*—was about one thousand times the concentration of her *beta* endorphin level. *Beta* endorphins are known to be high in comatose patients, and their levels were high in these patients, though somewhat lower than expected. This *sigma-b* endorphin was being produced by the enzymes in their brains at a phenomenal rate, to the exclusion of other related endorphins."

She paused. "What was each of the patients' behavior like while they were in the hospital?"

"Like any other patients with head injuries in the intensive care unit, frightened and confused."

"And prior to their head injuries?"

"We know they weren't schizophrenic. They were ordinary people without medical or neurologic histories of any significance."

"You said they were on the road to neurological recovery until each one suddenly went sour. Tell me about it."

"Well, with Jessica, both her vital signs and her level of mental alertness had been stable for about forty-eight hours. She became agitated in the middle of the night, presumably from a bad nightmare. According to the nurse on nightshift, she let out a shriek so loud it could be heard in the ward one floor below. Jessica became increasingly agitated, frightened, confused. Then several hours later she lost consciousness and had a cardiac arrest."

"How did her vital signs correlate with that?"

"That's the fascinating piece of the whole puzzle. Around the same time she had a sudden meteoric rise in the intracranial pressure, followed by significant elevations of her heart rate and blood pressure. Then she coded. The other two patients had their head bolts pulled hours before their bizarre behaviors, so we don't know what their intracranial pressures were like before they died."

"Any theories?" Suzanne asked.

"It's possible it was an adverse drug reaction of some kind.

At least in the girl's case, about an hour before all of this occurred, she was supposedly given chloral hydrate sedative by the night nurse."

"Supposedly given choral hydrate?"

"The nurse remembers receiving the ampule on the lift from the pharmacy, then drawing up the medication, but the pharmacy has no record of dispensing it."

Suzanne removed her glasses, massaged the bridge of her nose. "Hmm. Interesting. Chloral hydrate has been known to cause an idiosyncratic reaction that can lead to a similar picture, the agitation and elevated heart rate, but not the sudden rise in intracranial pressure. Especially to that level. It just doesn't fit, and the toxicology screen did not indicate any chloral hydrate in her system. What else could have caused the reaction? Think theoretical now. It doesn't have to make sense."

"An internally hemorrhaging brain tumor could do it, but nothing like that ever showed up on her MRI or PET scans."

"I've sliced the brain completely. No tumor."

"A ruptured aneurysm. Again, nothing on scans to correlate

with that."

"No aneurysm seen at autopsy, either."

"Brain infection like meningitis, maybe," he offered, shaking his head doubtfully. He was reaching.

"Nope, no signs of central nervous system infection. Anything else?"

"Not really. That list runs the gamut from the unlikely to the improbable."

Suzanne suddenly looked up from the charts at Geoff. "What about the head bolt?" she asked, a gleam in her eyes.

"Bolts can't cause the brain pressure to elevate. They're just pressure monitors, unless they become infected and cause meningitis. You said there was no evidence of infection."

"That's not what I meant. Did anyone check the bolt to see if it was working properly? I mean, what if the pressure never really spiked like that?"

"They're flushed and calibrated every night. Hers checked out fine. It's documented in the nursing notes."

"So you're sure the pressure spike was real?"

"Yes."

"You're becoming pretty trusting in your old age, Geoff."

"What are you getting at, Suzanne?"

"I guess that brings us back to the only way to figure out if *sigma-b* was a mutation or was somehow introduced."

Geoff leaned forward in his chair. "Their PET scans."

"That's right. We've got to review them right away and see how they correlate."

"I've got bad news, Suzanne. The hard copies are missing, the digitalized versions inaccessible."

Geoff thought of his meeting with Stefan. The information was out there in cyberspace.

CHAPTER 20

"At least *I* couldn't retrieve the data," Geoff said. "Maybe *you* can."

"I don't get it, Geoff," Suzanne said. "We're both physicians at the Trauma Center. We should both have the same access."

"We probably do, by and large, except for these cases. I think I've been selectively deleted from the loop on this stuff. If it's true, we've got a whole lot more to worry about than I thought."

Geoff walked over to the terminal in Suzanne's office, sat down. "Here, let me sign on, I'll show you." He entered the Traumanet system, signed on to Neurad. Each attempt to retrieve the PET scans on the three patients failed, "insufficient data" the response. Geoff signed off the system. "Now you try."

Suzanne leaned over Geoff's shoulder, a wisp of her hair brushing his face. She pulled her chair over, sat down beside him, signed on to Neurad. Suzanne entered Jessica's hospital number and waited. A digitalized image of a PET scan appeared on the screen.

"Damn. I knew it!" Geoff reached over and gave Suzanne a warm hug.

"Good going, Dr. Davis," she said.

Geoff leaned closer to the screen. "Mind if I do this?" He reached for the mouse.

"Be my guest. This is your territory anyway." Suzanne rolled her chair over a bit to make more room for Geoff.

Geoff checked the dates on each of the three images and

placed them in order: Jessica's admission scan followed by the scan right after her bolt placement, and finally, the last study, the one taken the night before she died.

He studied the first scan. "Looks like a radioactive carbon-11 study. This is the isotope I worked on in Balassi's lab. We used it to measure endorphin receptor saturation." Geoff traced the outer area of the brain, the cerebral cortex. "This royal blue indicates a very low level of endorphins in her cerebral cortex. No surprise. But look here in her deep, reticular area," he said, pointing out a small, linear region of fiery vermillion. "This saturation is consistent with her coma and a high level of *beta* endorphins."

Suzanne studied the film closely, repositioned her glasses. "I don't see any indication of a *sigma-like* endorphin here, do you?"

"No, I don't."

"Well, that's proof against the mutation theory. She obviously had no significant *sigma* endorphins on admission."

"Let's look at the second scan," he said, shifting his attention to the middle image. "If you look at the same cut of the reticular area, you can see that the *beta* endorphin concentration is fading. It's now a light red, consistent with when she started awakening from her coma."

"How do you explain this?" she asked, pointing to the third and final scan.

Geoff stared at the third image on the screen, his gaze riveted in astonishment. At the base of her brain, deep within her temporal lobes, blazed an iridescent red horseshoe.

"It can't be," he whispered in a hushed but incredulous tone. His attention jumped to the name at the top of the screen. It was Jessica's scan, her hospital number; the date and time were all correct.

Suzanne seemed to know the scan was abnormal, but not to

what extent. She looked to Geoff. "What does it mean, Geoff?"

"The amygdaloid horseshoe. It's a pattern we see only in schizophrenics or someone higher than a kite on angel dust."

Suzanne seemed confounded. "I thought you said she was a normal, healthy eight year old prior to the accident?"

"She was."

Geoff moved on to the next image. The bright amygdaloid horseshoe seemed larger and more intense. His gaze followed the sequence of slices. The enlarging horseshoe had encompassed her entire brainstem, like a rapidly expanding mass or a ruptured aneurysm. He studied the subsequent frames: first the adjacent temporal lobes were engulfed by the spreading firestorm, then the entire cerebral cortex. "I've never seen anything like this—or have I?"

The entire brain, from the brainstem to the cortex, was aglow a searing red.

"Does this mean her brain was supersaturated with endorphins?"

"That's right, Suzanne, but not just any endorphin." He pointed to the last image on the screen. "There's your *Sigma-b!* It's consumed her entire brain substance! Let's print this out." Geoff clicked on the print command.

Suzanne studied the entire sequence of frames carefully. "I know this sounds strange, but it almost looks as though her brain is pulsating."

Geoff grabbed the color printout of the PET scan, studied it carefully.

Pulsating. A pulsating brain. Geoff remembered his hellish nightmare. "Oh, my God," he whispered.

"What is it Geoff?" she asked in obvious concern.

"Kapinsky was right."

"What?" She leaned forward.

"The rabbi. Do you still have his chart?"

"Are you okay, Geoff? What's going on?"

"The rabbi, Suzanne. The chart I asked you to hold for me!"

"Yes, I have it. Now tell me what the hell is going on here!"

"I need another favor, Suzanne. See if you can pull up PET scans on a Jesus Romero and on the rabbi for me. The computer already denied my access to Romero's file. Do it right away while you still have access to the data."

"I think you've lost me, Geoff, and unless you fill me in on what's going on, I'm not doing you any more favors."

"Print out all the scans, and page me when you're done. I'll fill you in on everything, Suzanne, I promise." Geoff turned to leave the lab, the hardcopy of Jessica's PET scan in hand.

"Where are you going with that scan, Geoff?"

"I'm going to show this to Balassi. He's got some explaining to do."

CHAPTER 21

JOSEF BALASSI STOOD BY THE VIEWING BOX IN HIS OFFICE, studying the astonishing scan. His keen eyes darted from frame to frame, after a brief pause fixating on each one. When he reached the final frame, he scratched his beard, and with a nod of the head turned off the viewer, removed the scan from the box, placed it back on his desk.

Geoff stood beside Balassi, amazed at his apparent disinterest.

"How did you get these, Geoff?" Balassi asked with more than a hint of curiosity. He handed the scan back to Geoff. "We've been turning the film room upside down for almost a week trying to find the original hardcopies. I thought the digital images were lost as well."

"I retrieved them from the Neurad system. Not without some difficulty."

An awkward silence.

Balassi cleared his throat, motioned for Geoff to sit down. "Walter, Walter," Balassi said. "You know, it's hard to believe how someone so organized and thorough as Walter could be so computer illiterate at times! Some days I wonder if he remembers to screw his head back on the right way in the morning before he comes to the lab." Balassi chuckled loudly, then began tapping the table with his index finger. "I bet you're wondering about the unusual results on that final scan."

"That did cross my mind."

"Of course it did, Geoff, of course." Balassi reached over and gave Geoff a pat on the shoulder. "I can understand you're very upset by the loss of your patients, Geoff. First, the hang glider, then the little girl, now the cop. We've never had a patient jump out a window here before, at least not since the days when the psychiatric hospital was housed here. Tragic indeed, Geoff. But you must realize that patients with head injuries like these may have far more brain damage than we detect. It's not unusual for their conditions to suddenly go downhill."

"I suppose, in general, that may be true, but these patients were well on the road to neurological recovery."

Balassi's hard brown eyes showed a glimmer of compassion. He leaned back in his chair and clasped his hands together, staring at Geoff. "Well, tell me, what do you think it shows? You know as much about PET scanning as anyone, almost as much as I do."

"It doesn't take an expert to see that the brain's totally saturated with endorphins."

"It does appear that way, doesn't it? Quite a spectacular discovery, Geoff. A patient with a head injury coming out of a coma suddenly relapses with cerebral edema, and we document the underlying cause *as it's happening*, on a PET scan, a massive outpouring of the brain's endorphins. The correlation appears perfect, doesn't it? Do you have any theories?"

"Several."

"Let's hear them." Balassi settled back in his chair, his chin resting on his intertwined hands.

"The first possibility I considered was that the endorphins were merely the result of generalized brain swelling. Of course, such massive levels of endorphin from brain swelling have never been documented. It's really never been studied before in the lab or on PET scan."

Balassi studied Geoff carefully. "A credible theory, to be sure, Geoff, but you don't buy it, do you?"

"No, I don't. For her endorphin level to be as high as it appeared on PET scan, every neuron and support cell in her brain had to be totally geared up as an endorphin factory to the exclusion of any other cellular function. The only thing that could do that might be something like a very fast acting virus infecting her brain, but I doubt we've discovered a new virus here. Anyway, viruses infecting the nervous system tend to be slow acting."

"Highly unlikely, I agree. Go on."

"Also out is traumatic aneurysm or meningitis. The brain appeared structurally normal on autopsy, according to Suz—the pathologist."

"Ah, Dr. Gibson. A brilliant neuropathologist. She has done some excellent work on the brain's biochemistry, hasn't she?"

"That's what I've heard. Yes."

"Did she provide any insight into the girl's death?"

Geoff took a deep breath and paused. He didn't want to involve Suzanne, but a powerful figure like Balassi would find out sooner or later. Better he be told at least a partial truth of their discovery.

"The only logical explanation seems to be that it was drug-induced."

"Oh?" Balassi furrowed his brow in apparent interest.

"I think she was given something—intentionally."

Balassi's smile froze for an instant, then the corners of his mouth turned upward, and he let out a loud belly laugh.

"I'm sorry, Geoff, I really am," he said, obviously trying to harness his laughter. "You're way out in left field on this one. I'd have thought you'd be smarter than to let Howard Kapinsky plant his ridiculous ideas in your head. That mercy killing conspiracy nonsense, really. If I were Pederson, I'd have thrown the fool out of the program by now."

He shook his head, massaged his jaw. "Okay, let's look at this wild accusation. You have three questions to answer, and I'm anxious to hear your responses. Who, why, and with what?"

Geoff felt acutely uncomfortable. He believed he was onto something, but Balassi was a master at holding his cards close to his chest and at power plays.

"I don't know who or why, but I have a thought about what: some sort of an endorphin-inducing drug, a PCP-like compound."

"You seem pretty sure of yourself, Geoff. Tell me, were there any unusual drugs on the toxicology screen?"

"No. At least none that have shown up yet."

"Well then, your theory is blown out of the water for two reasons. First, and I'm surprised you haven't considered this, eighty percent of any endorphin or endorphin-like substance injected intravenously would be metabolized by the liver before it ever reached the brain. The small amount that might make it that far would be a thousand times below levels that would give a PET scan picture like this."

"True. But what if it was bound to a fat-soluble sphere like a liposome, then injected? The level reaching the brain would be much higher, wouldn't it?"

"A good thought, Geoff, but the endorphin would still not reach such a level of saturation as we viewed a few moments ago. I'm afraid the answer lies in the study, not in the patient."

"The study? What are you talking about?"

"The study was completely worthless! It was supposed to be a radioactive C-11 study of her endorphins, of course, but the entire batch of labeling compound was bad that day. All the scans done during the twelve-hour period had to be repeated. Unfortunately, she passed away before that could be accomplished. I was so furious with Walter and the lab tech I could have fired them both on the spot, but mistakes do happen now and then. Anyway, I had to forgive them. The cyclotron's cooling system had a leak, and no one else knows how to trouble shoot that damn machine better than Walter."

Geoff felt deflated, confused. He'd thought he had the puzzle of Jessica's sudden deterioration neatly solved, that Dr. Balassi would confirm his theory. "How does that explain the entire brain lighting up on the scan?"

"It's simple, really. The carbon atom was mistakenly tagged to glucose, and glucose, as you know, is ubiquitous throughout the brain. Hence, the spreading pattern culminating in the entire brain lighting up."

"I see." Geoff shifted uncomfortably in his seat. "That makes good sense, Dr. Balassi."

Balassi smiled. "I apologize for our isotope lab. Of course, I must accept complete blame. It won't happen again."

"No problem, Dr. Balassi. I understand. You're right about Kapinsky. I should stop listening to him. He's nothing but trouble."

Geoff wanted to get out of the lab quickly—with the scan—and compare it to the other scans Suzanne was trying to retrieve for him.

He was convinced Balassi was hiding key information from him. Balassi had not accounted for one major item: the *horseshoe*. The pattern was anything but random on Jessica's scan. He wondered if the same pattern would show up on the other scans as well.

Partial truths, deceptions. Geoff thought about Kapinsky's

comment regarding the pharmacy log, wondered if Balassi had betrayed his trust. Only two people had known, or so he had thought, Balassi and Pederson.

Geoff stood to leave, clutching Jessica's scan in his clammy palms.

Balassi stood as well, approached him. "So tell me, how were you able to retrieve this scan on the Neurad system when our own techs couldn't do it?"

Geoff tried not to break his stare, but faltered for a split second, long enough, he was sure, for Balassi to make a mental note of his reaction. "It was simple, really. I just signed on and entered the patient's hospital number. Just like I always do." Geoff smiled.

"Oh?" Balassi massaged his bearded chin. "Somehow, I don't think you're giving me the full story. This is beginning to sound like an Agatha Christie novel, Geoff! Accusations of mysterious mercy killings, unnamed accomplices delving for information. Well, I won't ask you to breach your code of confidentiality," he said with a paternalistic smile.

Balassi lead Geoff to the doorway, then paused. Geoff felt a pull on the scan.

"I'll take that back to the filing room myself. It may be the only hard copy we have until we find the original."

***

"I told you never to call me on this line unless it was an emergency."

"It is, in a manner of speaking, general," Balassi replied. "I need to speak to Bluebird."

Silence. He was only to use that salutation in the event of a condition red.

"Hold on. I'll get him on the line and scramble the transmission."

These government fools with their asinine names. Why had he let them stay involved?

Another minute passed, a dissonant whirring sound emanated from the phone. Reflexively, Balassi held the receiver a distance away from his ear.

"Bluebird's on the line. Go ahead," said the general.

"What the hell's goin' on down there Papa Bear?

"Why is it I always feel like I'm part of a children's fairy tale when I talk to you gentlemen?" asked Balassi sarcastically. No response. Totally humorless. They were all the same.

"The line is secure," said Bluebird.

"Then how about real names for a change?"

"I'd rather we didn't. Is the project in jeopardy?"

"Not yet, but we've got a serious problem that could jeopardize everything if it's not corrected right away."

"What the hell does that mean? I don't like surprises, Papa Bear. *The Sigma Project* is of the highest priority."

"We've got a loose cannon here."

"Is it the one we discussed last week?"

Balassi paused.

"Well?"

"The very same."

"And your solution?" asked Bluebird.

"I'm trying to steer him away from—"

"He must be neutralized."

"I really don't think that's necessary," said Balassi, his voice hesitant. "I'm sure I can settle him. We've got leverage that should shut him up."

"It's really out of your hands now, Papa Bear," interrupted Bluebird. "We'll take care of everything on this end. You just see the project continues. We don't want 1962 all over again."

"I won't allow it," muttered Balassi, staring at the photograph on the wall behind his desk.

"What was that?"

"I said, don't worry about it."

"I won't. Just let us handle it from here." A few seconds of silence passed. "And Papa Bear, one more thing."

"Yes?"

"I want that vial. Soon. Very soon."

CHAPTER 22

GEOFF SAT ALONE IN THE HOUSE STAFF OFFICE STARING BLANK-ly at the CRT. Things hadn't felt right since the day he started back from his year in the lab. He had wondered why he was treated so well by Balassi and Pederson after last year's pharmacy log incident, the accusations of drug abuse, though he passed the urine test. Now word of the incident had crept somehow to Kapinsky. The whole situation was beginning to smell rotten.

The e-mail icon flickered in the upper right-hand corner of the screen, indicating a new message had arrived in his electronic mailbox. His heart pounded, his palms felt clammy. Could it be another message from Proteus? Geoff maneuvered the mouse, clicked on the icon. There were three new messages.

MESSAGE #1

DATE: July 5, 2010

TIME: 13:38

FROM: Alpha Micronet.org/syssad

Received: NYTC.org, 5 July 2010, 13:37.

MESSAGE: Hi, big brother. Proteus routing messages through government and academic gateways, using expired addresses. I'm about halfway there. A few more messages and I may have point of origin nailed. He's a professional, but so am I! Don't forget, get a conversation going. Hold fast, and he may show his true self and answer your questions. I'll call you.

Stefan

Geoff smiled. If anyone could track down Proteus, Stefan could. He thought about how much closer he and Stefan had become. After all this was over, they'd spend more time together, just the two of them. Maybe go on that fishing trip to Alaska they'd always talked about.

Geoff had always been too busy. Not anymore. He'd make the time.

Geoff checked the second message.

MESSAGE #2

DATE: July 5, 2010

TIME: 15:45

FROM: S. Gibson/NYTC-P1/pthsjg

MESSAGE: I've got all the scans but Romero's. See you at my place 7 p.m. We'll make it a working dinner, okay?

Suzanne

Suzanne was nothing if not persistent. She was a bright, engaging woman, and Geoff had to admit he was attracted to her, though she did make him feel a little nervous. He hadn't been with a woman since Sarah. Meet at her apartment instead of the lab? Interesting. Her apartment was safer, more secure, at least for reviewing the scans. Whatever else happened maybe this was a good opportunity for him to move on, let go of Sarah more completely.

Geoff moved on to the third message.

MESSAGE #3

DATE: JULY 5, 2010

TIME: 16:44

FROM: Received by: Mercury, NYTC.org, 5 July 2010, 16:43; Received: Cobalt,telnet/locis.loc.gov, 5 July 2010, 16:41; Received: gopher/nih.gov, 5 July 2010, 16:38; Received: telnet/ info.umd.edu, 5 July 2010, 16:34; Received: telnet/nasa.gov, 5 July 2010, 16:31; Received from: ber2759.USDA.gov, 5 July2010, 16:28.

MESSAGE: When you have eliminated the impossible, whatever remains, however improbable, must be the truth. Proteus.

Great goddamn time for philosophy. He pondered the phrase. Truth, indeed. Who spoke the truth anymore around here? He read the message again, the familiar words nagging him. He knew the phrase from somewhere.

Geoff's finger trailed across the screen, sifting through the internet gateways for any deviation in routing of the message. At first glance it seemed the same as the routing of previous messages, a convoluted pathway of government and public agencies. He punched in a command, entered Stefan's email address, forwarded the latest message to him for analysis.

Geoff's hands rested on the keyboard, his gaze fixed on the message. Stefan's words tugged at him, egged him on. *Get a conversation going, hold fast and he may answer your questions.* Geoff made a decision, typed a reply.

What is the truth?

He sent his message, then waited. The odds of chatting real time with Proteus were slim. Particularly if he was as professional as Stefan thought he was. Geoff tapped his foot, checked his watch. Five p.m. He had to be at Suzanne's at seven to review the scans. Plenty of time. Suzanne said she was able to retrieve all but Romero's. Even with her sign-on, she couldn't access it. Maybe they were onto her, too.

Minutes passed. No response from Proteus to his question. Geoff's mind wandered back to Romero. Geoff needed hard evidence Romero had been a patient at the Trauma Center. He couldn't find Romero's scan or his chart, but there was one trail they might have neglected to cover up.

He toggled back to the menu screen and clicked on the appointment scheduling system, then the appointment history submenu. He entered Romero's full name and waited. The cursor blinked, teased him. Seconds passed. The screen flickered, came up blank. Geoff muttered, bit his lower lip. Damn.

One more thought came to mind. Geoff switched back to the Neurad system, entered the schedule sub-menu. He thought back to the period of time he remembered Romero had his scan, sometime around Memorial Day. He entered the date.

Patient names and numbers filled the screen, the record of patients scheduled for PET scans on May 23, 2010. Geoff scanned the names, his finger gliding down the screen. No Jesus Romero. He scrolled through the days, one at a time, each attempt coming up empty. Until June second, two p.m., the date and time Jesus Romero, patient number 257-368, had his PET Scan.

"Yes!" Geoff pounded the table. He returned to the screen, checked the descriptive entry next to the appointment time. Admission scan. He continued scrolling, day by day. June 15, ten a.m., discharge scan. Jesus Romero *had* been a patient at the NYTC. He had had two PET scans performed. Someone let the information slip through. Hopefully he or she would get careless again. Geoff would have to watch for any other slivers of information that might creep through.

An icon lit up, flickered on the upper right corner of the screen. E-mail received. Geoff toggled to the e-mail screen.

MESSAGE #4

DATE: JULY 5, 2010

TIME: 1708

FROM: Received: Mercury, NYTC.org, 5 July 2010, 17:07; received: telnet/info.umd.edu, 5 July 2010, 17:06; received: telnet/nasa.gov, 5 July 2010, 17:04; received: ber2759.USDA. gov, 17:01; received cobalt, telnet/locis.loc.gov, 17:00; received: telnet/glis.cr.usgs.gov, 5 July 2010, 16:58. Sent: gopher/nih.gov, 5 July 2010, 16:55.

MESSAGE: The truth is a seven percent solution. Similar but different.

They had communicated real time! Proteus was sitting at a computer terminal somewhere at this very moment. Geoff tapped his foot, thought about the cryptic message. *Seven percent solution*. What did Proteus mean? Again, the familiarity of the phrase vexed him. The message could mean any number of things. Geoff's mind raced through the possibilities. Seven percent of the internet gates? Maybe Proteus was trying to tell him something about a percentage of the isotopes on the PET scans, or a percentage of the neurosurgical patients on his service who would be in trouble. Nothing seemed to make sense.

Was Proteus simply playing games with him, stalling for time? Or was Geoff simply thinking too literally? If he kept the conversation going, held on, maybe he could find out more. Geoff typed another response.

Where can I find the seven percent solution?

Several minutes passed, another message arrived.

MESSAGE #5

DATE: JULY 5, 2010

TIME: 17:16

FROM: Received: Mercury, NYTC.org, 5 July 2010, 17:15; received: telnet/nasa.gov, 5 July 2010, 17:14; received: ber2759. USDA.gov, 5 July 2010, 17:12; received: cobalt, telnet/locis.loc. gov, 5 July 2010, 17:11; received: telnet/glis.cr.usgs.gov, 5 July 2010, 17:10; received: telnet/info.umd.edu, 5 July 2010, 1708; sent by: gopher/listserve.columbia.edu, 5 July 2010, 17:09.

MESSAGE: 221B Baker Street.

Geoff stared at the message, bit his lower lip. Two twenty-one B Baker Street? There was no Baker Street in New York, at least none he knew of. Geoff was getting tired of this game. So much for the real time conversation idea. Why didn't Proteus just come out and tell him what he wanted Geoff to know? Was he being toyed with, or could it be the communications were being monitored?

Geoff flipped through the messages one more time, read them over. So cryptic, yet so familiar. He tapped his foot, thought.

The realization smacked him in the face like a cold bucket of water. Of course it seemed familiar. Any high school student could have put it all together.

Excitedly, Geoff entered his response: *The Sign of the Four.*

Geoff hit the 'enter' key, bouncing the message back through the Internet gateways. He had to be right. And if he was, the treasure, in this case the truth, lay hidden in the one place truly fitting such a description.

Could he go there and simply explore unnoticed? It wouldn't be easy, but his navy training had prepared him for far more difficult missions.

Several minutes passed, another message returned.

MESSAGE #6

DATE: JULY 5, 2010

TIME: 1738

FROM: Received: Mercury, NYTC.org, 5 July 2010, 17:37; received: cobalt, telnet/locis.loc.gov, 5 July 2010, 17:35; received: telnet/nasa.gov, 5 July 2010, 17:31; received ber2759. USDA.gov, 5 July 2010, 17:28; received: telnet/info.umd.edu, 5 July 2010 17:25; sent by: telnet/sklik.mcgilu.edu, 5 July 2010, 17:23.

MESSAGE: Elementary, Dr. Davis. Be on your guard; it's a deadly game. No further communication possible for now. Good luck.

He was right. Geoff looked around, checked to make sure no one saw his communication. The room remained empty. He stared at the message, then forwarded it, same as the others, to Stefan. His mysterious electronic pen pal had to be close by, studying him, watching his movements. Proteus' words seemed to pulsate on the screen. *Be on your guard, it's a deadly game.* Geoff had held on long enough to get some answers.

It had been a deadly game already. Geoff couldn't imagine things getting much worse.

CHAPTER 23

As the elevator swiftly ascended to the twelfth floor of the PETronics Research Building, Geoff's mind raced. He tried to sort out the pieces of the complex puzzle. He wanted to review the PET scans in person with Suzanne, but this was far more important. He left her a message postponing their dinner plans. Her response indicated she wasn't thrilled.

Geoff had deciphered Proteus' cryptic messages and distilled valuable information from them. The clues were from Sir Arthur Conan Doyle's tale of Sherlock Holmes, The Sign of the Four, a story of murder, cryptic letters from an unknown sender, and a missing treasure, hidden in a laboratory.

It's a seven percent solution. Cocaine was a seven percent solution in those days. Same, but different. Cocaine was structurally similar to morphine; both stimulated endorphin production. It made perfect sense to Geoff to search Balassi's lab for the answers.

Proteus seemed to be an ally. Or was Geoff simply being set up, led down a path to slaughter? His instinct told him he was not.

Balassi was a man Geoff had known for five years and worked closely with for the past year. A man who knew the trauma of Geoff's personal life in detail and who nonetheless came to his aid and offered him a place in his lab. A man Geoff respected tremendously. A man he thought he knew as well as anyone did. Geoff could not believe if the Josef Balassi he knew suspected, or knew, anything about foul play with his research, he would tolerate it for a moment without calling for a massive investigation.

Geoff had made an accusation—indirect, but an accusation nonetheless—that the girl was injected intentionally. Balassi reacted as if it were a debate on grand rounds. Balassi's reaction to the other patients' bizarre deaths was strangely detached. That's what didn't sit right with Geoff. Balassi's facial expression. The laughter. This was not the old Josef Balassi. This was a man with something to hide, a genius playing games.

Geoff was beginning to feel he was being set up. The tailor-made lab research position, the chief residency. Why the red carpet treatment for a doctor suspected of drug abuse, even if he was innocent? All the more reason Geoff had to do what he was about to do. All the more reason to proceed with extreme caution.

Geoff knew if he was caught he'd be bounced from the program in a second, but knew the best place to find the answers and information he needed was in Balassi's lab. Balassi practically lived in his laboratory. It was where his research projects were developed and carried out, compounds stored, papers written, phone calls logged, even personal notes and appointments cleared though the lab's calendar. It was Balassi's inner sanctum.

The elevator decelerated and came to a halt with a slight bounce as it arrived at the twelfth floor. Geoff looked up at the cobalt blue, illuminated numbers overhead to be sure he was at the right floor, then remembered there was no need to check as the automated voice reminded him: "Floor twelve, PETronics Research Center. Please have your I.D. ready."

Geoff clenched his fists together and took a deep breath as the elevator doors parted and the refrigerated air from the corridor wafted into the elevator. He stepped cautiously, hands in his lab coat pockets, and looked around to see if anyone else was there. He didn't want to be seen, but if he was confronted he had prepared a story about a patient chart he left in the lab. That might buy him a safe ticket out, but he would not have accomplished his mission. He hoped he wouldn't have to use it. The odds of anyone walking the halls of the research lab at eleven o'clock on a Monday night were small, except for the guard. A year working in the lab, however, had made Geoff well aware of the fact the guards at the Research Building, like security guards elsewhere, took frequent coffee breaks and would rather be watching late night TV or surfing the web than stare at video monitors. Their routine was to make their rounds at midnight. Geoff checked his wrist, set the timer on his watch. He had fifty-eight minutes to get in, find what he needed, and get out.

He walked briskly down the long, starkly lit corridor, squinting his eyes to shut out the glare of the florescent lights. He felt like a bank robber in broad daylight. He wished he could shut the damn lights off, but doing so might attract more attention. Even more worrisome was the incessant squeaking of his Nikes on the polished vinyl floor echoing down the empty corridor. He slowed his pace, attempted to tread lightly, rolling heel to toe to minimize sound.

Geoff continued around the corner, then froze. He caught a movement in his peripheral vision. Instinctively, he flattened his body against the wall, his attention fixating in the direction of the movement. It was the security camera, a small, silver box mounted in the corner, rotating back and forth to scan the area. Geoff scurried into a shadowy doorway, his heart pounding, and held his breath as the camera aimed in his direction, then slowly rotated down the other hallway.

He slid out of the shadows and down the hall, parked himself behind a large grey trash can and slumped to the floor to catch his breath and get his bearings. He checked his watch. Fifty-three minutes remained. Only one short stretch of hallway to go, but he had already wasted five valuable minutes. He would have to move the next time the camera aimed the other way.

Geoff peeked around the edge of the trash can, his gaze following the camera. It had just made its pass in his direction and was starting back the other way.

Geoff moved quickly down the corridor to the lab. He breathed a sigh of relief seeing those familiar, black stenciled figures on the door, PR-217. Beneath it was a warning in bright red lettering: "Authorized personnel only."

Geoff reached into his pants pocket and removed a key marked "do not duplicate" and smiled at his cleverness for having kept it from his research days. Carefully, he put the key into the knob and slowly slid it in. He felt the tumblers click as they rolled over each ridge. He turned the key, but it didn't move. Geoff removed the key and inserted it again, going through the same motions. Nothing. He jiggled the key and the knob back and forth, the sounds echoing throughout the empty hallway. Still nothing.

The locks had been changed. When and why, he didn't know. A lost key, a routine precaution, or was it something more?

Geoff bit his lower lip as he pondered his next move, a move he would have to make quickly. There was only one other way to get in, and that was through the keyless entry using his ID card. Using the ID would be like leaving a calling card, but it was now or never.

He reached down to the breast pocket of his lab coat, removed the ID card and held it for a moment, studying the seven-year-old picture with a nostalgic smile. Life was so much simpler then.

Cautiously, Geoff raised the card to the slot on the door, paused to reconsider. Balassi would know Geoff had been there when he checked the entry log in the morning. But by then Geoff would know all he needed to know, and Balassi would either thank him for uncovering the problem in his lab or be implicated himself beyond doubt.

Having rationalized the situation as best he could, Geoff closed his eyes, exhaled and jammed the card home, awaiting the reassuring click indicating the door had been unlocked.

The shrill alarm that came instead caught Geoff totally by surprise and just about sent him through the roof. The siren reverberated up and down the hallway, and a strobe light flashed over the door of the lab, a beacon for security guards sure to arrive any minute.

Geoff's heart pounded so fiercely he thought his chest would explode. Chief Resident of the New York Trauma Center captured breaking into a research lab by the Keystone Cops.

No way he was going to let that happen.

Geoff looked around for a place to hide, tried a few doors. They were all locked except the men's room. The guards were sure to search there right away. All that remained was the elevator, but he'd be nailed there in a minute.

Large droplets of sweat poured off his glistening forehead and landed on the floor. His shirt was like a sticky, wet sheet against his chest. *Keep your cool, man.* This was a piece of cake compared to Navy Seals training exercises.

The green exit sign at the end of the corridor caught his eye just as he heard a faint whooshing noise that sounded like a wind tunnel. Only it was getting louder, closer.

"Shit!" he said loudly and bolted down the hallway. His feet squeaked loudly as he raced toward the stairwell. He heard new sounds down the hall behind him. The sounds of voices, muffled behind closed doors. They were still in the elevator. His legs carried him closer. The voices were now louder, closing in.

The wind whistled as it rushed under the elevator doors, and the bell rang faintly, indicating the elevator's arrival on the twelfth floor. Geoff heard the elevator doors part and several pairs of feet scramble onto the linoleum floor. He was just a few feet from the stairwell. There was no time to turn around and look back. If they saw him, it was too late. If not, he was home free.

His sweaty palm reached out and grabbed the handle to the door just as it burst open from the other side. It all happened so quickly that neither Geoff nor the tall black man dressed in blue had time to avoid the collision that knocked them both on their behinds.

Geoff was dazed, but conscious enough to wince as the cold metal handcuffs were snapped around his wrists.

"Hold it right there, asshole. You're under arrest."

CHAPTER 24

GEOFF LOOKED UP AT THE IMPOSING BLUE BLUR OF THE MAN above him, wondering whether or not this was all simply a hypnogogic hallucination, a terror too bizarre to be happening to him. He sat slumped on the floor of the stairwell landing, handcuffed like a common criminal, awaiting a swift kick in the ribs from the pissed-off security guard.

He was confused, hearing a familiar voice instead.

"Geoffrey Davis, what the fuck are you doing?"

"Randall?" asked Geoff, incredulous but elated.

"You're gonna' give my guards here a heart attack setting off all kinds of alarms and making them think there's a thief in here. Worse yet, you gonna' get hurt yourself," said PETronics Security Chief Randall Johnson with a grin.

"That sound sure will startle a man. Looks like it scared the bejeebers out of you!"

He reached down, offered Geoff a hand and pulled him up off the floor, then turned to the other guards. "Hey, undo these cuffs, will you, Jonesey, and turn off that fuckin' alarm. It's giving me a whopper of a headache."

Geoff brushed off his bottom and straightened his lab coat, trying to act as composed as a man who had been knocked on his butt possibly could. He was grateful that of all the security guards at the Research Center, Randall Johnson was the one he literally ran into. Jones removed the cuffs, and Geoff massaged his sore wrists.

"Well, I, uh—"

"Forgot to pick up the new key, did you doc?" Randall interrupted. "Yeah, we had to change the lock yesterday. Somebody got hold of a copy of the master, and we had to change all the locks in the whole goddamned building. You can't believe what a fucking pain in the ass that was, man!" Johnson shook his head back and forth in disgust.

Geoff felt the noose around his neck loosening, sighed, wiped the sweat off his brow. "I bet it was."

"Bet your ass, my friend." Johnson waved off the other guards and sent them back to the office. "Come on, doc, let's go open that door for you." He put his arm around Geoff's shoulder as they walked back towards the lab.

"I really appreciate it, Randall. You know, I've been meaning to call you for that lunch I promised, but I—"

"I didn't expect a call until at least Christmas. So, whatcha' doing coming to the lab at so late an hour, anyway? You should be home right about now. All work and no play's not too healthy. Take it from me." Johnson smiled.

"Yeah, you're right, but there's a chart in there I need for rounds in the morning. Pederson will kick my ass if I don't have it."

Johnson reached down to his belt and removed a jingling ring of keys. He honed right in on the proper one, and the door opened with a neat click. "Wouldn't want to see that man on anybody's butt. No,sir."

"Especially mine. You know how he is with the chief resident."

"I hear you," said Randall with a curious smile as he flipped the light switch and scanned the lab from the doorway. "Listen, after you find that chart or whatever it is, make sure you lock up, or it'll be my ass on the line with Doc Balassi, and he can be one bad Hungarian!"

"I'll take care of it," said Geoff. He extended his hand.

"I know that, doc," he replied. Johnson leaned closer to Geoff and spoke in a loud whisper. "Whatever it is you're up to, be more careful, next time, will you? There's people out there just waiting for you to screw up like you almost did tonight. Ol' Randall Johnson can't always be there to save your ass." He turned and left.

Geoff entered the lab and locked the door securely behind him. He slumped against the inside of the door and exhaled a huge sigh of relief. He had escaped a trip to the city jail only by luck and the good graces of Randall Johnson. The episode had almost cured Geoff's agnosticism. Nonetheless, his cover was blown, and even though he felt he could trust Randall, one of the guards was sure to talk.

Balassi, worse yet Pederson, would find out soon. Then he'd be in deep shit. He knew he had been granted only a temporary reprieve and the only way to save his ass was to get hold of the information he had set out for tonight. Then they *had* to believe him. Facts couldn't be denied. He'd be the hero, not the trouble-maker.

Geoff removed his hands from his lab coat and held them in front of his face. They were shaking. He tried to slow his breathing, keep from hyperventilating.

Geoff's sweat-soaked shirt stuck to his chest like a damp rag, made him acutely uncomfortable, so he removed his lab coat, set it down on the bench. He unbuttoned his shirt to cool off. Slowly, he looked around the familiar lab. There were many pieces of information he needed. He had to prioritize them in case he was interrupted and security returned to close up.

Geoff walked down the aisle between two cluttered lab benches, directly toward Balassi's office. He wasn't going to waste any more time. He was going to go right to the source, the main computer. Geoff tried the door, but it was locked. He rattled the knob in frustration, remembered Balassi's routine. Balassi always locked his personal office when he left for the night.

Geoff tried to gather his thoughts. He didn't believe Balassi's story about the bad isotope. He wanted to check the isotope maintenance log. Any other information he stumbled across was gravy. First things first.

He walked over to Walter's desk, situated in an alcove outside Balassi's office, checked the file drawer, expecting it to be locked. Amazingly, it wasn't. Geoff searched underneath the stack of files and papers for the log. Nothing.

Next, he looked through the neatly organized pile of papers and notebooks in the middle drawer. A notebook caught his eye, the type of binder Geoff knew was used to log in the isotopes synthesized in the cyclotron.

Geoff grabbed the familiar green binder and checked the inclusive dates on the cover. This was the one. Anxiously, he flipped through the pages to the date in question, 3 July, 2010. He found the entry he was looking for. At the top of the page, clearly underlined in Walter's distinct Germanic script was the entry: "C-11 Carfentanil." The next column indicated the amount synthesized—100 nanolitres, enough for five or six scans—and the following column, the time, 0730. The time was right, just before Jessica's final scan was done. So far it all fit.

Then Geoff's eyes jumped to the comment inscribed in the final column: O.K. He ran his finger down the page, looking for any indications of a failed isotope, just to be sure. Nothing. He flipped the page back and forth and checked again, in case there was an entry out of sequence. It all checked out. The isotope was not defective as Balassi had tried to tell him. Walter was compulsive. He'd never screwed up an isotope before. Jessica's bizarre scan was real.

He put the log book back in the stack of papers where he found it and closed the middle drawer, trying to make it appear as if it were never removed.

Geoff looked up from Walter's desk and found himself staring at his old work station, the place he'd spent so much of his time the last year. Long days, longer nights. Experiments sometimes ran late into the night. On those nights, he would often nap on the old, green couch in Balassi's office after having dinner alone with his favorite rhesus monkey, Jezebel. When the experiment was completed, he was often the only one left in the lab and would lock up, sometimes as late as two or three in the morning.

Geoff had been the only one Balassi trusted to stay in the lab unsupervised, the only one he trusted to lock up besides himself, the only one given a spare key to the inner sanctum. He had free reign in the lab and in Balassi's office, his personal computer files included.

When had things changed?

Geoff tried to think back. He could not pinpoint an event in particular, but it seemed as though Balassi became more guarded when the group from NIH started coming around asking questions and auditing lab results. He became secretive, wouldn't share things with Geoff the way he had before. They stopped going out for happy hour beers at the The Palomino. "Can't make it tonight, Geoff. Too busy," was often the excuse. "Have to work on that grant pretty late." Things weren't the same in subtle ways, ways Geoff couldn't put a handle on at the time.

Then Walter was moved into the lab from the PET scan room to supervise endorphin isotope research, and things got even worse. Geoff had been totally shut out from that point onward. Balassi become ever more distant, and it was not unusual for sparks to fly between Geoff and Walter.

Now, as a total outsider—worse yet almost a criminal—Geoff could hardly believe he had once been such an integral part of the lab team. He couldn't help but wonder whether or not it was all a lie from the beginning. Why, he had no idea. It just didn't make sense.

The spare key.

Geoff ran over to his old work station and reached underneath the stainless steel sink, his hand probing frantically for the magnetic key box he had hidden. Could it still be there? He ran his hand all around the bottom of the basin, expecting to feel the sharp metal edges of the small black box, but there was nothing.

Balassi was too careful to leave an extra key around, especially one that someone he obviously no longer trusted knew about. Geoff bent down to look into the cabinet and around the underside of the sink, just to be sure. Gone. The acrid fumes of phenol made his eyes water, his nostrils flare. He leaned back to stand up and hit the back of his head soundly on the edge of the cabinet.

"Shit." Geoff rubbed his head, but he was not too dazed to notice what was directly beneath him on the bottom of the cabinet wedged between two large brown chemical bottles.

"Bingo!" He reached down and picked up the familiar key box, shaking it with anticipation like that of a young boy on Christmas morning. Smiling, he pried the rusted edges of the box open. Inside was the now-tarnished brass key.

Geoff ran over to Balassi's outer office door and, just as he had done countless times before, slid the key into the lock. Geoff turned the key and felt the familiar click. He paused for a moment, opened the door just a crack, and peered into the black abyss of the outer office.

Leave now, and no harm done. But his cover was already blown. There was nothing left to lose.

Geoff cautiously entered the room. He switched on the light, looked around the outer office. The familiar moth-eaten green couch sat in the corner, its musty smell permeating the room. The computer table was overflowing with data printouts. On the other side of the room was the refrigerator, the one Balassi used to store his most recently synthesized compounds.

Geoff bypassed the computer printouts and decided to open the refrigerator. A sample or two for Suzanne to analyze in the path lab would be perfect. Geoff removed the tray marked endorphins from the second shelf and examined the vials, each labeled with a six-digit number and a Greek letter. He removed one marked "Beta-279823" and a second similar-appearing vial marked "Sigma-346891." Geoff paused and stared at the label. *Sigma.*

Geoff placed both vials in the small compartment of his fanny pack, returned the tray to the refrigerator and moved to the computer table. He picked up the most recent stack of printouts and flipped through the pages. What might appear to the untrained eye to be pages upon pages of mathematical equations, Geoff identified as permutations of amino acid sequences for new isotope configurations. He knew these were probably significant—new compounds—but realized he didn't have the time to sift through it all. He had to get want he needed and get out of there.

Geoff sat down at the computer terminal. He removed the black flash drive from his pocket and plugged into a USB port on the front of the computer. He booted the computer and waited for the prompt. He hoped Stefan knew what he was talking about.

Geoff entered Balassi's Traumanet ID, PETJFB. The computer

cursor blinked, requested the password. Geoff waited for what seemed like an eternal ten seconds. The response came.

Access denied. Please confirm correct ID and password.

Geoff checked the connection, made sure the flash drive indicator light was on. It was. He looked at the screen one more time. He had misspelled Balassi's ID. He keyed in PETJEB. He waited.

Welcome to the Traumanet System, Dr. Balassi.

Stefan's decoding program worked!

Using Balassi's ID and password, Geoff pulled up all of the PET scan files, including Romero's. All patterns were the same—the blazing red horseshoe—all the patients' brains super-saturated with endorphins. He didn't have time to check the medical records in any great detail, but verified both Romero and the rabbi had been patients on the neurosurgery service at the NYTC. Whoever was trying to cover their tracks hadn't done a very thorough job.

An icon flickered in the upper right corner of the screen. Balassi had just received an e-mail. Geoff debated whether or not to check the message. He could be thrown in jail for such an invasion of privacy, at the very least thrown out of the program. Geoff clicked on the icon. A strange screen appeared, not like any e-mail he had seen. The words at the top of the screen were bright red, flashed a warning.

"TOP SECRET/EYES ONLY"

52-08-02-02-12-06-03-20-18-27-05-12-05-03-12-27-04-26-
22-04-04-22-28-27-12-16-28-17-18-12-03-118-17-12-04-
22-20-26-14-12-01-03-28-23-18-16-05-12-22-27-19-22-25-
05-03-14-05-18-17-12-15-10-12-14-20-18-27-05-12-19-03-
28-26-12-22-20-04-12-28-19-19-22-16-18-12-26-28-27-22-
05-28-03-22-27-20-12-04-22-05-06-14-05-22-28-27-12-16-

25-28-04-18-25-10-12-27-18-06-05-03-14-25-22-13-14-05-
22-28-27-12-28-03-17-18-03-18-03-18-17

There were no other words on the page. The message was entirely encrypted, some sort of numeric cipher.

Geoff knew something about encryption. All mission directives were received encoded. There was a chance he might be able to break this code, but it would take time to analyze. He printed the message, and put it in his pack. He'd examine it later.

Geoff checked his watch. 11:51 p.m. Time to get moving. Randall Johnson would be back, wondering why it took him so long to pick up a chart.

Geoff removed the flash drive and was signing off the system when he was startled by a strange sound coming from Balassi's inner office. Geoff approached the door and listened, his sense of hearing hyper acute. Another sound. At first he thought it was the sound of his own blood pulsing through his inner ear. He remained still, listened further. It was more like a creaking sound, back and forth, like a rocking chair on a squeaky, old floor.

Geoff put his ear to the door. The sound was louder, reminding him of a hammock blowing in the wind. No voices, no footsteps, no drawers opening or closing. Was someone asleep in there?

Slowly, carefully, Geoff turned the doorknob. He could see the corner of the room illuminated by the dim glow of the monitor. Above that annoying creaking sound he could hear the hum of the computer.

Someone was in there. Must be asleep at the terminal. Had Balassi stayed late tonight? Geoff had to find out, even though his instinct told him to get the hell out of there. Now.

He opened the door a little farther. A dim shadow moved back and forth like a pendulum. All of Geoff's years of training could not have prepared him for what he saw as he entered the room.

Above Balassi's desk, suspended from the sprinkler pipe by a rope around his neck was Howard Kapinsky, eyes bulging and mouth open wide from what must have been his last, agonal gasp for air. Pink, frothy saliva dribbled from the corner of his mouth and nostrils, landed on the floor below.

Geoff covered his mouth, then not able to hold back, heaved until his gut was emptied.

CHAPTER 25

GEOFF TAPPED HIS FOOT NERVOUSLY AS HE SAT IN THE WING-backed chair in Pederson's office. He had been up the entire night being questioned by the homicide squad. He thought he had handled himself well. In fact, he was so jazzed up from the encounter he didn't feel fatigued in the least, yet. He didn't have the time to be tired now. The crash would come later when the adrenalin stopped flowing.

He was prepared to tell Pederson everything he knew: about his strange e-mail messages, Suzanne's discovery of the new endorphin on autopsy, Kapinsky's wild theory, the strange deaths of his patients, Balassi's evasive behavior regarding the bizarre PET scan, and the peculiar Dr. Zelenkov from PETronics, who frankly gave Geoff the creeps.

Everything indicated to Geoff that something strange was happening on a level far beyond his capacity as chief resident to understand or investigate. He needed a powerful ally and felt he could trust Dr. Pederson, if he could only convince him this wasn't all some paranoid delusion.

To Geoff, the interrogation session had been like something out of the movies, cops with their guns strapped in shoulder holsters, the air thick with smoke and the acrid smell of burnt coffee, phones constantly ringing, people yelling.

The head of the investigation was a Captain O'Malley, a recent transfer from the tactical response unit to homicide. At first he looked vaguely familiar to Geoff, but after pleasantries were exchanged, Geoff realized he had seen him briefly in the NSICU just a week before visiting Jessica in the hospital.

"How's that little girl doin', doc? Last I seen she was comin' around pretty good," O'Malley asked as he wedged a piece of Juicy Fruit in his cheek.

"She died a couple of days ago."

"Shame." O'Malley's green eyes shimmered with sadness, betraying his tough exterior.

O'Malley then proceeded with questioning, making it all seem pretty routine. He asked Geoff a lot of questions about Kapinsky's personal and professional life, but very little about his own or the antagonistic nature of their relationship that would suggest Geoff was a suspect. In fact, it seemed like the cops were already calling it a suicide. There were no visible signs of a struggle—though the autopsy had yet to be performed—and a suicide note was said to have been found in Kapinsky's apartment. O'Malley finished the session. "We may need to ask you a few more questions in a couple of days." And that was it.

Suicide? thought Geoff, as he sat stiffly in the chair. Kapinsky was too much of a self-centered asshole to commit suicide. Kapinsky had to be on to something. His behavior had become nervous, his reasoning erratic. He had spouted his wild theory of a mercy killer in the hospital just the day before.

If he had stumbled onto some proof, why hadn't he told anyone? What was he doing in Balassi's office, and how the hell did he get in without the guards knowing, without setting off the alarm?

Though there was no sign of a struggle, Geoff was sure Kapinsky was murdered. The whole thing seemed to have been carefully contrived, but he dare not mention that to the police for fear of drawing suspicion to himself. He didn't tell them about any of the strange happenings at the hospital either. They wouldn't understand, and they probably wouldn't believe him anyway.

So here he sat in the same chair he had started out in as chief resident a week ago, more anxious about his meeting with Pederson than he had been during his interrogation by the cops. It was reminiscent of his meetings with his commanding officer in the Navy, Major General Payne.

Geoff's wandering thoughts were interrupted by the shrill, but muffled tones of Lynne Evers. "Yes, Dr. Pederson, he's inside."

Geoff stood and turned towards the doorway.

Pederson smiled sympathetically as he entered the room. "Sit down, Geoff. Sit down." He motioned with his hand. "You've had quite a long night, I hear."

Geoff sat down, studied Pederson. His brow was deeply furrowed, his hooded lids heavier than usual, dark circles beneath them. His eyes did not radiate their usual glimmer. He looked aged beyond his years, like a general who had fought and won many battles in his day, but had stayed in command for one bloody battle too many. Geoff felt sorry for him.

Maybe it was the feeling as if the entire weight of what had happened was on his shoulders as head of the department. Or the paternalistic way in which he related to the residents. Or maybe it was Geoff's own feelings he had let him down with all of this by not filling him in along the way. He had to tell him everything. Geoff nodded his head. "Yes,sir. It has been a most interesting twenty-four hours."

"A poor choice of words. Tragic might be more appropriate."

Suddenly, the full weight of what had happened struck Geoff. He had been so distracted by surrounding events—his own brush with the security guards, his night with the cops—he hadn't really faced the enormity of what had happened. Was it denial?

His mind flashed back to the image of Howard Kapinsky in the lab the night before. The creaking noise of the pipe as his body swayed back and forth. Geoff's mind's eye scanned slowly upward from the shadows below. Howard was wearing running shoes, old jeans, his frayed Columbia t-shirt. He was off duty. Must have been at home before he came to the lab. No white coat. No I.D. badge. How did he get past security dressed like that?

Ashen skin, cool to the touch. The jaw froze open in anguish, the blood-tinged frothy saliva, the eyes popping from their sockets. Geoff's shock, his wave of nausea. He'd doubled over and vomited, then recovered.

Standing on top of the desk, he'd untied the rope from the pipe and set Kapinsky down on the floor. He was struck by the weight and stiffness of the body. Quickly, he checked for any respirations or pulse: none. He checked his pupils: pinpoint and non-reactive. No use doing CPR. He was long dead. How long, Geoff was not sure. Maybe half an hour. Dead. Howard Kapinsky was dead.

"Yes, tragic," Geoff replied softly.

Pederson leaned back in the chair and swiveled, looking out his window at the Hudson River. "You know, I never really understood what made Howard Kapinsky tick. On paper, he was a brilliant physician, but he just couldn't put it all together when it came to people."

"Except with kids. He was great with kids." Geoff remembered Kapinsky at Jessica's bedside, making balloon figures.

"The police are calling it a suicide," said Pederson, turning and facing Geoff.

"So they told me last night." Geoff poised to tell him everything. He was like a dam ready to burst. "There's—"

"Did they ask you any questions about your relationship with

Howard?" Pederson looked Geoff squarely in the eye.

Geoff hesitated. He was caught off guard, not sure of Pederson's intent.

"The way you two argued," Pederson said.

"No, they didn't."

"Of course they would have no reason to ask questions like that. It was a suicide, wasn't it? Note and all?"

"Yes." Geoff shifted uncomfortably in the chair. "That's what it appears to be."

"Good thing they found that note, or you might still be at the police station answering questions."

Geoff began to reconsider his plan to share the information with Pederson. He forced a smile and nodded.

Pederson leaned forward in the chair. "What the hell were you doing in the lab on a Monday night?"

Geoff was caught off guard once again. "I was looking for a chart I—"

"Do you realize what a commotion you caused? I know the alarm went off. Someone from security told Balassi the whole thing, and he hit the roof. I've spent most of the morning calming him down, telling him you must have had a goddamn good reason for doing that!"

"I did," Geoff said.

Pederson continued, his face now crimson. He lowered his voice, forcing Geoff to lean uncomfortably close in order to hear. "First, my senior resident wanders into the lab and hangs himself, then my chief resident breaks in like some cat burglar and sets off the alarms. Patients that should be in the rehab unit by now die suddenly, one jumping out the window, the first suicide at the NYTC in years. What the hell kind of department do you think I'm running here? This is the New York Trauma Center,

Dr. Davis, not an episode of Grey's Anatomy!"

"But—"

Pederson put up his hand, his voice a mere whisper. "It hurts me to do this, Geoff, but I have no choice but to put you on probation. You're suspended for thirty days, effective immediately. Stay home, spend some time in the countryside, get yourself and your priorities together before you come back. It's the only way to protect the interests and reputation of the department and the medical center. You should consider yourself fortunate to still be in the program."

Geoff could not believe what he was hearing. He had been wrong to break into the lab, but he was shocked at Pederson's implication about his having some connection with Kapinsky's death. Did Pederson really believe Geoff might do something so horrid? Was Balassi behind all of this?

Geoff looked down, his gaze coming to rest on Pederson's desk: the compulsively arranged desk photos, the Monte Blanc desk set, the Tiffany crystal paper weight. On the far corner, a stack of imaging folders that must have been covered up by the papers now on the floor. The computer generated name on the top folder came into focus.

Geoff closed his eyes, massaged them with his thumb and index finger. He could feel Pederson's ire from across the desk.

Consider yourself fortunate to still be in the program.

He opened his eyes, it was all a bad dream. Worse than that— it was real. The scan on top was Romero's.

CHAPTER 26

"Thanks for stopping by, Geoff. I've been very worried about you." Suzanne closed the door behind Geoff, invited him into the living room. The warm, sweet smell of fresh-baked bread filled the air. "When you left the message last night you couldn't make it over, I knew something bad had happened."

"It was bad, all right. Pederson placed me on probation today."

"What? Why would he do that?"

Geoff smiled knowingly. "For breaking into Balassi's lab. But it was worth it. Except for Kapinsky."

"*You're* the one who found Howard Kapinsky? That's awful." Suzanne touched Geoff's hand, furrowed her brow in concern. "I've never been able to understand a person's motivation to commit suicide, especially in so gruesome a way as he did. He must have been tormented by inner demons we never appreciated."

"I think his demons were external," Geoff said.

"You think he was pushed to the brink?"

"No. I think he was murdered."

A silent pause. Suzanne appeared momentarily lost in thought. "That's quite an accusation, Geoff. I have those scans you wanted to review. Can you stay for dinner?"

"I'd love to. It's been a hell of a day."

"How about a glass of wine?"

"Sounds great."

Suzanne walked to the kitchen, grabbed the chardonnay out

of the fridge, poured a couple of glasses.

Geoff remained in the living room, standing by a bookshelf. He browsed her CD collection, much of it jazz, then glanced at her framed photographs—the usual collection of graduation and family shots—resting on the shelf below. One in particular caught his attention. A black and white picture set in an antique pewter frame stood alone. A man and a woman smiled, cradled a beautiful, dark-haired baby girl between them. The man looked distinguished, hair dark with streaks of grey at the temples, starched white shirt, thin striped tie, knotted perfectly, stare intense. The woman tall, striking, could have been Suzanne's older sister, but by the clothes and hairstyles, Geoff dated the photo in the early sixties. He presumed the baby was Suzanne.

Suzanne returned to the living room, handed Geoff his wine.

"These your parents?" Geoff picked up the framed picture.

Suzanne appeared to tense momentarily, her eyes became glassy. She stared at the photograph, seemed to force a smile, took the picture out of Geoff's hands, and set it back down in its resting place. "My father died not too long after that picture was taken. Unfortunately, I never had a chance to get to know him. Mom's still alive, in a nursing home. She always told me what a great man he was. He was a political science professor."

Geoff realized he had over-stepped his bounds. He thought of the pain of his own father's agonizing death, how lucky he was. Though they had had their differences, he had a father while he was growing up. "Sorry. I didn't mean to pry, I—"

"Don't worry about it." Suzanne motioned him towards the couch, touched her glass to his with a clang. "To better days."

They each took a sip, sat down. "Couldn't be much worse than the last two," Geoff said.

Suzanne brushed back her long, auburn hair, extended her

arm across the top of the couch in Geoff's direction. "Tell me about your meeting with Dr. Pederson."

"Pederson's in on it," Geoff said. "I can't believe it." He shook his head in disgust. "He had Romero's scan, the one everyone has denied the existence of. The same one I was able to pull up on Balassi's computer. That's the *real* reason he put me on probation. He probably thinks I'll get scared and back off."

Suzanne smiled. "But you won't, will you? In fact, if he really knew you, he'd understand you'd see his ploy as a challenge." Geoff knew she was right, but wondered how she knew him so well. He felt suddenly uncomfortable. He stared at her chestnut eyes, searching for any hint of deceit. He was beginning to feel manipulated, but then again, he was using her to get the information he wanted. The thought assuaged him.

She returned his stare, her warm smile reassuring.

Geoff took a sip of the cold, dry wine. "Anyway, I've got evidence."

Suzanne leaned closer. "Let me play devil's advocate. You spot a missing PET scan of a crazy man on Dr. Pederson's desk while he's placing you on probation for illegal entry into Balassi's lab. While you're in the lab, you stumble upon a dead body, under mysterious circumstances, though they're calling it a suicide for now. The dead man and you never got along real well, and were often at odds in public. Tell me, Geoff, what are you going to do, call the FBI? Who do you think they'll arrest? Balassi and Pederson, or you?"

Geoff sighed, sipped his wine. "Doesn't look good, does it?"

"Quite honestly, it doesn't. Neither does your theory. Josef Balassi, world renown researcher by day, mad scientist by night, stalking the hospital and injecting patients with lethal doses of medication."

"I didn't say he was the one who did it."

"That's what your accusation amounts to."

"I said he was somehow involved in a cover-up."

"Your evidence is circumstantial. It would be thrown out of court in a second."

Geoff grinned. "I've got something a lot more than circumstantial."

"Besides sighting the mysterious scan on Pederson's desk? Like what?"

"A couple of things, actually."

"Well, let's hear it."

"I found Walter's isotope log book. There was nothing wrong with the isotope used for the PET scan on Jessica. Balassi lied."

"Hmm. They could say it was a mistake. Maybe Walter made the wrong entry, transcribed his initials in the wrong column or something."

"Maybe, though Walter's a pretty compulsive guy. I guess you're right. They could try and explain it that way."

"What else did you find?" Suzanne asked, her interest clearly piqued.

"Two vials of synthetic endorphins, one of which probably matches the substance found in the brains of three of the patients who recently died."

Suzanne's pupils dilated in surprise. "How did you—"

"They were in Balassi's refrigerator in his lab. I have them well hidden right now, but I'll get them to you tomorrow. Run the assays, and we'll have our smoking gun."

Suzanne tensed, leaned back on the couch. "Does anyone else know about this?"

"I haven't told a soul, Suzanne. You're the only one." Geoff thought about the e-mail messages, the encrypted message he

173

copied from Balassi's computer. He debated whether or not to let Suzanne in on the rest, then had second thoughts. Maybe after the assays were run and they had their evidence documented, but something told him not just yet.

"Then don't tell *anyone*. You're getting in pretty deep, Geoff. You just never know who you can trust." Suzanne straightened up, finished her wine.

Geoff looked at her warm, brown eyes, saw a hint of sadness behind them. She was holding something back. He leaned toward her, smiled, placed his hand beneath her chin, looked her in the eye. "I think there's a lot more to you than meets the eye, Suzanne Gibson."

"I could say the same about you, Geoffrey Davis."

Geoff brushed a wisp of hair off her face. A scent wafted by him. Fendi, Sarah's favorite. He pulled back, fought the urge to get up and leave.

"Something wrong?" Suzanne asked.

"Not a thing," Geoff said. He leaned closer to Suzanne, caressed her smooth cheek.

"Want to review those scans?" she whispered.

Their lips met, Geoff feeling a warmth he had not known in many months. He was unhappily certain he knew what the scans would show. "How about in the morning?"

CHAPTER 27

GEOFF LIFTED HIS HEAVY HEAD OFF THE PILLOW, REACHED over, and squelched the shrill buzz of the alarm clock. He managed to open his puffy lids just a slit, gazed at the time, the red glow of the numbers forcing his eyes to squint. Five-thirty a.m. One glass of wine too many had given him a hangover. He wasn't a big drinker and rarely had more than a couple of glasses, so the bottle of wine he had last night with Suzanne just about put him under the table, or on top of the counter, in this case.

His head throbbed and his thickened tongue was stuck to the roof of his mouth. He felt strangely uncomfortable this morning. It was something more than the hangover, more than a restless night of tossing and turning in bed. He felt as though he had betrayed Sarah, though he had no real reason to feel that way. He liked Suzanne, enjoyed working with her, was attracted to her. There was a sultry sensuality smoldering beneath her cool, intellectual façade. He needed her help, at least until the assays were run. Maybe the relationship would go somewhere, or maybe sleeping with her was part of breaking away from the past.

Geoff stared blankly at the ceiling, tried to replay his conversation with Suzanne. She had succeeded in planting seeds of doubt, warned him he was becoming too involved, suggested his conspiracy theory needed more proof. He thought about backing off, but quitting was something he hated more than anything. It was one of the few childhood lessons from his father, the renowned surgeon, that had stuck with him: never give up, even when the odds are stacked against you.

Geoff had been sucked into the vortex of the violent storm swirling around him. His involvement was beyond neutralizing, whether or not he stopped now, even if he returned the endorphins. He knew too much. Whomever was behind it all was clearly aware of that. He had to beat them to the punch, but first he had to root out the key players, and his plan to do that was already in motion.

All he had to do now was wait and watch—carefully. *Very carefully*. These people played for keeps. They had proven that with Kapinsky.

"Geoff, what are you doing up so early?" Suzanne said sleepily, as she reached over and gently stroked his inner thigh.

"I'm going to go for a run before heading down to the hospital to clean out my locker."

Suzanne snuggled up close to Geoff, her hand continuing to roam between his legs. "I could give you a better workout here."

He reached over and gave her a kiss on the cheek, then threw off the covers and sat up. "I really need to get back to my apartment. I need you to tuck the scans away some place safe for the day. Will you do that?"

"You're no fun." Suzanne frowned and pulled the covers up over her firm breasts.

"I had a really strange dream last night," Geoff said.

"Oh?"

"I dreamed we had wild sex on the bathroom counter." Geoff leaned over, his hand caressing her back through the sheets and kissed the back of her neck.

"That was great, wasn't it?" she purred with a satisfied smile. "I guess I'll let you go now, but you had better be prepared for tonight."

"Tonight?" Geoff wondered what he had gotten himself into. "What's it going to be tonight, the kitchen table?"

"Sounds exciting." Suzanne's smile faded as she reached out to grab Geoff's arm. She pulled him close. "You *did* have a strange dream last night, Geoff, but it wasn't about us."

Geoff noted the seriousness behind Suzanne's eyes. "Tell me about it."

"You kept repeating Sarah's name in your sleep. I've got a secure ego, Geoff, but I have to tell you, a woman doesn't like this sort of thing, especially after a passionate night of lovemaking."

Geoff looked away, tried to remember such a dream from last night, but he drew a blank. Was it his drunkenness that put him into such a deep sleep he couldn't recall it? He had felt uncomfortable when he woke up, feeling he had slept in the wrong bed with the wrong woman, but he had convinced himself it was just a hangover making him feel so down. He was at a loss for words. "I'm—"

Suzanne pulled Geoff down on top of her, kissed him full on the mouth. "It's okay, Geoff, I forgive you. Besides, I'm the one who did the seducing, not you."

"How can I redeem myself?"

"Two ways," Suzanne said. "Drop the vials by my lab this morning..."

"And..."

"Meet me on the kitchen table tonight. We still have those scans to review. And, yes, I'll keep them secure for you."

CHAPTER 28

THE RAYS OF THE EARLY MORNING SUN BARELY BURNING through the dense smog cast a surreal purple glow in the sky above. Temperature inversions were quite common in the city in mid-July, and this morning, New York was socked-in in a bad way.

Geoff climbed up the steps on 181st Street that lead to his apartment building, his mind filled with thoughts of Sarah. His conversation with Suzanne last night had stirred up the past. The day her anguish ended. The day his began. Intellectually, Geoff knew he had simply carried out her wishes and had done what was right, what she had wanted him to do, but he had never reconciled it with his heart nor his instincts as a physician.

It was climbing these very steps as Geoff returned from the hospital that day a year and a half ago that the realization of what he had done overwhelmed him. It *was* a mercy killing, the response to a dying person's last request, but murder was murder, plain and simple. He had done more than just put Sarah out of her misery.

It was one of those frigid January nights in New York when the icy wind howled and sheets of hail pelted the window of Sarah's hospital room like fistfuls of pebbles. Geoff had sat by the bedside, reading the *New York Times*, waiting patiently for Sarah's gynecologist, Carl Rosenberg, to return from the operating room. He had brought her into the ER early that evening after Sarah had complained of abdominal cramping, then doubled over in pain and began hemorrhaging.

Geoff was convinced it was a tubal pregnancy. They had been trying to conceive for months, and her period was late. Geoff remembered the look on Rosenberg's face as he entered the room. His expression was drawn, and his saddened eyes shifted nervously. Geoff knew right away something was terribly wrong.

"Geoff, I'm sorry to be the one to tell you this, but Sarah has an ovarian tumor. It's pretty large and must have been there for quite a while." The words came tumbling down, buried him like an avalanche.

"It can't be."

"We double-checked Geoff. It's cancer."

Cancer.

Months of radiation treatments and chemotherapy followed and the residual tumor at first appeared to shrink. They were hopeful until the next body scan was done. The tumor had seeded like dandelions scattered by the wind and was growing relentlessly throughout her pelvis. They tried to contain it with chemotherapy, what seemed like endless rounds of intravenous poison that slowly devoured both her body and her spirit, her thick, blonde hair falling out little by little.

Over the next few months, the vicious synergy of the advancing tumor and the chemical poisons insidiously zapped her vitality, despite her strong constitution and will. Jaundiced, gaunt, and in constant pain from the galloping cancer, Sarah began pleading with her nurses for her pain cocktails hours before her next dose was due. At first they gave her relief for a couple of hours, but after a while, the medication no longer worked. The cancer had spread too quickly.

The doctors suggested a trial of an experimental chemotherapy protocol from the National Cancer Institute, and Geoff tried to convince her to go ahead with it. Sarah refused. She knew the end was near, and she was ready to move on. She pleaded with Geoff to help her end her waning, pain-filled life. Geoff resisted at first. He thought she was delirious from her treatments.

One day, after a particularly rough round of chemo, he stared into her still beautiful, green eyes and saw what he had tried to deny for months. Her spark was gone, the flame doused; he could see the depths of her agony. She pleaded for him to end her pain and give her peace.

Geoff thought of his father, his agonizing battle with lung cancer a few years earlier. The proud and brilliant surgeon had wasted away, become a frail ghost of what he once was in a matter of months. Geoff had felt helpless watching him suffer, knew he couldn't stand by now and allow Sarah to suffer that way.

"It's time for you to keep your promise, Geoff," she said.

Geoff knew what he had to do as tears streamed down both their cheeks. Later that night he returned to her bedside and with a final kiss delivered the fatal injection of morphine he had spirited from the pharmacy by forging the medication log. He sat by her side and watched as she drifted away peacefully.

Sarah was gone.

His best friend, his lifeline to humanity had been taken away and a piece of him had died with her. Her death sent him into a deep depression. Distraught and distracted after Sarah's funeral, Dr. Pederson suggested Geoff take a leave of absence from the neurosurgery program for a year and do research in Dr. Balassi's lab, away from clinical responsibilities.

He kept busy in the lab during the day, but alone each night, the guilt of Sarah's death weighted heavily on his soul. His loneliness created a void in his heart he could not fill. Even his brother, Stefan could not break through. At least he wasn't a drinker—

alcohol or drugs were never things he had turned to in his life.

Geoff's despair reached its nadir one rainy April night.

He sat down on the side of the bed and opened a small wooden chest he hadn't looked at in years. After removing a stack of commendations, ribbons and medals he had earned in the navy, he retrieved a few photos from a much earlier, happier time in his life. He flipped through them, one by one. Geoff and his navy buddies after graduating from the academy. Geoff and Sarah when they first met, so young, fresh and in love, sitting on the beach in Maui on their first trip together. A bittersweet smile came to Geoff's face, but only for a moment.

Geoff reached deeper into the bottom of the chest for his service weapon, an M11 recoil-operated, semi-automatic pistol. Taking the pistol in hand he retrieved the clip, snapped it in place with a loud click. Never in a million years did he think he would contemplate suicide. It just wasn't in his DNA, or so he thought. His pain and loneliness could end tonight, he thought. He stared at the pistol for a long moment, set it down on the nightstand by his wedding picture with Sarah, stared at her image, her warm, happy smile. Geoff sniffed back tears. He grabbed the pistol in his hand once again, released the safety, his eyes staring blankly into space. His mind ticked off the path of the projectile. Tearing through the brainstem, his respirations and heart beat would cease almost immediately, his parietal and occipital cortices would be obliterated, a hole the size of a baseball would be blown out the back of his skull.....

Sarah would not want this!

Sarah's voice in his head jolted him back to reality. Slowly, he reengaged the safety, removed the clip, put the pistol back in the chest, and placed it back on the top of his closet shelf.

Geoff had tried to slam the door shut on that part of his life as well on that painful day. As he reached the top of the steps, he paused and closed his eyes briefly. He felt light-headed, short of breath. Then he remembered the report on the morning news about the inversion. It took his mind off Sarah.

Geoff stopped briefly in the marbled lobby of the building to check his mail, something he did regardless of the day. He looked through the window in the brass box, but it was empty. Odd. Yesterday wasn't a holiday, and his box was almost always crammed with something, at least a medical journal and some junk mail.

Geoff passed the stairs, deciding to take the elevator up to his third floor apartment. The old metal door slid closed with a loud clang, and the elevator departed with enough of a jolt to cause him to lose his balance. Amazing the old lift still worked.

As he walked down the dim hallway towards his apartment, something felt different. Just a feeling, nothing concrete, nothing he could put his finger on. He paused and looked up and down the hall, then looked at his watch. Six a.m. A strange silence enveloped him.

He paused by the door of his next door neighbor, Mrs. Lubka, and leaned close to listen for any sounds. Nothing. She must not be feeling well. Geoff couldn't remember the last time he entered his apartment without her opening her door and convincing him to come in for a cup of coffee and to check her blood pressure. He made a mental note to check on her later.

Geoff reached into his pocket for his keys, fumbled the keychain, and dropped it on the floor, the noise echoing along the hallway. As he bent down to pick it up, he heard a sound, not from the hallway, but from inside his apartment.

Was it his imagination?

He put his ear to the door and heard the sounds of cabinet

doors opening and closing, drawers sliding open and closed, what sounded like things being dumped on the floor. The door showed no signs of being forced open, and he didn't remember leaving any windows unlocked.

Geoff reached down to his shin, unsheathed his combat knife, and gripped it in his left hand. One swift pass with the blade could easily slit a man's throat. That would do nicely.

Slowly, he inserted the key into the deadbolt, tumbler by tumbler, unlocked it, turned the doorknob.

The door creaked as it opened. Geoff listened. The activity continued unabated. Whoever was inside hadn't heard him.

Geoff set his pack down by the door and walked toward the bedroom, from where the sounds were now coming. As he passed through the living room, a glimmer of something resting on the carpet reflected in the light and caught his eye.

Geoff bent down to pick it up. It was an old pair of glasses, frame bent and thick, bloodied lenses smashed as if they had been intentionally stepped on. Geoff bent down and studied them closely. They were cataract glasses. The only one he knew who wore glasses like those was Mrs. Lubka. A trail of dried blood lead to the broom closet.

Geoff's heart pounded so fiercely he wondered if it could be heard a room away. He tightened his grip on the cold metal weapon as he approached the threshold of the bedroom, peaked around the corner.

A man stood by the window, looking through Geoff's dresser. Geoff tried to get a better look, but could see the man only from behind. Tall and broad shouldered, he wore a running suit. A black ski mask covered his head and face.

This wouldn't be easy, but Geoff was trained for hand to hand combat. Geoff heard a murmur of frustration as the man threw down the dresser drawer. The intruder checked his watch, then looked around and paused. His gaze focused on the night stand.

The man bent down and opened the drawer. He removed a small, grey box and picked it open easily with a metal pin. Geoff could see the shadow of a smile as the intruder opened the box and removed two small glass vials.

He had found what he was looking for.

Geoff's heart pounded more loudly. His pulse raced wildly. He tried to slow his breathing. He shifted his weight, and the floor creaked.

The intruder set down the box after quickly slipping the vials into his pocket. He reached inside his jacket and removed a small, black pistol with a long silencer on the end of the barrel. He scanned the room, cocked the slide. Geoff backpedaled toward the living room.

The intruder reached the threshold of the bedroom, gun leading the way.

Geoff squeezed the knife handle, raised his arm.

Now, man, now or never! Geoff's knife came crashing down with great force and caught the man by surprise. It missed his neck, slashed his right arm instead.

The man howled, the gun flew out of his hand and bounced onto the carpeted floor with a thud. Quickly, the intruder regained his footing and held his injured arm, blood dripping on the floor. For a few long seconds they locked stares. Geoff examined the frosty eyes of the man behind the mask, his chilling stare hauntingly familiar.

Geoff summoned all his reserves and lunged toward the pistol. He was surprised he got to it first. He stood up ready to confront the intruder and pull off his mask, ready to shoot if he had to, but when he looked up the man was gone.

Geoff heard the front door open and close, then the squeaking sound of rubber soles skidding down the tiled hallway, down the stairs. He ran to the door, gun in one hand, knife in the other, thinking he'd chase him down, but realized the chase would likely be fruitless.

The peas. Check the peas!

Geoff ran to the kitchen and retrieved the bag of peas from the freezer. He ripped open the bag and spilled the contents into the sink, retrieving the two vials of endorphins. He sighed in relief as he clutched them in his hand.

His plan to root out the players had worked almost too well. It had almost cost him his life. Most difficult was the sense of betrayal, no one he could trust. He couldn't do this alone any longer, not with a professional hit man, or whatever he was, involved.

Geoff made another decision. He set the vials down on the kitchen table, removed a card from his wallet, and dialed the phone.

"Detective O'Malley, please. Tell him it's Dr. Geoff Davis from the New York Trauma Center. No, tell him it can't wait."

CHAPTER 29

"Well, doc, that's quite a story," said Detective O'Malley as he chewed on a fresh piece of gum, the stub of his unlit cigar dangling from his lips. O'Malley leaned back in the recliner, gazed at Geoff, who was seated in the overstuffed couch opposite him.

"They say truth is stranger than fiction."

"They do, don't they, doc? I must admit, after twenty-two years on the force with all I seen, I'd have to agree with you. I mean, I could've written ten books by now. They'd all be bestsellers, nobody'd believe the stuff was true. You hear what I'm sayin,?"

O'Malley paused for a moment, glanced at his note pad, then peered up at Geoff with a slight squint. "Even so, doc, what you're saying is far-fetched. Don't get me wrong. You seem like a pretty sharp guy. No reason I know of to think you got a screw loose or anything like that. Still, you've had a busy few days yourself, to say the least."

"That's very true, detective."

"There's that word, again, doc. *Truth*. That's really all I think we're both after here, isn't it?"

O'Malley turned on his recorder and placed it down on the coffee table. "Let's recap today's events first. Interrupt me if I say something wrong."

Geoff nodded.

"You say you left your lady friend's apartment about six o'clock this morning and came straight home. You didn't stop anywhere on the way. After entering the building you took the elevator up to the third floor. You didn't see or hear anything unusual—no sounds, no strangers, nothing out of the ordinary—except of course that there *were* no sounds, nothing going on, which you say is unusual at that hour.

"You go to open your apartment door and two things strike you: your neighbor, Mrs. Lubka, doesn't open her door to see what's going on as she usually does when you come home—because she's stuffed in your broom closet with a bullet in her head—and you hear sounds in your apartment." Again, Geoff only nodded.

"You sneak in and find a guy going through your night table and see him steal a couple of dummy vials you planted there. You sneak up on the fellah and slash his arm with your knife."

O'Malley picked up the plastic bag containing Geoff's standard issue combat knife and held it up. "Correct?"

"What are you doing with that?" asked Geoff, grabbing the bag, "That's mine."

O'Malley reached over and pulled the bag out of his hands. "Evidence, doc. I'm goin' to have the boys in the crime lab check it out. I'll make sure you get it back when they're through with it."

O'Malley leaned back in the chair. "Now where was I? Oh, yeah, so you grab the gun, face each other off. You don't recognize him because he's wearing a ski mask, but you *do* notice his eyes, like you've seen him before but aren't sure where or when. He runs out the door. Sound about right?"

"All except the face-off. That was *before* I grabbed the gun off the floor."

O'Malley wet the eraser with his tongue and made the correction. "Good doc, real good. But the incident does pose a number of questions that make me uneasy, as I am sure you are about this whole thing."

O'Malley replaced the unlit stub of the cigar in his mouth. "Don't worry, doc, I won't light up. I never do when I make a house call."

He removed the stub, examined it fondly, placed it back between his teeth. "Lots of people, my wife included, find these things offensive, though I'm not sure why."

O'Malley gazed back down at his notes. "Now, if no valuables were touched in here, as you say, it's apparent the perpetrator was after only one thing, the vials you acquired. If that's the case, someone had to know you had them. Correct?"

Geoff exhaled loudly, briefly closed his eyes, trying to shut out the fact he knew he had to face. "To the best of my knowledge only one person knew. Suzanne Gibson, a pathologist at the Trauma Center. That's not to say others didn't find out." Geoff fidgeted in his chair under O'Malley's watchful eye.

"Of course, one never knows for sure, but let's assume she was the only one who knew. What motive would she have to tip off a professional hit man—and that's what he had to be judging by the methods of entry and the single bullet in the old lady's head—to break into your apartment, steal those vials, and wait for you to arrive to knock you off the same way he neatly finished off the old lady?"

Geoff sat in stunned silence, his hands clasped in front of him. He had assumed the man was there only to get back the vials. It had never crossed his mind he might have been sent for another purpose as well.

"Suzanne is the one who brought the whole thing to my attention. She discovered the strange endorphin in the patients' brains on autopsy."

"So, this Dr. Gibson, she drew you in, involved you more deeply?"

"I guess you could say that, but I pressed her to look for anything unusual when she did the autopsy on the girl."

"You said the test she ran was not done routinely?"

"That's right. It's more of a research test. Besides, when she isolated the compound, she was genuinely excited and thought she had made a remarkable discovery, something that might win a Nobel Prize. I find it hard to believe she was acting," said Geoff, his voice trailing off.

"Maybe so, doc, maybe so. But you haven't convinced me she's innocent." O'Malley took a sip of water and cleared his throat. "Did Dr. Gibson—Suzanne as you call her—and you have any interpersonal involvement other than of a business nature?"

Geoff was caught off guard. He wasn't sure where O'Malley was leading him. "No, not really. Not until last night."

O'Malley's ears perked up a bit. "In my business, that usually means yes." He leaned forward and patted Geoff on the knee. "It's okay, doc. This isn't divorce court, and you aren't married, anyway."

"It's not like that. We've worked pretty closely lately on these strange cases I've told you about. I was at her place to review some scans, had a bit too much to drink, and ended up spending the night. That's all."

"Did she suggest you break into Dr. Balassi's lab?"

Geoff's heart skipped a beat. "What do you mean?"

"Sorry, I forgot the official report said the security guard let you in, even though it was after you tried to break in and set off the alarm in the process."

O'Malley smiled and put up his hand. "I got my sources, you know. Don't worry, nobody's filed any charges, so I couldn't do anything about it even if I wanted to."

"No, she didn't."

"So you came up with the idea on your own?"

"In a manner of speaking."

"Is that a yes or a no?"

"The anonymous e-mailer steered me in the general direction." Geoff felt a bit embarrassed as he said the words aloud. Had he fallen into a trap after all?

"Got any hard copies of the e-mails you've been sent?"

"No."

"What else did you find in the lab?" O'Malley asked.

Geoff hesitated. "A copy of a PET scan that had been missing."

O'Malley made a note on his pad and nodded his head in feigned disbelief. "First CAT scans, now PET scans! Are you guys takin' care of animals or people in that place?" He leaned forward and slapped his knee. "Just kiddin' doc, just kiddin'."

O'Malley continued to nod his head, amused, then settled back in the chair. "So this PET scan suddenly reappears after a center wide search turns up nothing?"

"That's right. I was able to pull it up from the computer's data bank."

"What did it show?" O'Malley held up his hand. "In laymen's terms doc, if you don't mind."

"It was consistent with the scans on the other patients, as well as the brain chemistry studies. It showed the man's brain was totally saturated with the endorphin Suzanne had discovered in the lab."

"Meaning what?"

"Meaning that was probably why he and the other patients acted as if they were crazy."

O'Malley shook his head, unwrapped a piece of Juicy Fruit.

"Lord knows he was crazy. I'll never forget that day." He stuffed the gum in his cheek. "Anyone else see this scan?"

"The only other place I know it existed, other than in Balassi's computer, was on Dr. Pederson's desk. I assume he had reviewed it. I know Dr. Balassi saw similar scans on the other patients. I think Kapinsky may have seen the one on the girl at some time before he was hanged."

"Was hanged? Interesting choice of words, doc. We'll return to that one." O'Malley made another notation on his pad. "What did this Balassi say about the scans?"

Geoff sneered. "He said all the scans done that day were like that, that there was a problem in the lab and all the compounds were bad."

O'Malley grinned broadly, his teeth clenching the cigar. "And you know that's not true, don't you, Detective Davis?"

"That's right. I reviewed the day's log, as well as the entries on the day of Romero's scan. All the isotope compounds were fine. There was no problem in the lab. Balassi lied. He's covering up something."

"That may be true, doc. But let's get back on track here for a moment. This pathologist friend of yours, Dr. Gibson, says she discovers a new compound, arousing your interest and pointing you in a very clear direction. All the makings of a set-up, if you ask me. She drew you in, then got you to do her dirty work for her."

"You're forgetting one important thing. She knew I was going to give her the endorphin vials later this morning. Why would she go to all the trouble to send someone to break into my apartment to get something she was going to be handed hours later?"

"Think about it, doc. You're a smart fella." He paused for a moment staring at Geoff. "This Gibson's a smart gal. My guess is she didn't want to take any chances with you or the vials."

Geoff sat stiffly in his chair, annoyed at O'Malley's cockiness. As if the New York cop understood what a goddamned endorphin or a PET scan really was!

"Hey, Doc, don't get defensive about your lady friend. I gotta ask certain questions, ya know, chase down every possible connection."

"Sorry."

"How well do you think you know her?" O'Malley asked.

Geoff thought of their night together, Suzanne's baby picture, her pained expression when he asked about her family. "We work together, and we've become friends lately. Fairly well, I guess."

O'Malley sat back in his seat and flipped pages back and forth, then rubbed his forehead as if he was trying to make sense of it all. "Let's move on to the big picture now. I want to be sure I have this right, because the chief's gonna' look at me like I'm a loony toon—and maybe I am—but I gotta have my facts in order here. Interrupt me if I say something wrong. Science ain't exactly my strong point. Fact is, I flunked biology in high school."

Geoff nodded, wondering why he had wasted his time trying to explain it all to this fool.

O'Malley flipped the pages back to the beginning once again. "In a nutshell, you say there's some kind of secret experiment going on at the New York Trauma Center—the foremost medical center of its kind in these United States of America—where patients, including that little girl and maybe the cop who jumped out the window, are being injected with a new chemical that makes them crazy, then kills them."

O'Malley paused for a moment and looked up at Geoff. "Is this statement accurate so far?"

"That's correct."

"Further, you say Dr. Josef Balassi, Director of Research, and unknown others, possibly including Dr. Pederson, Head of Neurosurgery, are involved in the project, as you call it, or in a cover-up of some kind."

Geoff nodded in agreement.

"You also state you believe Dr. Howard Kapinsky did not commit suicide but was murdered."

"He was too much of a self-centered asshole to commit suicide," Geoff responded with conviction.

O'Malley looked up at Geoff and said in an amused voice, "Doc, even assholes commit suicide. Besides, there was a suicide note that appeared to be written in his own hand, full of talk about some homosexual relationship and rejection. A pretty standard note. So, you have another reason? Because if you do, I'd like to know."

"Howard Kapinsky, gay? I don't believe it. He was about as sexual as a eunuch."

"Believe it, doc."

"Has the note been analyzed by a graphologist?"

"It's in the process." O'Malley voice hardened. "Do you realize if it turns out to be a homicide, you're at the top of the list of suspects? I'm aware of the nature of your relationship with Kapinsky, the fact you two couldn't stand each other and that the day before he was found dangling from the rafters like a side of beef you came close to punching him out in front of several witnesses."

"My feelings toward Howard Kapinsky were no secret, but I think he was onto something. He had developed a theory of a mercy killer at the medical center. I thought he was crazy at the time. He was acting anxious, and his medical decisions had become erratic. I think he was murdered by the people behind the experiments, to send me a signal to stay away, or to make me a suspect and keep me from getting any closer. Either way, they'd achieve their goal."

"That they might have, doc." O'Malley eyed him up and down, as if committing Geoff's body language to memory. "You would certainly be high on the list of suspects, though my instincts tell me you probably couldn't do it. Well, let's move on here." O'Malley made a few corrections on his pad. "You suspect one Jesus Romero, the crazy Puerto Rican who held that little girl hostage at the zoo, was given the same drug when *he* was a patient at the Trauma Center, months before the incident, and that's what made a previously normal Joe flip out and do such a terrible thing."

"That's right."

"And an anonymous pen-pal named Proteus has been dropping hints only to you about everything that's been going on?"

"I don't know if anyone else has received any messages. I can speak only for myself," Geoff said.

"Finally, the fanatic Hasidic Rabbi on the subway train—the same train you were on—who blew away poor, innocent people on their way home from work, got the same drug, probably given to him when he was a patient at the Trauma Center."

Geoff nodded. It all seemed so clear. It made perfect sense. "That's right."

"Do you have a *motive*, doc? I mean if this is truly goin' on—and I'm not saying it is or it isn't at this point—what's the reason? And you better have a good one you can back up, because there are some pretty powerful people involved here with a lot more to lose than yourself."

"Not yet."

"Do you know what common thread seems to connect all of these incidents? What one thing is always right there at the center of the action each time, right there in the eye of this hurricane, so to speak?" O'Malley asked, raising his brow.

Geoff felt O'Malley's sea-green stare burn through him like a laser beam from across the table. He returned the stare without hesitation. "Yes, captain, I do."

O'Malley removed the cigar from his mouth and pointed it across the table. "You."

CHAPTER 30

GEOFF HAD BEEN SO CAUGHT UP IN THE EVENTS OF THE LAST few days, he'd barely had time to go to the bathroom, let alone attempt to decipher the encrypted message he'd printed in Balassi's office. Now that he had returned from the Trauma Center after dropping off the vials for Suzanne, cleaned out his office and checked for any more e-mail messages—there were none—he had some time on his hands.

O'Malley had given him food for thought, and he began questioning Suzanne's motives. Perhaps she had used him—why, he wasn't sure—to get those vials for her, but he had used her in a sense, as well. She had risked her fellowship position by running the autopsy assays, retrieving the PET scan data from the computer, pulling the rabbi's chart, all at his request. Geoff had to wonder what stake she had in all this. Was it simply intellectual curiosity, their mutual attraction, or something more?

Geoff assumed one of the security guards tipped off Balassi, who noticed the missing vials and simply put two and two together. Geoff felt the intruder was connected to other events, through Balassi not through Suzanne, as O'Malley had suggested.

Geoff dismissed the police guard O'Malley had posted in the apartment and locked the door securely behind him. He entered the living room, checked his voice mail on his cell phone. There were two new messages. He sat down on the couch, listened to the first message.

"Hi Geoff, Suzanne here. Just wanted to let you know I found those theatre tickets I told you about. I think they're a matched set, just like we said they would be. I should know for sure by seven-thirty or eight tonight. I'll be working late in the autopsy room, so stop by. Eight o'clock, okay? I'll be waiting for you. See you tonight."

At first Geoff wondered what the hell she was talking about, then realized she was trying to be discreet about the endorphin vials. She must have gotten some heat about them from her department head and was trying to keep a low profile. He shook his head, checked the next message.

"Hi, big bro, Stefan here. I've got good news and bad news regarding the, uh, project I've been working on. How about the good news first? Proteus sent those messages from within the NYTC. No surprise, huh? But he's a real pro man, I mean, he has to be someone with big, big time resources and government connections. But even professionals screw up from time to time, and I think I caught one. Interesting routing pattern. Seemed random at first, but there's always a pattern, even to randomness.

"The bad news I have to tell you in person. I don't want to say more over the phone. You never know who might be listening. Meet me at the same place as last time. Tonight. Ten o'clock. Later. Hey, be careful, okay?"

Geoff replayed Stefan's message to be sure he hadn't missed anything. Stefan hesitated and cleared his throat between words, something he did only when he was nervous. Geoff felt concern for his brother, knew he felt like he was sitting on a time-bomb, knew he might in fact be doing just that. He hit speed-dial, tried to call Stefan. No answer, just voice mail.

It was only five o'clock. Geoff had a couple of hours to try and crack the coded message. He moved to the kitchen table and removed the sheet from his fanny pack. He placed the message on the table in front of him, pad, pencil and day timer alongside it, sat down. He studied the message.

Geoff had read coded messages before. It was a standard part of Navy Seal training, how mission directives were sent. Though the battalion commander read most of the messages, it was essential for every member on a mission to be able to decipher coded messages in case of injury, death, or separation from the commander or communications officer.

Geoff studied the pattern carefully, made notes on his legal pad. The smallest number was a 01, the largest a 52. The vast majority of the numbers were between 01 and 28. He concluded these must each represent letters of the alphabet, 52 probably the number that oriented the reader to the layout and pattern of the coded message in some way.

Geoff scanned the lines with his pencil, looking for any repeating patterns. He noted the frequent use of the number 12, and deduced this number probably represented a space between words. Some senders chose to use these, others did not. Looked like this one did. The trick to decoding was knowing the pattern and which number started the sequence of assignment with which letter of the alphabet.

Intelligence officers—at least in Naval Intelligence—had developed a number of ways to throw off anyone trying to break a code. Since there was no way, even with the use of a computer to know which of these tricks were being used in this case, Geoff fell back on what he knew and began trying familiar ciphers, those related to the monthly calendar. A recent day timer or calendar was essential. This process could take hours or days. Hours he had. Days he did not.

Geoff thought back to the code most commonly used in the Navy, the January Cipher. The sequence of number assignment was set by the January calendar of a certain year. Geoff glanced back at the first few numbers in the message. 09-08-02-02-12. He ignored the 12 and assumed that the first four numbers set the sequencing, 09 probably indicating the year and the orientation, horizontal or vertical. Since the message was printed horizontally, he made the assumption "9" in the right column of the digit indicated vertical, "0" horizontal. The number 09, then, must indicate the calendar year 2010.

Usually codes were assigned from current year back, not forward, since not everyone had a calendar that included dates two years ahead. Geoff flipped to the front page of his day timer. It contained a 2010 calendar. He then examined the month of January and tried to apply the other principals of ciphering he knew.

The second number, 08, was the day of the message. The month was assumed to be the current month. The third number, 02, how many days to subtract from the second number to find the true date of the message. The fourth number, 02 again, was usually the critical one, indicating with which Friday of the month—that was the convention used—to begin the sequencing, assigning the letter of the alphabet corresponding to that date as the number 01.

Geoff penciled in his first attempt to crack the code. July 6, 2010. X-U-J-H-N-W. He came up with nonsense, knew he was wrong. Geoff paused, considered an alternative. Maybe he had the "09" backwards, the "0" representing the 2010 calendar year and the "9" demonstrating horizontal orientation of the message. R-T-P-E-W-F. Gibberish once again.

Geoff considered different months to orient the sequencing. First he tried December, using both 2010 and 2009 calendars, then he tried June. Both were months he knew were used in ciphers. Each drew a blank. Geoff stared at the message, bit his lip in frustration. He had to break this code. He knew it contained valuable information.

Then he tried the month of February. The February cipher was the code he'd learned encryption on, but he'd assumed it had long since been discarded. First 2010. Nothing. Then 2009. Geoff jotted down his results. T-Q-F-D-M-S. Shit. He'd thought he was onto something.

Geoff closed his eyes and tried to visualize the last time he had decoded a message. He had been having a problem and had gone to the communications officer, who gave him a few helpful hints. What were they? One had to do with ordering of the letters to assign the code, the other with spaces.

Z. That was it. The ordering began with the letter Z at the front of the alphabet, not A! He tried it again, this time starting with the letter P as number 1, since it was the seventeenth letter of the alphabet, corresponding to the date of the second Friday in February, 2010, when Z was before A.

Z A B C D E F G H I J K L M N O P Q R S T U 11 13 14 15 16 17 18 19 20 21 22 23 24 25 26 27 01 02 03 04 05 06

V W X Y

07 08 09 10

URHFOT TRBOSNJSSJ__O

Geoff recognized a pattern. The message was beginning to take shape. He was close, but the sequence was off by a letter or two. Somehow, it had to relate to the other hint his old navy buddy had told him about. Something to do with spaces.

Geoff looked over the entire message once again, and noted the number 28 was used several times, though not as often as the number 12, which he was still sure corresponded to a space between words. Two numbers, not just the number 12, had to have specific purposes. What could it be?

Numbers. Of course. The February cipher indicated a number would be coming instead of a letter after the number 11 was seen in the message. 12 indicated a space, 11 a number. Geoff reordered the sequence, this time skipping 11 and 12.

Z A B C D E F G H I J K L M N O P Q R S T U 13 14 15 16 17 18 19 20 21 22 23 24 25 26 27 28 01 02 03 04 05 06

V W X Y 11= number to follow 12= space

07 08 09 10

Then he deciphered the encrypted message:

URGENT TRANSMISSION CODE RED SIGMA PROJECT INFILTRATED BY AGENT FROM THE IGS OFFICE MONITORING SITUATION CLOSELY NEUTRALIZA-TION ORDERED DO NOT ATTEMPT TO INTERFERE BLUEBIRD

Geoff read the message over, exhaled to release the tension. He tapped his foot nervously. What he had been calling experimentation with his patients was an organized conspiracy—*the Sigma Project*—with Balassi and whoever Bluebird was at the center. Pederson had to be in on it. Lord knew who else was involved.

They had tried to take Geoff out of the loop by suspending him. If an agent from the IG's—Inspector General's—office was infiltrating the project, something big was happening here. That much was obvious. So was the term "neutralization." He had to do something to contact the agent, find out who it was. Could it be his anonymous pen pal, Proteus?

It was worth a try. Stefan said he'd have information for him tonight.

The problem was, the message was already over twenty-four hours old. The agent, whoever it was, might be dead by now.

CHAPTER 31

GEOFF CHECKED HIS WATCH AS HE WALKED DOWN THE DARK and musty corridor to the autopsy lab: 7:54 p.m. Better to be a few minutes early, get what he needed and get out so he could head downtown and meet Stefan. Geoff was worried about him. He had left him a message to rendezvous at nine instead of ten o'clock. With the order to neutralize the agent foremost on Geoff's mind, every minute counted. He reached down to his left calf and checked to be sure his Colt was in its holster. It was. O'Malley had taken his combat knife, but not his pistol.

The autopsy lab, located in the basement of the old wing of the hospital, was not one of Geoff's favorite places. He had wondered why Suzanne wanted to meet him there and not her research lab, but concluded it would be more private. So much the better.

Geoff approached the autopsy room, inserted his ID card into the slot. The door opened with a soft whoosh. A waft of moist, acrid air smacked him in the face. His nostrils flared. His eyes watered. Nothing else smelled quite like a room full of stiffs in various states of pickling and dissection.

Expecting Suzanne to be sitting at the desk just inside the doorway, Geoff was struck by the room's eerie silence. No saws were buzzing, no voices dictating notes. Not a *living* creature was in sight or within earshot as he scanned the room. Ten autopsy tables, four of them occupied. He checked his watch again and verified the time on the wall clock: 7:56 p.m.

Geoff walked over to Suzanne's desk and sat down. He hunted

around, looking to see if she had left the information she had promised. Nothing but scattered papers and research grant proposals. He scanned the room to be sure no one was watching, then searched her desk drawers one at a time. Nothing in the top three, but the bottom drawer was locked. He glanced up at the clock: 8:02 p.m. Suzanne was nothing if not punctual.

Geoff picked up the phone and dialed her research office, let it ring ten times. He was beginning to feel uneasy. He looked around the dimly lit room again, thought he heard a sound. He waited. No sound. No movement.

Geoff began to wonder whether Suzanne was playing games with him, testing him. He stared at the locked drawer and was somehow sure the information he was after was inside. He rummaged through the other drawers for a key, found none. He had to get into that drawer.

Geoff took a letter opener out of the top drawer and forced it in the crack between the drawers. He fiddled it back and forth, trying to force open the lock, but it would not budge. He grabbed a paper clip and tried to pick it the lock, but to no avail. In frustration, Geoff pounded the drawer with his fist. A metallic clink from beneath the desk echoed through the room. Geoff looked down and found a small key. Couldn't be that easy. He tried it anyway. The drawer opened.

He found a large, thick manila envelope, clearly marked: "Theater tickets for Geoff Davis. Hope you enjoy the show!" Geoff looked around the room again to make sure he was alone, then ripped open the envelope. Inside was an SD memory card, a flash drive, and a stack of papers. Geoff rummaged through her desk for a handheld digital recorder and found one. He put the memory card in and turned on the recorder.

"Hi, Geoff. I don't have much time..." Suzanne's voice had a sense of urgency and echoed through the room. Geoff instantly switched off the recorder, placed the contents back in the envelope. Suzanne was obviously in trouble, and he was convinced he had to get out of there right away. He'd listen to the rest of the recording when he got back to his apartment.

Geoff scanned the room one more time. He listened for any sounds, his hearing hyper acute. Nothing. The morgue was often the most private place in the Trauma Center.

I don't have much time...

The words jolted him like an electric shock. Who knew he was coming here besides Suzanne? Where was Suzanne? He looked at the clock: 8:17 p.m. His mind raced with options.

It was past time to get the hell out of there. Geoff stood and stuffed the envelope into his pants, covering it with his sweat shirt. He reached down his leg, removed the Colt from its holster, and slowly walked away from the desk, weaving his way between the autopsy tables.

Geoff heard a strange sound to his right, the sound of water dripping onto the floor. His gaze darted from table to table, searching for any sign of an intruder. The dripping sound became louder.

Slowly, he moved past the last table, toward the exit, revolver drawn. Geoff found himself standing in a puddle of blood. He turned, almost lost his footing, tried to stabilize himself by grabbing the edge of the table. Instead, he grasped the body's arm and pulled its dead weight on top of him, landing on the floor with a crash.

Covered with warm blood, Geoff jumped up, lifting the freshly autopsied body off of him in the process. Geoff forced himself to look down at the body as he tried to wipe himself clean.

He gasped.

"Oh my God, Suzanne!"

Suzanne Gibson, her skin chalky white, her belly slashed cleanly, surgically—*professionally*—was lying on the floor in a dark crimson lake of her own blood. Geoff grabbed Suzanne's face, looked at her lifeless eyes, checked her carotid pulse. She was still alive, gasping for air, her pulse barely palpable. Geoff grabbed a towel from the table and applied pressure to her oozing abdominal wound, trying to stop the bleeding. Suzanne had lost a lot of blood and Geoff knew he didn't have much time. He had to get her to the ER right away so they could stop the bleeding and replace her lost blood volume.

Suzanne opened her eyes, stared at Geoff, tried to speak, but no words flowed. Geoff's eyes were glazed, somewhere between sadness and anger.

"Who did this to you, Suzanne, *who?*"

Suzanne whispered a response, nothing Geoff could understand. Geoff bent down, kissed her cool, waxy lips. "Stay with me Suzanne, I'm taking you to the ER. You're going to be O.K."

His instincts told him to get them out of there as quickly as he could. Geoff placed his arms beneath her, lifted her carefully and turned to run but something blocked his path.

A tall, broad-shouldered man in a ski mask stood in front of them, holding a large autopsy knife dripping blood. Suzanne's eyes widened with a flash of terror. Geoff set Suzanne down as quickly and carefully as he could. He was breathing so hard his ribs hurt. His heart felt like it was going to burst. He started to reach down for his gun, realized it had fallen on the floor by the autopsy table. Once again, he and this masked man stood across from each other, facing off. Only this time, there would be only one survivor.

"What the hell do you want?" Geoff demanded.

Ice blue eyes, set deep in their sockets deflected Geoff's anger, gazed at a limp Suzanne now moaning on the floor nearby. The assailant approached, knife in hand, slashed at Geoff, who dodged the lunge, then ducked under one of the autopsy tables.

Geoff ran from table to table, knocking over buckets of body parts, staying low to the ground, out-maneuvering the less agile killer.

A foot kicked in from the side and connected with Geoff's ribs. A sharp pain radiated from his side around to his back. The foot came swiftly again, but this time Geoff was prepared. He grabbed it and flipped the man to the ground with a loud crash.

The knife bounced to the floor, and both men scrambled to get to it. Geoff was just a foot away from the weapon, when the man grabbed his leg with a grunt and pulled him away. Geoff kicked fiercely, heard a loud crunch as his heel connected with the man's nose.

Geoff broke free, grabbed the knife, turned and lunged. He put the knife to the man's throat. Though Geoff had been trained to kill as a Navy Seal, he was a healer, not a killer.

"Who sent you?"

Silence. Geoff reached to rip off the mask, but the killer grasped his hand and squeezed. The knife dropped to the ground.

The man seized the knife again, thrust it at Geoff who had stood to run toward Suzanne, then collided with one of the autopsy tables. The slashing knife missed its mark, but the man's momentum carried him forward, the weight of both combatants knocking table and corpse to the ground.

Geoff's head hit the ground, and he was dazed briefly. He looked up just in time to see a glimmering reflection coming at him. He rolled to his right, the knife whooshing by his ear and piercing the dark flesh of the supine corpse.

Geoff felt something fine and cold against his face. He grabbed an autopsy knife that had fallen off the table and plunged it through one side of the assailant's neck and out the other, just as the man freed his own knife from the cadaver's chest. Blood pumped fiercely from the neck wound at first, then slowed to a trickle.

Geoff rolled the man's body over on its back and removed the knife from his hand. He checked for any signs of life. The man had stopped breathing, and there was no pulse. Geoff took a deep breath and exhaled loudly. He studied the man's lifeless eyes, eyes just moments ago full of cold-blooded hatred.

Geoff knew who it was, who it had to be. Slowly, Geoff removed the mask.

Walter Krenholz.

Sweat poured down Geoff's chin onto the lifeless body beneath him. Geoff dropped the mask, stood, ran toward Suzanne. Her pulse was fainter, her eyes now closed, but she still breathed. Geoff lifted her slowly off the floor.

"You're safe now, Suzanne. I'm taking you to the E.R."

He was halfway to the exit when he froze in his tracks. His Colt was somewhere in the bloody mess on the floor.

Geoff cursed himself for his carelessness. Military issue guns were easily traced. He bent down, looked underneath the autopsy tables, scanned the floor. Tables turned on their sides, partially dissected corpses, their parts strewn on the floor, trays of instruments scattered about.

Geoff peered farther across the room toward the table Suzanne's body had been resting on. Geoff had slipped there, hit the ground hard, Suzanne's body falling on top of him. That's where the gun had to be.

A chill crept up his spine. He had no choice but to retrieve the gun and he didn't have much time—Suzanne was hemorrhaging to death. A security guard, morgue tech, someone who heard the commotion, would be here any moment. He had to get the gun and get the hell out. *Now.*

Geoff stood, took a deep breath, looked at Walter's dead body, then back towards the door. All clear so far. Still cradling Suzanne's almost lifeless body, he slid between the overturned tables, made his way to the table he had found her on. Geoff paused, looked around the area one last time. Nothing. The gun had to be somewhere in the vicinity.

Commotion outside the main door, loud voices calling, legs moving quickly toward the morgue. Geoff glanced at the door. Someone, probably security, was heading toward him. Shit. He had to get his gun back!

Geoff's gaze darted all around the chaotic mess on the floor. Nothing. He walked towards Walter's body, rolled it over with his foot. No gun.

The sounds were now louder, whoever was approaching just outside the door. Geoff had to give up the search.

Where the hell was that gun?

He looked beneath the nearest autopsy table, looked around the room one last time, peered between the table supports. A shimmer of light drew his attention. Jutting out from beneath an overturned stainless steel basin was the blue steel grip of his Colt—near the front of the room, by the entrance.

The automatic doors parted with a whoosh, four guards entered the room, guns drawn. *Goddamnit!* Suzanne's life, or the gun. Geoff slid softly to the back corner of the room and bolted out the fire exit to the emergency room.

CHAPTER 32

Trauma doc Brian Phelps was sitting at the ER nursing station finishing a chart note when Geoff burst through the doors of the emergency room bloodied and frantic, carrying his precious cargo still clinging to life.

"I've got a knife wound to the abdomen here, massive blood loss, severe internal injuries! Call the OR and have them get the trauma surgery team mobilized!" said Geoff.

Phelps jumped up from the station, ran towards them, motioned to the gurney in the entranceway. "Geoff? What the hell—?"

"—It's complicated, Brian. Just get her volume up fast until you can stop the bleeding, Goddamnit!"

A flurry of activity, nurses and technicians, now surrounded Suzanne placing monitors, IV's, hanging bags of blood. Geoff grasped Suzanne's hand, leaned in close to her, whispered in her ear. "Hang in there Suzanne, you're going to pull through. I'll take you to see that show when you get back up on your feet." Oblivious to the hive of activity around him, he kissed her forehead gently. "I have to go now, but I will be back for you."

Geoff turned and slipped out of the emergency room, into the darkness.

CHAPTER 33

GEOFF SAT IMPATIENTLY IN THE SAME BOOTH OF THE SMOKEY coffeehouse on Houston Street, waiting for Stefan to arrive. It was nine forty-five and he had left a message for Stefan to meet him at nine. Maybe he never picked up the message. Geoff tapped his foot, scanned the crowd for anything irregular. He had to be on his guard. They tried to kill Suzanne. Walter Krenholz had been eliminated. They—whoever they were in a broader sense—wouldn't take kindly to that.

"Get you another one?" asked the waitress.

"Sure," Geoff said. He lifted his shot glass, drained the last few drops of Stoli.

The waitress smiled, cracked her gum. "Looks like you could use it. Rough night with the girlfriend or somethin'?"

"Something like that."

Geoff didn't realize he looked so bad. He had run home from the autopsy lab, showered, changed, bagged his clothes and sent them down the incinerator shoot.

The only thing that had worried him besides Suzanne was the gun. It wasn't a good situation, but neither was getting caught with blood stained hands alongside a murder victim, even if it was self defense. Geoff had taken a cab downtown, looking out the back window the whole way to be sure he wasn't being followed. He'd tried to look like a regular guy out for a drink, but the worry behind his eyes must have given him away.

The second Stoli arrived and Geoff downed it quickly. He

checked his watch again: 10:05 p.m. He left a twenty dollar bill on the table, left the bar and walked east to Third Avenue towards Stefan's apartment, looking over his shoulder all the while.

The vodka had taken the edge off his anxiety, the nightmarish image of Suzanne nearly bleeding to death burned into his visual memory, but Geoff remained keenly aware of his surroundings. His only weapons now were his mind and his hands. Brian Phelps had sent Geoff a text message a short while ago Suzanne made it to the OR and the trauma team had stopped the hemorrhaging. Her spleen was ruptured and her liver badly lacerated, but it looked as though she'd make it.

Geoff turned up Third Avenue, crossed to the east side of the street. Red lights flashed two blocks north. Cautiously, he approached the corner of Third Avenue and Beekman, then stopped dead in his tracks. Police cars and an aid unit, a crowd of onlookers, massed outside Stefan's building. Yellow police tape cordoned off the area. An orange body bag on a stretcher was being wheeled to the ambulance parked at the curb.

Frantically, Geoff searched the crowd for Stefan. He moved through the throngs, checking silhouettes of faces in the red strobe lights of the emergency vehicles. Voices crackled over the police band. Television crews arrived. Vans set up their equipment. The faces of the crowd would be blasted into daylight with bright halogen lights any minute. Geoff had to find Stefan and get them out of there, quickly.

If he couldn't find Stefan, maybe he'd recognize a friend, a neighbor, someone who knew where Stefan was, *someone* who could tell Geoff he was okay.

Geoff felt a hand on his shoulder, heard a man's voice, spun around.

"Hey bro, sorry I'm late!" said Stefan.

Geoff grabbed Stefan on each shoulder, looked him squarely in the eyes. "Where the hell have you been? I've been worried sick about you!"

"Some little old lady set her kitchen on fire in my building and apparently died of smoke inhalation. The fire department made us evacuate." Stefan eyed Geoff at first taken aback by Geoff's urgent tone, then sensed Geoff's exhaustion. "You look like shit."

"Thanks. I feel a lot worse than that. Let's get out of here and go somewhere we can talk more freely. I've got a lot to fill you in on."

CHAPTER 34

GEOFF FLED TO KAPINSKY'S APARTMENT. HE DIDN'T KNOW where else to go, any other place no one would think to look for him, at least not right away. He was fortunate enough to find Kapinsky's spare key in the same hiding place he had left it in the past when Geoff and he had socialized.

First his patients, then Kapinsky, now the attempt on Suzanne's life. If they had been killed so readily, Geoff could be eliminated just the same. With murder all around him, bodies stacking up like cord wood, there had to be a reason his life had been spared.

The prestigious position in Balassi's lab, the chief residency on a silver platter, all for someone who forged a drug log. It never felt right, never made sense. Until now. *He had been set up.* A goddamn, brilliant scheme. He was to be the fall guy. Geoff was, as O'Malley had put it, *at the center of it all.*

Geoff was devastated by Suzanne's assault. He felt totally responsible, having drawn her into a danger zone to solve his own problem. Suzanne had trusted Geoff completely, and Geoff had betrayed her trust, however unintentionally. He didn't want to make the same mistake with Stefan and endanger his life any more than he already had, but he was the only one Geoff could completely trust. After staying up most of the night talking and recounting the night's awful events, Geoff felt he had no choice but to send Stefan far away from the city to the family compound in Connecticut where he'd be safe. A kind and gentle soul, he had never been in combat like Geoff, never even been involved in a fist fight, even as a kid. Geoff had always bailed him out of trouble, protected him. And he would protect him again at all costs.

Geoff collapsed on the bed, sat head in his hands. He thought of Suzanne lying in a dark lake of her own blood on the floor of the autopsy room.

Those assholes would pay for what they had done and pay dearly. He didn't care if it was the CIA or even the goddamned President of the United States. He'd see to it. Nothing mattered greatly to him at this point except that he stay alive long enough to bring a certain end to the Sigma Project. It seemed unlikely he would survive his own accomplishment.

Right now though, he knew he needed to sleep to keep functioning. Geoff was physically exhausted and emotionally drained from the encounter in the autopsy lab. Sleep. The great escape, if only for a little while.

Geoff awoke abruptly at four a.m., body drenched with sweat, his heart racing as he tried to shut out the nightmarish images of grotesque corpses bursting with dancing snakes that slithered out of orifices and bloody wounds. He wiped his forehead with his hand, calmed himself. He needed a plan, and he had to be quick about it. He couldn't afford to make an error in judgment now. He shut out horrible images of the autopsy room, of Suzanne, chalky white and near death in the emergency room.

Geoff sat up in bed, turned on a small night light. He glanced at the envelope from Suzanne resting on the coffee table. He threw off the bedcovers, walked to the table, grabbed the envelope, sat down at Kapinsky's desk and emptied the envelope's contents. Recorder, flash drive, electrophoresis printouts, endorphin vials. Geoff flipped through the printouts, noted the sigma endorphin patterns, assumed they were from the vials he had given her earlier.

At the bottom of the stack of printouts were two newspaper clippings, yellowed with age, edges frayed.

The first one was from *The Washington Post*, September 13, 1962.

"Professor Jumps to his Death. In an unfortunate incident today, Georgetown University political science professor Cameron Daniels died after jumping from the window of his seventh floor room at Bethesda Naval Hospital. Daniels had been hospitalized for depression. He leaves behind a wife and an infant daughter..."

At the bottom of the page was a picture, the professor's family, a handsome man with streaks of grey in his hair, a starched white shirt with a perfectly knotted striped tie, his striking, young wife and infant daughter cradled between them. Geoff dropped his jaw in astonishment. He remembered seeing the same photo in an antique pewter frame resting on Suzanne's bookshelf. Suzanne's reaction was one of tension tinged with sadness. *He was a political science professor, died not too long after that picture was taken....*

Geoff flipped to the next article, from the same newspaper, dated November 23, 1962. "Family Sues Intelligence Agency, Wins Settlement. In a landmark decision, the First Circuit Court of Appeals upheld a judgment against the Central Intelligence Agency in which the family of a professor with ties to the CIA had claimed his suicide was the result of CIA experimentation..."

"Oh, my God," Geoff whispered. Until now, he had not understood Suzanne's involvement, his feeling of being prodded along, used by her. Now it all became clear. He set down the articles, turned on Suzanne's recorder.

"I assume you're listening to this message in a private place and that you're alone. If not, turn this off immediately until you can safely listen to what I have to say without being over-heard." Geoff switched off the recorder, scanned the room. Silly, almost. He turned the device back on, volume down, his ear close to the speaker.

"You have stumbled into something that is way over your head, Geoff. Your life is in danger. I urge you to leave the medi-cal center immediately and don't tell anyone where you're going. *Not anyone!* Do not trust even those you think are closest to you." There was a pause of several seconds followed by clicks as if recorder was being switched on and off.

Geoff took a deep breath, looked around, listened. He flipped on the recorder again.

"Now that you think I'm crazy, or simply trying to manipulate you, take a careful look at the papers in this envelope."

Geoff removed the papers one at a time as she described them.

"The assay of the sigma endorphin you left me earlier today is an exact match with the one I isolated from Jessica's brain tissue. It's a synthetic *sigma* endorphin analog, one so potent it is capable of altering a person's mental status and inducing a violent state of schizophrenia. Injected, it is like a ticking time bomb ready to go off. The other vial contains a *beta* endorphin analog, probably just an extremely powerful euphoria-inducing substance with some hallucinogenic properties, similar to, but much more potent than, morphine. I have placed both in this envelope. Keep them in a safe place as evidence.

"I have enclosed digitalized copies of the girl's and Smithers' PET scans and those of the rabbi and Jesus Romero. I was able to obtain them from the computer's data banks. They tried to lock the files, but I was able to break the code.

"I know you are aware of Balassi's involvement, but it goes

much, much deeper than that. PETronics Corporation, the government. It's all encrypted on the enclosed flash drive.

"Listen, Geoff, I'm sorry to draw you into this, but it was the only way. We needed an outsider to break this thing, and you were identified as the one with the knowledge and skills to do the job. You must, I repeat *must*, get this information to Dick Bennington at the CIA, Langley, Virginia, soon as possible. He can help protect you and break the project before it gets further out of control.

"Find a public phone and call this number, 703-235-0339. It's a secure line. Tell him you have urgent information for him about the Sigma Project."

There was silence on the recording, followed by a knocking sound. "Gotta go now. Remember, *when you have eliminated the impossible, whatever remains, however improbable, must be the truth. Good luck, Geoff.*"

Geoff sat in stunned silence. Suzanne was Proteus, the agent from the Inspector General's office slated to be neutralized. Geoff had known Suzanne for over a year and had never observed even the slightest inconsistency in her behavior. They had even spent the night together. She was a doctor, a pathologist, not a spy. Or so he had thought.

Leave the Medical Center immediately. Don't tell anyone where you're going.

Geoff felt angry, manipulated, used. She knew *exactly* what she was doing, lured him with clues dropped like crumbs along the path, allowed him to feel as though she was helping him, cared about him. O'Malley had been right.

Geoff thought of the articles, the man who was obviously her father committing suicide, the experimentation. He thought of his own patient, Smithers, suddenly psychotic, jumping out a window, the endorphins. There were no synthetic endorphins in 1962, but there were other drugs. Geoff remembered the army MK Ultra LSD experiment scandal. Could this be related? The connection was there. Now forty years later, another generation. Suzanne's motivation was clear: avenge her father's death. Geoff thought of Stefan and understood perfectly. If something had happened to his brother, he'd probably react the same way.

You have stumbled into something that is way over your head.

No shit. Whoever was behind this, and it did indeed have to go far deeper than Balassi, was willing to kill anyone who stood in the way.

Who else was involved? Pederson. He and Balassi had known each other in their early days at the NIH. Geoff couldn't pinpoint anyone else at the Trauma Center. PETronics Corporation? Suzanne had mentioned it on her recording. Someone else on the neurosurgery service had to be involved besides Pederson. Someone with day-to-day patient contact, someone who could identify the patients and administer the endorphins.

Someone like Kapinsky.

CHAPTER 35

It had to be Kapinsky. Kapinsky was always the first one there, long before rounds in the morning, the last one to leave at night. He had been there at Jessica's bedside the night before she coded, had examined Smithers before he was discharged to the seventh floor. Kapinsky was the resident on the service when Jesus Romero was admitted with his head injury; Kapinsky had had contact with the rabbi when he was a patient at the Trauma Center as well. Kapinsky, the fucking fly in the ointment, whose fumbling hands were a hazard in the operating room, who should have been bounced by Pederson from the program, *but never was.*

If Kapinsky had been part of this thing, why was he murdered? Had he had second thoughts, threatened to expose the conspiracy, or did he just screw up somehow? Who else was in on the project?

His mind racing, he got up, walked to the kitchen without turning on any lights. Geoff was ravenously hungry, so he made himself a peanut butter and jelly sandwich on stale white bread and popped the tab on a Budweiser. The head from the beer foamed out of the can and spilled down the sides, forming a large puddle on the countertop. Geoff looked around for a sponge or a paper towel, using the refrigerator light for illumination, but could not find one. "Didn't Kapinsky ever clean this dump?"

He opened a few drawers and came upon a pile of neatly folded dishtowels. That was more like it. It seemed like Kapinsky to have folded them so neatly. Geoff's thoughts returned to Kapinsky's role in all this, his murder, the suicide note. He still couldn't believe Kapinsky had written the note, nor that he was gay, as asexual as he had known him to be. If Geoff was wrong, if that was all true, there had to be some kind of evidence here of a relationship, something indicating his despair, his depression. Letters, notes, *something.*

Geoff walked back to Kapinsky's desk, searched the drawers with a penlight. He came across three by five cards on neuro-anatomy, class notes, research papers, nothing personal.

Geoff got up, moved to the dresser, examined the photos resting on top. Kapinsky with his sister and mother at med school graduation. His hair was not as thin, no mustache. Geoff smiled. Without the mustache, Kapinsky looked a lot like his mother.

He searched the drawers, top down. Nothing in the top two but a silver dollar collection hidden in a sock, a small switchblade pocket knife. Geoff placed the knife in his sweat pants pocket. It might come in handy. Geoff tried to open the bottom drawer. It was stuck at first, but he managed to jiggle it open. Running shorts, a jock strap, a box of condoms. Not so asexual, after all. Nothing else of note. No hidden envelopes, photos, notes. Nothing. Geoff was disappointed.

He tried to close the drawer, but it jammed on the track. He jiggled it again. Geoff heard something drop to the floor behind the drawer. He pulled the drawer off its track and out, got down on the floor, searched with the penlight.

Geoff was startled when he saw a small, bound, composition notebook. Geoff held up the book so he could see the writing on the cover in the penlight's dim light. In Kapinsky's hand was scrawled the simple word, "Journal."

Geoff stood up, walked over to Kapinsky's desk and sat down.

He was hesitant to turn on the lamp and instead continued using the penlight, though it was beginning to flicker.

The first entry was dated July 1, 2003. Geoff tried to think back to that period of time and reconstruct his own life. He had been working like a dog as a second-year resident and had been happily married to Sarah for two years. Happy times.

The penlight flickered and went out, the room now illuminated only by the dim rays of slivered moonlight streaming between the slats of the window blind. Geoff played with the penlight until he got it to work again and returned to the first entry.

For Kapinsky, the rookie, it was the first day of his internship.

"Started my internship in Neurosurgery at the New York Trauma Center today. I can't believe I'm here! Spent last night wandering the halls of the Center. Came back to my apartment so charged up I finished reviewing my neuroanatomy book again. Everyone else was out partying. I'm sure I got a good head start on them all! Hundreds of young doctors from around the country would die to be here, and here I am. Howard Kapinsky from Queens at the fucking New York Trauma Center. It's going to be great. I'll show them all!"

Kapinsky's boyish excitement brought a smile to Geoff's face. He scanned down the page. "I've been assigned to a team lead by Dr.Geoffrey Davis. He's a tall, good-looking gentile—G-d, even the name is blue-blooded—athletic, smart, charismatic. Probably a great surgeon. A real lady-killer, at least that's the scoop here among the staff in the hospital. He's everything I wish I were. Maybe if I stick with him throughout this residency some of it will rub off."

The reflection of Kapinsky's deep-seated insecurity and envy was unsettling. Geoff weeded through the pages one at a time, looking for the slightest inkling of anything to do with endorphins, the project, spies, *anything* relevant.

Geoff found it strange Kapinsky never wrote about relationships with any women in his life, except his mother of course. There was a detailed cataloging of interesting cases, almost verbatim transcripts of his ongoing verbal battles with Geoff at rounds, further signs of Kapinsky's deep insecurity. It was all very personal, and ultimately it felt to Geoff like a violation to be sorting through another person's innermost thoughts and feelings, especially when Geoff himself was so much an issue.

Until Geoff came across the entry dated November 25, 2009. "Had another big problem in the O.R. today. It was finally my opportunity to do a case as the first surgeon, a simple burr hole in the skull to relieve a sub-dural hematoma, and I drilled right into the brain tissue. I felt awful, but Dr. Pederson, though he was angry at first, was very understanding. He took me to his office after the operation and let me know it was obvious I didn't have the manual dexterity to be a surgeon. He said I had two choices: leave the program, something I could never do, or do medical neurosurgery (Is there such a thing?) and get involved part-time in an exciting research project he and Dr. Balassi had been working on jointly. Geoff worked with Balassi for a year, so I think I'll take Pederson up on it."

Geoff read on. January 10, 2010. "The project is exciting. It has to do with new endorphin analogs to be used for pain control in head injury patients. It's all pretty hush-hush, though, and I was warned by Balassi not to talk about it with anyone. His assistant, Walter, keeps an eye on things constantly, and I catch him checking on me now and then. That guy gives me the creeps! It seems there's a lot of industrial espionage going on in the biotechnology industry, and PETronics Corporation wants to be the first to hit the market with the new drug before anyone is even aware of the possibility. It's great to be involved with something like this.

"January 19, 2010. Great news! We completed synthesis of an endorphin analog today, and according to Balassi, we were given the okay by the FDA for human trials. And guess what, little Howard Kapinsky from Queens is to be the one to administer this breakthrough drug!"

Geoff nodded his head in dismay, then continued reading. "It has to be given in a special way, since it would be broken down rapidly in the bloodstream, but I dare not mention it, even here. No one's to know about any of this. PETronics Corporation is still paranoid about someone stealing their idea."

"How'd you inject it, Kapinsky? How'd you inject it?" Geoff whispered as he bit his bottom lip and flipped forward searching for the answer.

"March 16, 2010. I've been very busy on the wards during the day and in the lab at night. Geoff and I have been at odds, and it's very upsetting, more than he knows. I've come to a realization as to why there's so much friction between us, but it's difficult for me to write. I've told no one..." The entry trailed off at the bottom of the page.

"Come on, Kapinsky, get it out!" Geoff muttered in frustration. He turned the page.

"It's, and this is difficult for me to admit even to myself in my own journal, that I'm attracted to him, that I'm... I'm...gay."

No shit! Just like O'Malley said. Geoff read on.

"That's right—gay. Besides my fantasies about Geoff, I had my first sexual relationship with another man last month. His name is Ricardo, a very hot Puerto Rican lab tech working with Balassi. It was very satisfying, much more so than it has ever been with a woman, though there haven't been very many. No pressure, no expectations, nothing. It's the best I've ever been treated, by man or woman. I'm worried, though, about people at work finding out. It probably wasn't smart to get involved with someone at work. But it gave me pleasure. Something I haven't had much of in my life.

"April 3, 2010. It was one of the worst days of my life. Dr. Balassi called me into his office and showed me photographs of me and Ricardo last night. My G-d, does Pederson know, too? Balassi wants to meet with me tomorrow. I'm scared shitless. My life could be ruined."

"Son-of-a-bitch," Geoff muttered. "One of the oldest tricks in the book."

"April 4, 2010. Shock and surprise! I saw a side of Josef Balassi today I never dreamed existed. He was understanding and sensitive to my situation and promised not to tell Pederson or anyone else. He said my secret was safe with him. In fact, he said I could stay with the lab. Now that he knew something so intimate about me, he felt as though he could trust me more and would let me in on a new aspect of the project."

"May 12, 2010. No entries for a while. Things have taken a turn. Walter's peering at me strangely these days. He gives me the creeps. I think Balassi must have told him. I'm being black-mailed to remain with the project and do more than I want to, more than I should do as a physician. I don't think Balassi would do it, but, G-d, if those photos get out about me, and my family found out, I don't know what I'd do! Balassi's not what I thought he was. I've totally fucked up my life."

Geoff continued reading. He noted a definite change in the tone. Despondent was a good description. Kapinsky's handwriting, normally akin to Chinese, had become total chicken-scratch, barely legible. Fortunately, Geoff was used to deciphering it in patient charts.

"May 25, 2010. I was told to inject a new compound today into a patient named Jesus Romero. Carried it out per instructions, but no effect noted yet. I think the stuff has a delayed reaction. The new analog they're working on is going to be more immediate. I've had it with this! I didn't spend my whole life training to become a slave! I'm going to do some snooping around on my own and see what's really going on, what Balassi's hiding.

"July 03, 2010. Snooped around Balassi's desk after he left for dinner. The lab was empty. Found a list of what appears to be patient numbers under the heading Sigma Project. Balassi's getting careless in his arrogance. There's big time involvement here. Is this a James Bond movie or real life? Sometimes I think it's all just a bad dream. How did I let myself get involved in all this? I must have been set up from the beginning. Shit, I'm scared!

"The numbers under the Sigma Project match patients I injected already in the NSICU. The other is a little girl who was just admitted a few days ago. I won't do it even if he threatens to announce my secret on the reader board in Times Square!"

"Kapinsky, you coward, how could you?" Geoff swore under his breath.

"July 05, 2010. I tried to refuse, but Balassi brought Pederson in and showed the photographs to him right in front of me! I've never been so humiliated in my life. They forced me to carry it out. They said it was a newer analog and would bring her further out of her coma, that it wouldn't cause any harm, that it was part of a classified experiment backed by the United States Government,that it would be tantamount to treason to refuse. Well, I could live with that, but I removed myself from the situation in a way they'd never know. I left it there at her bedside in a syringe marked "irrigation." The nurse did the job for me without realizing it. My G-d, what have I become?"

When you have eliminated the impossible, whatever remains, however improbable, must be the truth.

Of course! The only way to reach the deep brain tissue was to deliver it *directly*, and the only way to do that and evade detection was to deliver it with an entry site that was already there: *the ICP bolt!*

Every one of those patients—Romero, the Rabbi, Jessica, DeFranco, Smithers—had ICP bolts drilled through their skulls that communicated directly with the space around the brain to measure the pressure in their heads and monitor their levels of injury. The lines were flushed daily. It was not a difficult chore to substitute the endorphin, or any substance for that matter, with the saline irrigation. The nurse on shift that night delivered the substance without knowing it when she irrigated the line.

Geoff resumed reading. "After she coded, they said it must have been too potent to inject directly into the brain. They would have to refine the analog further. I was instructed by Balassi to start raising the suspicion of a mercy killer on the loose and plant evidence to implicate Geoff. Tie it in with a drug problem. Balassi told me Geoff had had one in the past. I was supposed to accuse him of forging medication logs. At first I refused, then Walter—I hate that man—came to visit me at my apartment that night and...it was awful."

"That son-of-a-bitch, Balassi. A drug problem?" Geoff's mind was whirring at a fast clip. He had forged that pharmacy log, but not because of a drug problem. The morphine was for Sarah, poor suffering Sarah. But he had never told anyone that.

CHAPTER 36

GEOFF SLAMMED THE JOURNAL CLOSED AND PLACED IT ALONG with the documents and Suzanne's digital recorder memory card in the manila envelope. He had to act right away, get this incriminating information to someone who could help, someone he could trust.

There are some pretty powerful people involved here with a lot more to lose than yourself, doc.

Geoff pondered that statement over and over. Should he call O'Malley and hand over all the information to him, and let him deal with it? What the hell could this New York cop do against the CIA, a huge multi-national corporation, and the Director of the New York Trauma Center? Would he even understand it all?

Geoff made a decision. He reopened the envelope and removed the piece of paper on which he had jotted down the phone number of the person Suzanne told him to contact. Suzanne was in the ICU still critical. He had to trust she was telling it to him straight when she thought it was over for her. It was Geoff's best bet.

Geoff dialed the number and waited. Strange electronic tones, then a women's voice came on the line. "Are you calling for Director Bennington?"

Geoff was shaken by the unexpected female voice on the other end. He hesitated, hoping Bennington would pick up. He didn't.

It's his private, secure line Geoff. He'll help you.

"Yes, I am."

"The Director is out of the country right now. Please identify yourself."

Geoff's heart sank.

The voice on the other end persisted. "Excuse me, sir, did you say something?"

"Uh, no, I didn't."

"Perhaps Deputy Director Lancaster, his assistant, can help you? Your identification, please."

Geoff was desperate. If the man was his assistant, he had to know what was going on. "The Sigma Project. Just tell Mr. Lancaster it's about *Sigma*."

"One moment, please, sir."

All of the sudden, Geoff wasn't feeling so secure, and the line didn't seem so private. More electronic sounds, then an icy male voice on the other end. "Code name?"

"I have information on the Sigma Project. Do you want it?"

Seconds passed in silence. "Who is this?"

"A friend of Suzanne Gibson's. She was murdered and asked me to deliver the information she had acquired to Director Bennington."

"Director Bennington will be unavailable for an extended period of time. I've assumed his responsibilities. Tell me where you are, and I will have a courier pick up the information."

Suzanne hadn't said anything about his being unavailable.

Geoff felt increasingly uncomfortable. Was the call being traced?

"Is there any way he can be reached? I was instructed to speak with him directly."

"I've told you that's not possible." Lancaster's voice had lost its hardness. "It sounds by your tone like you're doing more than conveying information. Sounds to me like you're in trouble, in need of assistance. I can help you. Just tell me who you are and where I can find you."

Geoff hung up the phone. He held onto the receiver and stared at it, waiting to see if it would ring back, if they had traced the call. Seconds, then minutes passed. Nothing.

They must have gotten to Bennington.

CHAPTER 37

GEOFF NOW HAD NO OTHER OPTIONS. HE NEEDED AN ALLY, AND O'Malley was the only one left. He reached into his wallet, retrieved the card O'Malley had given him, punched in the number, took a deep breath, waited.

"Yeah, O'Malley here."

Geoff paused, then answered. "Detective O'Malley, this is Dr. Geoff Davis." He exhaled.

"Well, doc, you've had a pretty busy twenty-four hours, haven't you now?"

"That's an understatement, detective. Listen, remember the conversation we had at my apartment the other day? The endorphin conspiracy I told you about? I've got some pretty incriminating evidence about who's behind it all, the same ones who tried to murder Suzanne Gibson."

"I'd be very interested to see your evidence, doc, but first I've got a question for you." O'Malley's tone changed, became more grave. "Where were you between the hours of eight and ten p.m. last night?"

The question was not unexpected, but Geoff didn't know what to answer. "Waiting for Suzanne Gibson and my brother Stefan. I think you must know the rest of what happened."

"Doc, my instincts tell me I have no good reason to believe you to be a murderer, no *motive* to explain the deadly assault on your friend Suzanne Gibson. I have a few problems with this situation, though, that the chief keeps bringing up to me, and I don't know how to explain them. Maybe you can help me out."

Geoff didn't like the way the conversation was heading. He wondered if they were tracing his call. He checked his watch. He'd been on about a minute. He'd have to hang up before another minute passed. "I'll try."

"My first problem, I should say *your* first problem, has to do with why your ID badge was found in the morgue in a pool of Suzanne Gibson's blood. She was carved up pretty skillfully, like whoever it was knew what they were doing, you know?"

Geoff knew all right. He had been so worried about finding his gun, he hadn't even realized his ID badge was missing as well.

"The second dilemma, the unfortunate murder of one of the security guards who was near the morgue at the time. You see, the murder weapon was a Colt 45, registered to a Lieutenant Geoffrey Davis, military issue."

Oh, my God. Balassi's cohorts must have picked it up from the morgue. Geoff felt his face flush with anger. "What the—"

"I'm sure you have a good explanation for these things, doc."

Goeff thought about Walter. Surely, finding his body there would help support Geoff's explanation. "Walter Krenholz savagely attacked Suzanne and left her for dead. He attacked me in the morgue after I discovered her near death, tried to kill me as well. I killed him with his own knife in self defense. My gun fell out of my belt during the struggle. Surely your forensic team is sharp enough to confirm this as the cause of Walter's death. "

"Doc, I'd have a hell of a lot easier time believing you if you'd tell me where his body and the knife you speak of are."

Silence. "What do you mean?" Geoff asked. "He was on the floor near the front of the morgue with a knife in his neck."

"The only fresh stiff in the whole place was the dead guard." O'Malley cleared his throat. "What do you say you and I get together here at the station house and talk about it all over a cup of coffee? You might want to call a lawyer, but that can probably wait until we chat a bit. If these people are as dangerous as you say, you'd be a hell of a lot safer here than wherever you are. Where's your brother, Stefan who you say you were with later that night? And where are you, anyway, doc?"

Geoff hung up the phone. Shit. It was a tight, professionally orchestrated scenario. They had set him up without leaving an escape hole big enough for a lab rat.

CHAPTER 38

GEOFF WALKED THE FIVE BLOCKS FROM KAPINSKY'S APARTMENT in the shadows, his hooded sweatshirt bunched up around his neck and the side of his face, concealing his identity as best he could without looking too suspicious. It was five-thirty. Though sunrise was just a half-hour away, the thick cloud cover gave Geoff a little more darkness than he would have had otherwise.

Geoff crossed Cabrini Boulevard and stayed about ten paces behind an old man walking his dog, then stopped in front of the Cabrini Arms apartments. Geoff scanned the area. He was alone. He walked to the entrance, climbed the three steps leading to the stained glass door, quietly turned the brass handle. Locked, as he thought it would be.

Geoff slipped into the shadows around the east side of the building, looked up. The fire escape was his only ticket into the building. Only problem was, the bottom of the ladder was at least ten feet off the ground.

Geoff continued to the service entrance around back, looked for a large box, a small step ladder, *anything* that could give him a few feet of reach. He searched the area around the dumpster. Nothing. Quietly, he lifted the metal lid, looked inside. The stench made his nostrils flare. A large plastic milk crate caught his attention. Geoff reached in, pushed aside a foul-smelling garbage bag, pulled out the crate, set it down. Perfect.

Geoff carried the crate to the east side of the building, placed it beneath the fire escape ladder. He stood on the crate, extended his reach as far as he could. His fingertips scraped the rusted bottom rung, but he couldn't grab hold.

Geoff relaxed his outstretched arm, shook it off. He took a breath, bent down, and with a grunt jumped as high as he could, knocking over the crate in the process. "Yes!" he said as his hand gripped the fire escape ladder.

Geoff pulled himself up and climbed the stairs to the fourth floor. Short of breath, he paused, listened for any activity. No sounds, no movement.

He followed the fire escape to the back of the building. Apartment 4G. Geoff paused, felt for Kapinsky's switchblade, removed it from his pocket. Geoff looked through the bedroom window into the familiar apartment to be sure he was at the right place. The target was sleeping soundly in bed.

Geoff used the knife to pry open the window, slid into the room, landed quietly on the floor next to the dresser. The man snored, shifted in the bed. Geoff approached from the back side, knife in hand. He inched closer until he could hear his target's respirations, then put the knife to his neck, indenting the skin.

Josef Balassi raised his arm to swat away the object on his neck, awoke with a start. He tried to turn his head around to look at his assailant, but Geoff pressed his face into the pillow with his opposite arm.

"What the hell—"

"I wouldn't make any sudden moves, if I were you." Geoff released him slowly. "Now get up. Very slowly."

Balassi sat up, turned toward Geoff, looking dazed, confused. "Geoff? What are you doing in here? How'd you get in?"

"Thought I'd drop by for a cup of coffee, talk about the Sigma Project."

Balassi's pupils dilated in surprise. "Ah, you've heard of the project. Must have been through Suzanne Gibson. You two were quite close in the end, weren't you?"

"Cut the bullshit, Balassi."

"Patience, Geoff, patience. We have all the time in the world here." He smiled.

"Have you ever heard of the MK Ultra experiments, Geoff?"

"Can't say I have."

"In the late fifties, a visionary group within the CIA formed a top secret research project known as MK Ultra. The Agency, at the height of communist paranoia, wanted to develop mind-control drugs that could be unleashed to reach the populace of the Soviet Union and perhaps ultimately their leaders. An admirable goal at the time. The strategists behind this project went to Montreal and recruited a young neuroscientist, an émigré from Yugoslavia."

"You?"

"That's right, Geoff. I was a foreigner in a strange land. U.S. Immigration had turned me away in New York, and like many others I was sent to Canada. Well, these men from the Agency—I didn't know who they were at first—offered me a position as assistant director of a new research facility called the Human Ecology Institute and connected me with a brilliant neuropsychiatrist, Dr. Rudolph Schmidt, who was studying the chemical basis for schizophrenia.

"He had discovered that LSD given in high doses could induce a schizophrenic-like condition and wondered whether giving this drug at varying doses could bring the neurotransmitters in the brain to normal balance. Dr. Schmidt had a sizeable clinical practice in Maryland, and we had plenty of subjects on which to try out our theory.

"The Human Ecology Institute was the control center of this

project, but MK Ultra had tentacles that extended throughout the U.S. and Canada. There were over eighty sites, some at major universities, Geoff,that participated in one way or another."

"Well, as I said, we experimented primarily with LSD at the time. Only we were haphazard and crude in our methods. We had no way to physiologically monitor our results. We didn't have the PET scanner we have today. Short of normal subjects we could monitor closely, we tried our theories on some of our own agents, who were slipped the drug at a CIA retreat. One poor fellow had endless hallucinogenic flashbacks and eventually committed suicide by jumping out a window."

The newspaper clipping of Suzanne's father's suicide burned through Geoff's consciousness. Now another generation carried the torch. Balassi had to be stopped. Death was too high a price for scientific advancement. With Suzanne in the hospital recovering from her injuries, Geoff felt he was the only one left to carry out the mission, to stop it all for good. Suzanne's brush with death had sealed that for him.

Balassi gave a morbid laugh, then his tone suddenly became serious. "The higher ups in the Agency got wind of what happened to that agent and abruptly closed down the project—or so they thought."

"So you gave people who were normal or simply a little depressed LSD, made them crazy without their knowledge, then tried to make them normal again?" Geoff was incredulous, the story so horribly fantastic he could barely believe what he was hearing. Even knowing what was happening now.

"In a manner of speaking, that's correct. I know the whole thing seems ridiculous, and it was a ridiculous failure on one hand. It was doomed from the beginning. But at the same time, it was a great success. It failed because we really didn't know what we were doing. We didn't know exactly how we were altering the brain. Schmidt died a short while later, but I preserved his files in spite of the Agency's directive, and a core group of us who were involved went underground. We kept in touch, indirectly at times, until it was safe to resurface.

"A short while later, with the help of those connections I went to the National Institutes of Health in Baltimore, where I developed the PET scanner and created one of the greatest advances medical science has known! With PET, we study the living biochemistry of the brain. We can actually *see* the neural pathways for love and hate, determine the brain patterns of a future concert pianist or a serial killer, make the necessary corrections early in life to either foster or suppress these potentials. Perhaps with proper resources we can develop a substance to change the brain's chemistry to create a class of strong political leaders, another for brilliant physicians, and so on. It's a window to the workings of the human brain like no other, Geoff. PET's potential is limitless."

"Who else is in on this with you, Balassi?"

Balassi brushed his disheveled hair back with his hand and continued, his dark eyes dancing with excitement. "The core group of MK Ultra is still together, Geoff. It never truly disbanded. We now have support from people higher up in the CIA and more powerful government agencies than we ever dreamed possible.

"They've funded my research for the last thirty-five years, created a corporation—PETronics—solely for this purpose. Without them, PET would not be here today. There's no way I could have developed the sophisticated technology to this level in that short a period of time through the usual means, begging the NIH for piddley handouts, living from year to year, not knowing whether or not I would have to close down a project, justifying my research.

"PETronics has given me complete control over my research with unlimited funds funneled through the corporation and all they ask in return is for me to develop and test compounds for them, leaving me to spend the majority of my energies on the PET scanner. It's the ideal situation."

"You're mad, Balassi."

"You think small, Geoff, like most physicians. Why don't you join us? We can be even greater with you on board. You can remain on staff here and follow Pederson as Chairman of the Department. We can see to that. The professional rewards will be great, not to mention the phenomenal financial return."

"Dr. Pederson had so much more to lose, Balassi. Why did he do it?"

"Ah, what do you think, Geoff? Ego, of course. He wanted to have his name associated with these new endorphin compounds we're working on, ones that will cure chronic pain and schizophrenia. You see, Geoff, we can do so much good."

"Except you have to induce these conditions in innocent people before you can study them and find a cure."

"Don't be a simple-minded fool, Geoff. The testing phase of the study won't go on forever. Oh, the Agency may want us to periodically synthesize and test a new neurotransmitter here and there—"

"Talk about simple-minded, don't you realize you're the one being manipulated by this renegade group? They jerk you around like a puppet on a string. You've prostituted yourself to them."

"I guess that means no, doesn't it?" asked Balassi with regret.

"Kapinsky didn't commit suicide did he?"

"According to the police, you killed him," said Balassi with a smile.

"You ordered Walter to kill him, didn't you, and forged the suicide note? He was just an innocent fool. Or was he about to spill the beans and expose you? I know how you and Pederson blackmailed him, how you held the constant threat of exposing his homosexuality over him."

"I'm impressed with your resourcefulness, Geoff, I really am. You must have a good source for such private information. Was it personal experience?"

"Far better than that. I came across Kapinsky's personal diary. It spells out your involvement and Pederson's all too clearly. I also have—*had* I should say—a packet of information given to me by Suzanne Gibson before Walter tried to butcher her."

"Excellent work, Geoff. You'd be a real asset to the project. She could have been, too, but like you, she was a small thinker."

"Not as small as you might think, Balassi. You almost destroyed a second generation when Walter tried to kill her."

Balassi's eyes narrowed. He seemed confused. "What are you talking about?"

"Cameron Daniels was her father," Geoff said.

The blood drained from Balassi's face, leaving his complexion a chalky white. His jaw dropped. It was a name he had not heard in many years. "That's not possible," he whispered.

"It's true, Balassi. Suzanne Gibson, Daniels at the time, was just an infant when her father jumped to his death. I've seen the newspaper clippings, Suzanne's documents."

"This, this evidence you speak of, it must be in a secure place—"

"All of the information is on its way by courier to Washington as we speak." Geoff's thoughts returned to Stefan. He had to know. "Why did you have the security guard killed, Balassi? He had nothing to do with this."

"He simply stumbled into a scene he should have not been a witness to and needed to be taken out of the picture. When your gun turned up in the morgue, well, it was felt to be too good an opportunity to miss."

Geoff tensed. "Pity about Walter."

Balassi grimaced in anger, his fist stabbing the air. "The project will continue, Geoff, regardless of what you do! There are very powerful people involved, not only here but in Washington. We have the support of visionaries at the highest levels of government, Geoff, far beyond just the CIA. They will be able to make your piddley evidence disappear."

Director Bennington will be unavailable for an indefinite period of time.

"You had great promise, Geoff. It's truly a shame to waste your life in prison. Two murder convictions, more if they find enough evidence to link you to Walter, the little girl and Smithers. You'll be put away for well over a hundred years!" He gave a loud belly laugh; his dark eyes shifted in their sockets. "They have quite a watertight case against you, Geoff, dating back to the mercy killing of your beloved wife—"

"You filthy scum!" Geoff lunged toward Balassi, grabbed him by the shirt, slammed his back to the wall.

"What's another thirty years behind bars, eh Balassi? The judge will just tack it on." Geoff rammed the point of the knife firmly under Balassi's chin. "I wonder what a knife track in the brainstem would look like on PET scan."

Balassi stared at the knife. Beads of sweat formed on his forehead, ran down the slope of his nose, landing on the coarse, grey hairs covering his upper lip.

Geoff pushed the knife further upward, causing Balassi to let out a choking sound. A drop of blood trickled down the blade, landed on the carpet.

Balassi struggled to get out the words. "Please, Geoff. Please. We can work—"

A police siren sounded faintly in the distance.

"I don't make deals with the devil. I should kill you now and save humanity, but I'll let you bring yourself down. It's only a matter of time."

Geoff withdrew the knife and bolted out the window and down the fire escape.

CHAPTER 39

As Geoff ran up the steps to Kapinsky's apartment, his anger gave way to determination. He entered the building, paused, looked around. No one seemed to pay any attention to him or the ubiquitous sirens. New Yorkers were used to sirens and emergency lights, especially near a hospital. He thought he'd be safe here for a little while longer. All he needed was an hour to plan and regroup. But pretty soon the police, or worse the group from the Sigma Project, would come looking here. Then he'd have nowhere to go.

Geoff carefully opened the apartment door a crack, peering through the opening to make sure no one was waiting for him.

It appeared empty. Things were just as he had left them earlier. No movement. No sounds. Once again he looked over his shoulder, then slithered inside and double-locked the door. He leaned his sweat-soaked back against the wall, took a long deep breath, removed the digital recorder from his pocket, placed it on the coffee table along with the pocketknife. He slumped down on the couch and rested his head in his hands. The tight knot in his stomach confirmed this wasn't just a bad dream.

Balassi was finished. Geoff had gotten the entire conversation on disk. But who could he trust with the evidence? He had to think things through clearly. He must have one ally in the midst of this hornets' nest, but who? Was Suzanne the only one? There had to be a back-up. There just had to be!

Geoff realized his next move would be the most important

one of his life. It was like diffusing a time bomb without instructions or training. Two wires—one red, one black. Pull the right one and the trigger is deactivated. The other blows you to hell in a thousand pieces. Still, he had to be decisive and act quickly.

Faces popped in and out of his mind's eye. If Balassi and Pederson were in on it, then no one at the Medical Center could be trusted. How about Spiros, Director of the ER? A man who had dedicated his life to patient care. It was hard to fathom, but he had to be in on it too. Who else could have directed the patients to Pederson and Balassi for their studies? The Medical Center had to be permeated and controlled by agents of the Sigma Project. Zelenkov and his group of international scientists, Trauma Center orderlies, nurses and technicians, infiltrators *everywhere*, at every level, all part of this vast, international conspiracy.

Geoff sat up abruptly, stared at the envelope containing the information given to him by Suzanne. He would have mailed it, but he didn't know to whom to send it. Bennington was unavailable, and Lancaster couldn't be trusted. The contents of the envelope could be Geoff's ticket to freedom, or his death sentence. He couldn't let the information fall into the wrong hands.

Geoff bit into his lower lip, drawing blood. The salty taste was strangely reassuring. He looked across the living room, his gaze coming to rest on Kapinsky's computer. If he couldn't get through to Bennington at the CIA by phone, what about sending the information by e-mail? It was worth a try.

Geoff sat down at the desk, flipped the power switch on, booted the old Dell computer. The welcome screen appeared after what seemed like an eternity, prompting Howard Kapinsky for his password. Damn.

Geoff looked over towards the couch for his fanny pack containing Stefan's decoding flash drive, then realized he had left it back at his apartment last night. He was on his own.

He closed his eyes, tried to remember Kapinsky's password at the hospital. He had seen Kapinsky log on the computer to check lab results and remembered it was a strange one. Something to do with food, his favorite food. Geoff tried several. Deli, corned beef, matzo ball. All were negative. Then, an epiphany.

"Knish," he whispered aloud.

Welcome flashed across the screen. Geoff maneuvered through the internet, found a government directory. There wasn't much listed under Central Intelligence Agency other than a central clearinghouse. Geoff felt it would be too risky. He couldn't get it directly to Bennington that way.

What about the FBI? They'd probably sit on it.

Geoff took a deep breath, logged out, turned off the computer. He still had the matter of what to do with the vials. He needed a back-up. There was only one solution. He'd turn himself and all the information he had into the police. Deliver it all on a silver platter to O'Malley, make the captain the hero of the day.

A street-wise, free-spirited cop like O'Malley couldn't be in with the CIA. He might be on the take, like a lot of cops in New York, but Geoff couldn't believe O'Malley would take kindly to an order from above, especially one from outside the department, about how to handle an investigation.

There was only one problem. O'Malley was a cop out to solve a murder—*several murders*—and all the evidence pointed towards Geoff. And it wasn't just circumstantial. O'Malley had told him as much over the phone. They had his ID covered with Suzanne's blood, and his gun had been used to murder the security guard. Walter's body conveniently disappearing would make Geoff's version of the truth seem like pure fantasy. No, even though he thought O'Malley would listen, he was just a small fry in the NYPD.

The tape of his conversation with Balassi was powerful evidence in Geoff's favor, but it could easily be made out to be a fake, or simply disappear. There'd be pressure from high up to scapegoat Geoff and cover up anything else.

But at least he'd have half a chance, especially with the files he had from Suzanne and the conversation with Balassi on disk, which was more than he would have trying to run from the CIA. He'd probably be safer in jail.

Geoff picked up the phone and punched in O'Malley's number.

"This is Captain O'Malley. I'm away from my desk right now. Please leave a message after the tone, or hold and a dispatcher..."

Voice mail. Shit. The tone came. Geoff hesitated, then put down the receiver.

The sound of the phone ringing just about sent him through the roof. His pulse raced. His heart pounded. Someone had discovered him. Trying to send the e-mail had tipped off whoever was monitoring the phone lines that someone was in Kapinsky's apartment. Goddamnit.

Geoff stared at the phone as it continued ringing. Maybe it was the wrong number. Maybe they were just checking to see if he'd go for the bait, if he was really there. Whatever the case, he had to get the hell out. Now.

Geoff ran to the kitchen, grabbed the two vials of endorphins out of the freezer and placed them in the envelope. He picked up a marker from Kapinsky's desk and wrote "Confidential—Hand Deliver to Detective Donald O'Malley, NYPD, only," on the front in thick black letters, underlined the word "only" in red. He folded the envelope in half, tucked it into his running shorts. He was going to deliver it directly to O'Malley himself.

CHAPTER 40

GEOFF'S PULSE RACED AND HIS HEART POUNDED FIERCELY AS he maneuvered through the underpass and headed up the backside of Fort Tryon Park. The shortest route to the precinct house was straight up Fort Washington Avenue from Kapinsky's apartment to the south, but he would fool them all by coming down out of the park from the north.

It was a scorcher of a day, and Geoff's side ached sharply, but his legs continued their pace, carrying him ever closer to his destination. The hill was a killer, but he was in great shape and loved the challenge. His breathing was fine. No tightness.

Geoff could see the exit from the park at Cabrini Circle off in the distance, about a hundred yards away. The path looked clear, no one ahead or behind him, no helicopters overhead. No sign he was being followed.

His feet pounded the hot pavement as he kicked up his pace for the final sprint, the last twenty-five yards. Sweat poured off his head, drenching his body. His shirt clung to him like a second skin. Ten yards to go, then he would bolt as fast as his legs could carry him to the stationhouse just a few blocks down from the park. It would all be out of his hands.

Geoff closed in on the exit, picked up his pace, pushed himself to the limit. The exit was wide open, Cabrini Circle just about empty. No blockades. No police cruisers. He gave it all he had, sprinted past the gate out onto the cobblestone street.

The unmarked Ford that struck him from the left side came

seemingly from nowhere as he exited Fort Tryon Park onto Cabrini Circle. He felt crushing pain in his left hip as he was flung onto the hood of the speeding car, his bloodied face flattened against the windshield. Their gazes met. Even in his semiconscious state, Geoff could not mistake the cold-blooded stare of an assassin. The driver slammed on the brakes, throwing him off the hood onto the ground like a limp ragdoll.

Then all was blackness.

CHAPTER 41

THE AMBULANCE CAME TO A SCREECHING HALT JUST OUTSIDE the entrance to Fort Tryon Park at Cabrini Circle. An unmarked grey patrol car had arrived at the scene first and cordoned off the area, plainclothesman kneeling at the side of the victim, making feeble attempts to assess injuries. The paramedics bounded out of their vehicle, equipment in hand, and rushed to the victim lying motionless in a pool of blood on the hot pavement.

"'Bout time you guys got here," said the cop, shielding his eyes from the sun as he looked up at the medics.

"Took three minutes from the time we got the damn call," shot back Enrique Santos. "What took so long to call it in?"

"Had to shoo away a couple of grave robbers lookin' for money, jewelry, stuff like that. These animals don't care there's someone dyin' out on the street. Think they'd maybe lend a hand, do somethin' good-Samaritan-like? No way. It's a fuckin' jungle out here. If you find anything on him, bag it and give it to me."

"Yeah, sure boss. Good thing we got here when we did, or maybe you would've robbed him yourself. Now how about gettin' out of the way so we can save this man's life?" Santos said, getting down on his knees to get to work. He closed his eyes, crossed himself, then opened his box and grabbed his stethoscope.

The cop stood up abruptly. "Okay, wise ass, but don't forget there's gonna be an investigation here and we need every piece of evidence—wallet, papers, anything—just like I said."

He paused and looked back down at the victim on the ground.

"I think this one's gonna' be needing a priest, not a medic. Pretty bad hit and run." The words trailed off as the cop stepped back out of the way and started walking across the street.

Santos carefully rolled the victim on his back and set him on top of the backboard. His face was swollen, bloody and bruised, but not beyond recognition.

"*Dios mio*, Rosey. It's Geoff Davis!"

"What?" Rosey Ceravolo placed her stethoscope to the patient's carotid artery. She raised her hand to Santos to keep quiet so she could listen carefully for any sounds. "Got a pulse! It's a bit thready, but it's there."

With precision and speed, she cut open Geoff's blood-soaked t-shirt with her bandage scissors, then placed the stethoscope on his chest. "Respirations shallow, but regular. Both lungs inflated. I think he'll make it, at least to the ER." She looked up at Santos. "What'd you say?"

"I said this is Geoff Davis, *Doctor* Geoff Davis, Chief Neurosurgery Resident at the Trauma Center!"

"What?" she asked in disbelief.

"You heard me right, Ceravolo."

"Shit," said Ceravolo in disgust. "Ain't fair."

"No, it ain't." Santos quickly inflated the blood pressure cuff. "BP 80/30. Looks like he's lost a fair amount of blood here," Santos said, gingerly checking Geoff's head. Bad head injury, real bad. Damn."

Santos pried the lids open and checked his pupils. They were almost pinpoint, but reactive.

"That crazy son-of-a-bitch drivin' that car must have been going ninety miles an hour! Had to be on drugs or somethin', man!"

Santos shot a glance at Ceravolo. "Whoever hit him knew what they were doin'. Look at those skid marks over there. They overlap and go in both directions." He nodded towards the pavement as he wrapped Geoff's head with gauze. "That driver kept at him, back and forth, back and forth. He was aimin' for him."

"The cop didn't say anything like that. What makes you such an expert?"

"I know a hit when I see one, Ceravolo. This was a *hit*, not a hit and run. Same thing happened to my little brother. Drug dealer finished him off. A hit. Skid marks looked just like that."

She paused as she ripped off a piece of tape with her teeth. For a moment she was speechless. He had never told her that before. "How come our cop friend over there didn't say anything like that?"

They looked up briefly, glanced over at the tall, pock-marked plainclothes cop, who was awkwardly looking through the low hedges and flowers in the center island of the traffic circle across the way.

"Looks like our friend over there has more interest in finding what he's lookin' for than skid marks, Rosita."

"Yeah, well, maybe you're right. So what if this was no ordinary hit and run. Especially now that you tell me who this is. Maybe it had somethin' to do with the attempted murder of that lady doc at the hospital. Maybe it was revenge or somethin', you know what I mean, like the papers are sayin'?" She looked up at Santos. "You think he did it?"

Santos threw her a scornful glance. "No more than I think my own mama did it! No fuckin' way! It ain't in him to kill someone, especially the way they tried to kill that lady doc. Forget it."

"Hey, just askin', Santos. You know him as well as anyone, just thought I'd ask."

"Let's move him. Ready on three."

They hoisted him up onto the stretcher. As they did so, something fell to the ground. Santos picked up the manila envelope and examined it, puzzled.

"What the fuck is that?"

"What the fuck does it look like, Ceravolo?"

"Well I know what it *is*, Santos, but what's it doin' in his shorts? Funny place to keep your mail, don't you think?"

"Doesn't look like mail." He held it up to the light, then shook it back and forth. Something other than papers slid around inside. "Looks like some papers, a computer disk of some kind. Couple of small plastic vials, too."

The envelope was sealed with packing tape and had a name written in black marker on the outside, but no address, no stamps. The word "URGENT" was scribbled underneath, underlined in red. "He was probably going to deliver it himself. Maybe he was on his way there when he got hit. Probably felt it was too important to trust to the post office," he said as they lifted the stretcher and slid their patient in the back of the ambulance.

"What are you going to do with it?" she asked as she climbed inside.

"Hand it over to Detective O'Malley, 22nd Precinct, NYPD."

"Maybe you should just give it to that guy in the unmarked car over there. He'll get it to him. I mean, this looks like police stuff, Santos. Evidence. You know what I mean? Maybe this is what the cop is lookin' for in the bushes over there. We're medics, not detectives. We're not supposed to get involved in this kind of thing."

Santos looked over at the detective walking back in their direction. "That jerk? No fuckin' way, babe. I don't know him, and I don't trust him. If I handed this envelope over to that bozo, this O'Malley might have it by Christmas, if he was lucky. No, this one's being hand delivered by Enrique Santos. I'll take the heat."

He looked up and grinned. "Besides, you never saw it."

"Saw what?"

"Didn't think so." Santos slammed the back door and climbed onto the driver's seat. "Now let's get this man to a doctor."

CHAPTER 42

"WHAT THE HELL'S GOING ON UP THERE, PAPA BEAR? HAVE YOU lost control of your senses?" Bluebird was fuming, his usual controlled demeanor fallen by the wayside.

Balassi's hand squeezed the receiver tightly, his jaw tense. "Quite the contrary, Phillip. I've just taken into my own hands what you and your team obviously couldn't handle. Things are under perfect control now, let's cut the fairy tale code names. I've had enough of this game."

"You're not paid to take *anything* into your own hands, Balassi! You're paid to do research. Rather handsomely, I might add. That's all! You should have stuck to your lab work and left the rest to us."

"I would have if I could trust you'd have handled it, Phillip, but obviously that didn't happen. I refuse to let thirty years of brilliant research go down the drain as a result of sheer incompetence!"

"Research you could never have done without our help, you fool. You scientists think you know everything about every fucking thing! Well, let me tell you what you've done. That pathologist you tried to have killed, Gibson, she was an agent working for the CIA Inspector General's Office. The Inspector General! Do you know what that means?"

Balassi moved the receiver away from his ear as Lancaster raised his voice.

"We were watching her so closely she couldn't change a tampon without us knowing about it. She hadn't conveyed anything to the IG's office, Balassi, not a goddamn thing. We were damn close to recruiting her to the project, and you had to have her sliced and diced.

"Now I have the boss looking into every crack and crevice, my asshole included, trying to find out who tried to knock her off! He's been rattling cages like a mad gorilla, and someone's gonna' talk. It's just a matter of time. The Sigma Project, your ass included, is in jeopardy, you idiot."

No one calls me an idiot!

Balassi moved the earpiece closer. He could hear Lancaster panting heavily on the other end, visualize his jowls quivering. He smiled to himself. "She knew more than you think, Phillip. She passed some very incriminating evidence to the one she had recruited as her courier, Dr. Geoffrey Davis. He was becoming as much a loose cannon to the project as Kapinsky was before.

Balassi thought back to what Geoff had told him about Suzanne's background, her father, her obvious motivation. How could Lancaster not have known? "Do you know who she really—"

"I know what she *did*, Balassi."

"Then you know who her father—"

"—I don't care if her father was the goddamned pope! That Davis boy called me, and we tracked him down. We had him followed and were about to pick him up and reclaim the information when you interfered."

"You don't have to worry about him anymore," Balassi said triumphantly.

"Oh?"

"He's been eliminated. One of my associates took care of it." His thin lips formed a self-satisfied smile.

"I'm sorry to disappoint you, good doctor, but my sources tell me he's alive and in the emergency room of your very own medical center as we speak. And the information you speak of is still not accounted for. Our man at the scene combed the area and couldn't find a fucking thing."

"It's impossible, I—"

"That's right, Balassi. Alive. You fucked up big time. So big, I have no choice. It's really a shame I have to do this. For forty years the—"

"I, it's, it's impossible."

"There's no way out now, Balassi. I have no choice but to pull the plug like I did forty years ago. Only this time, it's for good. As of now, the Sigma Project is shut down. Forever. Too many careers, too many lives, are at stake. You know how high up this thing goes."

Balassi sat in stunned silence. He thought of 1962, Cameron Daniels jumping to his death, the cablegram to Dr. Schmidt, ordering him to shut down MK Ultra. "You can't do that, Phillip."

"There is no other way, Balassi. My advice to you is to keep a low profile. Take some time off. Pack up today and go to your house in the country for a couple of weeks."

"You can't—"

"It's over. Keep clean, or I'll bring your head in on a silver platter and serve it to the IG myself."

A loud click, and the line went dead.

Balassi continued to hold the phone to his ear, staring off into space. He had invested his entire adult life in this project. He *was* the Sigma Project. No one could take it from him.

CHAPTER 43

"WHERE ARE THOSE GODDAMNED UNITS OF WHOLE BLOOD?" barked George Spiros, Director of the Trauma Unit. "The patient was typed and crossed over twenty minutes ago. Doesn't the blood bank realize we have a doctor's life on the line here?"

"They're on the way, Dr. Spiros," answered Jan Creighton.

Spiros was tense. Jan had known him for seventeen years and rarely had she seen him lose his cool during a trauma. *After*, maybe, but not *during*. Not since the assassination attempt on the governor had she seen him in a state like this.

"Run in both bags of normal saline full bore. Let's get a third IV line going for the blood. Stat!" He turned to Flynn, the trauma doc, who had just tapped the peritoneal cavity with a large syringe. "How bad's he bleeding?"

Flynn held up the syringe filled with dark blood. "Pretty badly. Probably ruptured his spleen. If we can keep up with it and maintain his blood pressure while we're waiting on the OR, we'll be okay."

Beads of sweat formed on Spiros' upper lip. His gaze darted nervously back and forth between his patient and the monitors. Geoff's heart rate had reached 120, his blood pressure was 90/50 and dropping. Spiros knew he was hemorrhaging faster than they could replace the lost volume. It was a race against death, and it was pretty tenuous.

"Don't breath him so fast," he barked at the respiratory tech squeezing the black ambu bag. "Turn up the oxygen, six liters.

Somebody get another blood gas!"

The tech nodded, slowed down the respiratory rate.

"Jan, what's holding up the OR?"

"The room's almost ready, Dr. Spiros. Anesthesia said they need about five more minutes—"

"Tell anesthesia if we have to wait five more minutes, we won't need the OR!"

"Yes, sir."

"Choy, how's his neuro status?"

Karen Choy had just finished the most difficult neuro exam of her short clinical career. She had seen worse: mangled car accident victims, the cop, Smithers. But she had never had to work on someone she knew so well.

She looked at Geoff, his battered, swollen face, the raccoon-like dark circles around his swollen shut lids. She couldn't believe it was the same living, breathing, handsome Geoff Davis she had worked with.

"Well, uh, the patient's—Dr. Davis'—deep reflexes are intact, and he responds to pain."

"His pupils, Choy, how are they?"

"His pupils, yes, sir. His pupils are small, about two to three millimeters. They react equally. The small pupils seem a little unusual given the extent of the head injury. Eye movements are intact, too, Dr. Spiros. That's good, isn't it?"

"That's very good, Choy. A good assessment by you, even better for our patient. At least his neurons seem intact."

Karen Choy nodded.

"And the PET scan?"

She hesitated. "Well, it wasn't really a good study, Dr. Spiros. They, didn't have much time because—"

"I don't care how good it was, Doctor Choy. Just tell me what you found!"

"It was consistent with mild to moderate coma, prognosis good—"

"Blood's here!" came a voice from the doorway. The tech carrying two bags of dark blood held them up triumphantly.

"Dr. Spiros, Dr. Pederson's on line two," yelled the ward clerk.

"Tell him Dr. Davis' neuro status is stable."

A moment passed while the message was communicated to Pederson.

"He wants you to make sure the OR knows he's coming down himself to put an intracranial bolt in when the surgeons finish working on his belly."

Spiros glared at the clerk. "Jesus Christ! My patient's hanging on by a thread and Pederson's worrying about drilling a hole to put a fucking monitor in his head? Tell him to call the OR himself. We're busy trying to save a life here."

"BP's dropping, seventy over palp, pulse thready. Hang the other unit of blood, stat!" Flynn blurted out.

Then the monitor sounded its high-pitched alarm. "He's in V-tach!" Karen Choy yelled.

Spiros rushed to the crash cart. "Give me a gram of epi!"

All eyes were on the monitor as he squirted the ampule of epinephrine through the IV line.

They watched and waited.

"No change." He turned to Flynn. "Give me those paddles!"

"Shouldn't we give the epi a few more seconds to work?"

"I said give me those goddamn paddles!" Spiros grabbed the paddles from Flynn and put them on Geoff's chest. "Ready at two hundred. Stand away!"

Geoff's body arched violently upward, then fell back on the bed board with a thud.

Jan Creighton covered her mouth with her hand.

Nothing.

"Again! Get back."

Spiros readied the paddles again, then fired.

The monitor was eerily silent for what seemed like forever. Nothing. All eyes remained fixed on the screen. Then a blip.

"He's in sinus rhythm!" Flynn yelled. "His heart's stabilized!"

"Thank God," said Karen Choy.

"Dr. Spiros, the OR is ready," said the clerk.

"It's about fucking time. Let's go!"

CHAPTER 44

THE ORANGE GLOW OF THE SUN FADED QUICKLY, GIVING WAY TO darkness much earlier than usual for a mid-summer night. A billowy layer of black storm clouds had rolled in late in the afternoon, and a nasty summer storm drenched the streets of New York.

Inside the protective walls of the Neurosurgical ICU at the New York Trauma Center, however, all was quiet. Two patients had been discharged to the floor earlier in the evening, and only one remained. Jill Aker, the rookie nurse on nightshift had just received report from Cathy Johannsen. The ICU was required by law to have at least two RN's on duty, even if there was only one patient. Jill had met Geoff only once, on his first day as chief resident. She was sure he had barely noticed her, but here she was with his life in her hands. It made her more than a little nervous.

"Eight hours in surgery? Jeez," Jill said.

"Takes a long time to do what they had to do. Ruptured spleen, lacerated liver, shattered thigh bone, fractured cheek, not to mention various lacerations that needed suturing. Oh, yeah, the head bolt—the pressure monitor."

"Isn't that important?"

"Depends who you ask. I think they put them in way too often around here. Supposed to be just for comatose head injury patients to monitor their level of pressure around the brain, their level of consciousness and all that, but Geoff was responsive to pain even in the ER. He hasn't fully awaken yet, opened his eyes or said anything, but he's definitely not in a coma. I don't get it." Cathy stared over in Geoff's direction, frustration in her voice.

"Aren't they doing a study on that? That's probably why they all get the head bolts put in," Jill said.

"There's a study, all right, but he's no guinea pig!"

Jill wanted to ask Cathy what she thought about the murders. Did she really think he was guilty? She was dying to know, Cathy being his friend and all and the announcement this morning that the charges had been mysteriously dropped. It all seemed so bizarre. But she sensed this was the absolute wrong time to ask.

"They must be treating him overcautiously. It happens all the time, because he's a doctor." Jill put her hand on Cathy's reassuringly. "Listen, I know you're upset about this, that you're a friend of Geoff's. Why don't you go get something at the snack bar."

She looked at her watch then reached into her purse. "Look. It's midnight, cheeseburger time at Randy's Bar-B-Q pit. I think we could both use a good greasy burger and a shake to take our minds off things. My treat."

Cathy forced a smile and took the money. "Sure. Thanks for the words of encouragement, Jill." She stood to leave. "Keep your eyes on our VIP. Anything, I mean *anything*, seems out of the ordinary, page me."

"No sweat, Cath. Trust me. He's in good hands."

The doors of the NSICU closed with a whoosh. Jill sat alone at the nursing station, the eerie stillness of the room pierced only by the constant beeping of the monitors. She couldn't believe she'd sent Cathy off like that. She was jumpy enough about the whole situation with her around, let alone by herself in this big, dark, empty ICU.

But she wasn't alone. Geoff was there. Maybe he'd wake up on her watch. She decided she'd keep him company until Cathy got back.

The phone rang, just about sending her through the ceiling. Jill jumped on the receiver before the first ring was half-way through, her heart racing.

"NSICU!"

"Jill?" It was Cathy. "Everything okay?"

Silence. Jill took a deep breath. "Of course everything's okay. Your call just about gave me a heart attack, that's all," she said with a nervous laugh. "Our patient hasn't stopped talking since you left."

"Very funny. How do you want your burger?"

"You mean how well done? I've never seen a Randy burger anything but charcoal broiled!"

"Guess you're right. I'll tell him to make it crisp. See you in a few minutes."

Jill put down the phone and walked over to bed one. She stood at the bedside for several minutes, simply staring at Geoff, the casted leg suspended by a wire from the frame above the bed, the shaved and bandaged head sprouting a bolt and accompanying tubing, the swollen and bruised face, his handsome features blunted but recognizable.

Her gaze shifted to the monitors: heart rate seventy-five and regular, BP 120/80, normal cardiac rhythm, brain pressure normal at sixteen. Every system was being monitored, everything under complete control. Amazing. If she was ever in an accident, the NYTC was where she'd want to be.

She could see Geoff's eyes darting rapidly back and forth beneath his closed lids. He must be dreaming, maybe lightening up. REM sleep was lighter than deep, stage four sleep.

Carefully, she placed her thumb and forefinger on his upper lid and tried to gently open it. She met some resistance.

"Geoff," she whispered. She moved in closer. "Geoff, can you hear me?"

A sound. A deeper breath. Perhaps a grunt? She forced his eyes open. More resistance, she was sure of it this time. His eyes continued to dart around, taking no particular notice of anything, let alone her. It gave her the creeps, so she let go. She tried another strategy, pinching his arm, squeezing it hard, hard enough to make any conscious person complain.

A movement. He moved his head. A moan. He was waking up!

"Geoff, this is your nurse, Jill. You're in the NSICU at the Trauma Center, Geoff. Everything is okay. You're going to be okay. You've been in an accident, a bad accident, and you had surgery—"

A word came softly from between his dry, sticky lips.

Jill reached down to squeeze his hand. She leaned in closer. "What, Geoff? What did you say?"

"Oma..."

"Oma? What's Oma? Geoff, try to open your eyes. Look at me. Say it again, please."

His puffy lids twitched, then parted, not fully at first, the room light overwhelming his eyes.

Geoff clamped them shut, then slowly tried to open them once more. Again he spoke. "O'Malley. Call O'Malley."

A whooshing sound was heard, the sound of the NSICU door opening. Jill could barely contain her excitement. She continued to hold Geoff's hand, gazed at him as she called out, "Cathy, over hear, quick! Hurry up, girl. Drop those burgers! Geoff's awake, and he's trying to say something! Something about someone named O'Malley."

Their gazes met. Jill leaned in closer, her eyes studying his.

What she saw in those crystal blue eyes was not pain, but fear. Mortal fear.

"Nurse Akers, why don't you go take a break. I'll keep an eye on your patient for a little while."

Jill startled, turned around to see where the authoritative voice came from. "Oh, Dr. Pederson, it's you!" She took a deep breath, tried to relax. "Are you sure? There's always supposed to be a nurse on duty in here. Medical center rules—"

Pederson held up his hand, smiled, spoke in tones so soft Jill had to strain in order to hear him. "Don't worry about it. How could our patient be any better off than with the chairman of neurosurgery and the director of research at his bedside?"

Jill looked toward the doorway, saw Joseph Balassi enter the NSICU, approach the bedside. "Well, whatever you say, Dr. Pederson. You should know. Is fifteen minutes okay?"

"That would be perfect."

Jill Akers left the room.

Pederson and Balassi stood over Geoff, glanced down at him. Pederson looked at the ICP monitor, turned to Balassi. "He seems to be rousing. You can take it from here. Call me when you're done."

Pederson left the NSICU.

Geoff's eyes widened. Was he still dreaming, or was this a hallucination?

"Geoffrey, Geoffrey, so good to see you again. I heard you were in the hospital, so I thought I'd pay you a visit," Balassi said. "You and I have been through so much together lately.

"Balassi approached the bedside, stood directly over Geoff, casting a shadow on his face. "Roles are reversed this time, aren't they?"

Geoff tried to muster whatever strength he had. He shifted his position, attempted to roll out of bed to his right, but a searing pain shot from his right leg and jolted his spine. Then he realized why. His leg was tethered to the frame above the bed. He was dead in the water, trapped. This couldn't be happening, not here, not now after all he'd been through. He hadn't survived so much for it to end this way.

Fear transformed to hatred. "Asshole," he mumbled hoarsely.

"I see illness hasn't changed you, Geoff. Here let me help you out," he said as he released the wire holding up Geoff's leg, sending the cast crashing to the bed. Geoff let out a scream and was momentarily blinded by the excruciating pain.

Balassi smiled and continued, ignoring Geoff's writhing. "Often major life events—illness, injury, a death in the family will do that to someone. Change them, that is. It's true. Really it is. But there are other ways to change a person, Geoff. You know what I mean. *Really* change them, their personalities, their intellect, their abilities. I gave you a chance, an opportunity of a lifetime, Geoff, to be a part of this great discovery, and you turned me down.

"You tried to destroy me. You didn't understand this discovery is greater than either of us. It will live on, Geoff, be picked up by others, the project passed from one generation to the next as it has been. The seed that was planted forty years ago as Project MK Ultra has blossomed and become the Sigma Project. Under our care it will be carried to fruition."

Balassi's piercing brown eyes danced wildly. "I had no choice but to do what I did, Geoff. I am the agent of mankind's next great leap in evolution: *neurochemical evolution*. As the guardian of this historical advance, I simply could not let you get in the way."

"There is someone else who knows, someone who can stop

you." Geoff coughed out the words.

Balassi laughed derisively. "You mean your detective friend, O'Malley? The one you went to all that trouble to get the information to? You must be kidding."

"You can kill me, but he knows everything. They'll be coming for you Balassi. You're insane."

Balassi continued to laugh. "Detective O'Malley won't be coming after me or anyone else, Geoff. The ignorant fool came to see me in my office earlier this evening, played me a recording of the conversation you and I had in my apartment. That was good, Geoff, very good! He threatened to take me down to the stationhouse. Can you believe it?" Balassi snickered. "Let's just say your detective friend is tied up with other business right now."

Geoff's eyes narrowed in disbelief. "You're lying."

"I'm so sorry, I really am. I know he was your only hope and without hope the human spirit withers away, dies a slow death, Geoff, but it's true. See." Balassi held up O'Malley's badge and I.D.

"So, where do we go from here, hum? I'd still like to give you a chance, a chance to be part of this. I think there's still a way we can work together." He reached into his pocket and held up a syringe filled with an amber solution.

"This syringe, Geoff, contains the most powerful sigma endorphin known to man. Oh, we thought that of the other sigma analogs we developed, but the compounds were unpredictable. Their half-lives either too long or too short, their structures unstable, short-circuiting the brain's neurochemical pathways. Like early LSD, far too crude."

Balassi rolled the syringe between his thumb and index finger and held it in front of Geoff's face. Geoff sank back into the pillow, tried to push himself away. Beads of sweat formed on his brow.

"I've honed it down, Geoff. I've finally identified the exact location of the receptor imbalance that causes schizophrenia. Your patient Smithers helped me with that. Of course he didn't know it at the time. Do you understand what this means? The elimination of this crippling mental illness from the human race, vaccinating against it like polio or small pox, eliminating it entirely! This is only the beginning, and I have chosen *you* to play a major role."

"You're mad," gasped Geoff.

"Not as mad as you will be shortly." Balassi unsheathed the needle and leaned over, holding it in front of Geoff. He squirted out a few drops of the endorphin, the drops landing on Geoff's lower lip. Instinctively Geoff spit, his saliva and the endorphin catching Balassi in the eye.

"Really, Geoff," he said with disgust. "You needn't be so crude and ungrateful." He wiped his face with a handkerchief. "It's far better than dying, you know. They'll take good care of you in the institution. You'll get visits from your friends on the weekends, care packages from the family. It won't be so bad."

Balassi laughed loudly, then became deadly serious. "Enough nonsense. It's time. Congratulations, my friend. You'll go down in history."

Slowly, Balassi reached over the top of Geoff's head and grabbed the tubing that connected to his head bolt. He found the injection site, pierced it with the needle. Geoff felt the pop as the needle was inserted into the transducer. Balassi pinched off the tubing with his thumb.

Geoff looked up at Balassi's hand on the syringe. Sweat poured down Geoff's face. His heart was racing, his breathing labored. He could handle the pain, even the thought of death, but the notion of insanity brought unbridled terror. He closed his eyes and prepared for the dazzling lightshow as his brain's receptors became saturated with the endorphin. Would he know what was happening? Would it be instantaneous, or would he have to live like a human time bomb, insanity ticking away slowly, unpredictably, inside him. That alone might be enough to make him go mad.

A voice jumped out of the darkness from across the room. "Hold it right there, Balassi. The party's over!" The voice was commanding, reassuringly familiar.

Geoff opened his eyes. Standing between the bed and the nursing station, a service revolver aimed directly at Balassi, was Detective Donald O'Malley.

"Take your hand off that syringe and put both your hands on your head. Now!"

Josef Balassi's jaw dropped in disbelief. "Well, Detective O'Malley, nice of you to come to visit Geoff."

"Better know how to tie knots, next time, Balassi. You'll have time to learn, where you're going.

"I'm not fucking around anymore. Now put your hands up and walk towards me. Slowly!"

Balassi laughed derisively. "You must be kidding. I have connections in higher places than you think, detective. Take me in, and your career will be finished."

"Who said anything about taking you in, Balassi?" O'Malley smirked, cocked the hammer on the revolver. "Your connections have been severed, Balassi. Your endorphin conspiracy, the Sigma Project, is finished. CIA Director Bennington is back, the group that infiltrated the CIA, Lancaster included, your phony PETronics Corporation—everyone's been busted. They're all gone. No one cares what happens to you now, except me and the good doc, here."

Balassi's pupils dilated. He took his left hand off the syringe and slowly reached down into his lab coat pocket with his right hand. "Now, now, detective, no need to do anything rash. Maybe we can work something out, a deal or—"

"You mean like the deal you had worked out for Doc Davis, here?" O'Malley glanced at Geoff, back to Balassi, grinned. "I don't think so. Now move it!"

Geoff's eye caught the movement of Balassi's right hand. From his angle he could see the gun. His gaze darted to O'Malley, whose eyes were fixed on the hand that had been holding the syringe. O'Malley obviously hadn't seen Balassi's right hand move.

Balassi's hand now gripped the pistol in his coat pocket, and he was pointing it in O'Malley's direction. He slowly moved around the bed. Geoff had to do something! He'd get only one chance.

He took a deep breath. Summoning every ounce of strength he could, he swung his casted leg into Balassi's knees, throwing him off balance. "Look out!"

Seeing the glimmering metal in Balassi's right hand, O'Malley fired his weapon. He aimed high, not wanting to endanger Geoff, grazed Balassi's lab coat. Balassi fell to the ground, but he scurried around the head of the bed, using Geoff for cover, then stood. His left hand reached up to the syringe still dangling from the IV tubing, his right hand held onto the gun.

"Don't do it!" O'Malley yelled, his revolver aimed at Balassi.

Balassi saw O'Malley's gaze shift to the hand holding the syringe, fired twice, one bullet hitting O'Malley in the shoulder, the other in the chest. O'Malley winced in pain, fell to the ground.

"You filthy son-of-a-bitch!" Geoff yelled. He rolled to his right off the bed, his casted leg making a loud crack as he fell to the floor, taking Balassi down with him. Geoff grasped Balassi's right hand, slammed it on the floor. The gun popped free and slid across the room.

Balassi tried to stand up, lunge for the gun, but Geoff grabbed his leg, his grip tight around Balassi's ankle. Balassi fell to the ground again, this time on top of Geoff.

Balassi straddled Geoff's chest, punched him in the face, again and again. Geoff, already in severe pain, was dazed. The room swam in and out of focus. Geoff felt he was on the edge of losing consciousness. He thought of Suzanne's brutal assault. Kapinsky, his patients, murdered. The madness had to end.

Something glistened next to Geoff's face, caught his attention. The syringe had popped out of the IV tubing and fallen on the floor beside him. He mustered what little strength he had left, grasped the syringe in his hand and swung his arm in as high and fast an arc as he could. The long needle pierced Balassi's left eardrum, entered his brainstem.

Balassi shrieked in pain, grasped for the syringe in vain, then fell to the ground, landing on the plunger and sending the sigma endorphin home.

Balassi was dead.

EPILOGUE

It had been over a week since the day it all came to an end. The bolt had been removed from his head, and his hair was growing back. Geoff found himself oddly amused by his buzz cut look. It reminded him of his childhood. His wounds, both physical and emotional were healing, and his doctors were talking about discharging him from the hospital in the morning. Stefan had arranged for a private nurse to care for him so he could go home early. He couldn't stand to be here one day more than he had to be.

Geoff had made up his mind he wasn't coming back here. Too many painful memories, too much horror. He was going to finish his residency, but it would have to be somewhere far away from the New York Trauma Center. Somewhere he could smell the grass, feel a salty ocean breeze, stay in touch with what was truly important in his life—his brother and Suzanne. They were all he had left. The thought of recuperating with Suzanne at his family's estate in Westport brought a smile to his face for the first time in weeks.

Perhaps it had taken such a horrible experience such as this to make Geoff realize his own caring nature, his basic humanitarianism were what had kept him going, from closing his eyes and turning away. He was, after all, a healer.

His thoughts were interrupted by a knock on the door. He wasn't expecting any visitors. Suzanne was barely mobile herself and was being discharged tomorrow as well.

"Come in." Geoff turned to face the doorway. Someone holding a bunch of Mylar balloons stood by the door. "This place is starting to look like a carnival." Geoff cleared a table. "You can set them down over here."

The balloons didn't move.

"Hello over there," Geoff called. "You can come in."

"Hi, doc. I'm happy to see you're up and around." O'Malley grinned, set down the balloons on the table by Geoff's bed. "Thought you might want a little company. How are you feeling?"

"Not bad for someone who's been battered and abused. How about yourself?"

O'Malley lifted his right arm. "Shoulder's coming along. My ribs are pretty sore, though. Thank God for flak jackets." "I have to admit, you had me believing you were dead when Balassi shot you."

O'Malley patted his chest. "Takes more than a couple of slugs to knock off a tough old Irish cop like Donald O'Malley."

"Guess so. Is this a social visit, or an official visit from the homicide squad, detective?"

"A little of both, I suppose. I wanted to stop by and say thanks. You saved my life, you know."

"I did what I had to do."

O'Malley opened his tweed sport coat, reached into his breast pocket, removed a well worn leather flask and a couple of shot glasses, set them down on the table. He filled each glass to the rim with an amber fluid. "Mind if I pull up a chair?"

"Be my guest." Geoff motioned to the side chair with his hand. O'Malley slid the chair to the side of Geoff's bed, raised his shot glass, waited for Geoff to do the same.

Geoff hesitated at first. His conscience told him he shouldn't be drinking in a hospital room, particularly given the medications he was taking.

O'Malley must have sensed Geoff's hesitation. "Don't worry, doc. It won't kill you. Glenlivit, single malt, aged twenty-five years." O'Malley winked, sniffed the vapors. "Only the best. As we say down at the station house, L'Chaim."

Geoff smiled, clanged his glass to O'Malley's, downed the whisky.

O'Malley did the same, slammed down the glass, settled into the chair. "Another round?"

Geoff nodded as O'Malley poured. "Tell me something, detective. Did you really think I was involved in all those murders? Kapinsky, the security guard, my own patients?"

O'Malley stared at Geoff, his emerald eyes smiling warmly. He removed a piece of Juicy fruit, crumpled the wrapper, put the stick of gum in his mouth. "Of course not, doc. I never thought you had it in you to do any of that stuff. Besides, you didn't have a reason. No motive."

"So why did you act like you believed otherwise?"

"Had to play my role, smoke out the perpetrators," O'Malley said. "I knew sooner or later, someone'd screw up. They always do. I just sit and wait, catch them as they float down the river, so to speak."

"Tell me one more thing, captain. Ever read any Sherlock Holmes mysteries?"

O'Malley's eyes twinkled, his lips formed a deeply creased smile. "A few."

"How about *Sign of the Four?*"

"You mean, the one where Sherlock Holmes says to Watson, 'when you have eliminated the impossible, whatever remains, however improbable, must be the truth?' That one?"

Geoff returned the smile. "That's the one."

"You'd make a damn good detective, doc, you know that? If you ever decide to make a career change, call me. We'd make a pretty good team, you and me."

"How about another round, Detective O'Malley? I've got a few more questions I'd like *you* to answer."

ABOUT THE AUTHOR

FREDRIC A. STERN, M.D., WAS BORN IN NEW YORK CITY AND attended Tufts University, where he majored in Greek and Roman Studies. He received his medical degree from Columbia University College of Physicians and Surgeons.

A cosmetic surgeon and enologist, Dr. Stern currently practices in the Seattle area, where he lives with his wife. He is currently writing his next medical thriller, *Genome*.

Made in the USA
Charleston, SC
13 April 2014